SECRETS OF THE WHIPCORD

'Do you like what you see?' she asked, her forefinger describing small circles about her love-bud.

Peter nodded. Small beads of sweat had broken out on his forehead and the bulge in his pants was growing larger by the minute.

'Would you like to touch?'

Once again he nodded.

Jo reached for his wrist with her free hand, guiding it up to her breast. She placed it over the soft flesh, loving the sensation of having his hand close about her firm globe.

D1638218

SECRETS OF THE WHIPCORD

Michaela Wallace

This book is a work of fiction.
In real life, make sure you practise safe sex.

First published in 1997 by
Nexus
332 Ladbroke Grove
London W10 5AH

Typeset by TW Typesetting, Plymouth, Devon

Printed and bound by
Caledonian Books Ltd, Glasgow

ISBN 0 352 33188 7

One

Jo never really knew what it was that drew her into the antique shop that morning. It wasn't as if antiques were really her thing. During her nineteen years she had always thought of herself as a modern girl and, since leaving home, she had surrounded herself with the trappings of the nineties. There had never seemed any point to her in dwelling on the past. Yet here she was, in this dark and rather dusty shop, surveying the Victorian china and tarnished cutlery as if it really mattered to her.

In fact, if she was honest with herself, Jo's mind wasn't on the establishment's wares, but elsewhere. The shop had simply been somewhere to go whilst she turned over in her mind the events of the previous twenty-four hours. Twenty-four hours that had seen yet more disasters in the lovely youngster's sex life.

Sex life, she reflected bitterly. Sex was not really the word for it. In fact sex was something that seemed to have been eluding her all her life. She wandered amongst the dusty cabinets, idly fingering the pieces of china and trying to work out just what it was that was wrong with her, and how it had managed to spoil such a promising evening only the night before.

It all should have been so different. She had looked forward eagerly to the dinner date, and had dressed as sexily as she knew how. The evening had started promisingly enough. Her date, Peter, had been a handsome and personable young man, and he had taken her to a pleasant Italian restaurant where they had enjoyed fine wine and an excellent pasta, after which they had strolled down by the river, savouring the balminess of the summer evening. She had found herself warming to him as the evening wore on, and had readily agreed when he had asked her back to his flat for a cup of coffee.

It was then that it had started to go wrong. Sitting on the sofa beside her, he had placed an arm about her shoulder. It was a simple enough act, and one which her previous demeanour had not discouraged, yet her whole body had gone tense the moment he did it. Later, when he kissed her, she had experienced none of the passion that she knew that she was supposed to feel, keeping her lips firmly closed against the insistent probing of his tongue. When he had tried to slide his hand inside her bra she had instinctively withdrawn, hugging her arms about her chest and pushing him away.

Peter had persisted, but each advance had increased her resistance until the inevitable row had ensued, and she had ended up walking out. And so had followed another night in her lonely bed, cursing her inability to form a sexual relationship with a man.

Why was it that she seemed quite unable to respond to a man's advances, she asked herself for the umpteenth time. It wasn't as if she was physically unattractive. Only that morning, on emerging from her bath, she had paused naked before the mirror and critically examined her body, unable to find any fault in her appearance.

Jo was not tall, only about five feet four inches in height, but her lithe young body was perfectly proportioned. The image that had confronted her in the bathroom would have pleased any woman. She had firm, plump breasts, the size and shape of ripe grapefruits, with long brown nipples that pointed upwards from her pert mammaries, as if inviting potential lovers to caress and suck them. Her waist was slim, her belly flat, her mons covered in a dark fleece, beneath which her thick, pink sex lips were prominent. Her legs were slender, tapering to small, neat ankles, and she moved with the grace of a gazelle.

Her eyes had drifted from her body to her face, still searching for something that men might find unattractive. But there was nothing to concern her. Her features were classically beautiful, with high cheekbones and a small, eminently kissable mouth, the whole framed by dark tresses that hung to her shoulders. It was her eyes that men noticed first, though. They were the brightest green, and seemed to sparkle with life, giving her an air of youthful exuberance that was at once innocent and alluring.

In the drab confines of the antique shop the recollection of standing before the bathroom mirror sent a sudden shudder through Jo's body. It brought back an even fresher memory, and one which she had yet to come to terms with. She tried not to think about what had occurred between her and her flatmate that morning, but still the images kept coming back, bringing with them the embarrassment of yet another failed encounter.

It wasn't as if she hadn't tried to get aroused, she told herself. She thought of how, still standing before the mirror, she had run her fingers over her breasts, then slid a hand down between her thighs. According to all the magazines she had read this should have been a delicious feeling, yet she experienced nothing. It was so damned frustrating. She longed to enjoy the pleasures that she had read about and heard other women talk of. It was just that her body didn't seem to respond in the right way. With a sigh she had wrapped a towel about herself and headed back toward her bedroom.

Halfway down the corridor something had made her

3

stop and listen hard. There was a strange buzzing sound coming from somewhere. As she strained her ears, the noise seemed to become alternately louder and softer. There was another sound too. A faint gasping, as if someone was out of breath.

She crept forward. It was coming from a door about halfway down the hallway. This was the door to her flat-mate Lucy's room. Lucy had been sharing with her for about a month now and, whilst the two girls were friendly enough, they weren't particularly close. Lucy worked in the evenings at a café and Jo's job at the bank meant that they didn't have a lot of contact with one another.

Jo stood outside Lucy's door, listening hard. Still the noise continued, a kind of whirr, its tone continually changing. As well as the rasping breath there was another sound too, a sort of low moaning.

Unable to contain her curiosity, Jo pressed at Lucy's bedroom door. It opened slightly and she placed her eye against the crack. What she saw almost made her exclaim aloud.

There, stretched out across her bed, was Lucy. She was quite naked. Jo's eyes drifted over her bare flesh, taking in the large breasts that rose proudly from her chest and the wisp of blonde curls at her crotch that matched the colour of her long mane of hair.

But it wasn't just her nakedness that held Jo's attention. It was what she was doing.

In her right hand, Lucy held something long and pink. From what Jo could see of it, it was a replica of a man's erect penis, bulging with veins and emitting the strange buzzing sound that had first caught her attention. She couldn't see all of it, however, since Lucy had the object buried deep in her vagina, her legs spread wide, her backside clear of the bed as she thrust the object into herself urgently, small groaning sounds escaping from her mouth as she did so. At the same

4

time, her other hand was caressing her breasts, the nipples standing out like hard brown nuts.

Jo was spellbound. She had never seen a woman masturbate before. In fact, come to think of it, she had never seen a mature woman naked before. Lucy was about a year older than her and had an almost flawless body that never failed to draw stares when she was out. Jo knew little of Lucy's love life, but she knew the girl was asked out often, and had occasionally glimpsed young men slipping out of her room in the early morning. Jo had long been certain that Lucy had the natural desires of a woman, a fact that was confirmed by the sight that met Jo's eyes now. The younger girl found herself unable to take her eyes off the whirring dildo as it slid between Lucy's sex lips, its shaft gleaming with moisture.

It was at that moment that Lucy looked up and saw that she was not alone.

'Jo!'

Jo's face blushed scarlet.

'Lucy I . . .'

'How long have you been standing there?'

'Not long. I'm sorry I . . .'

'You were watching me?'

'I didn't mean to. I heard the noise. I just wondered what it was.'

'And now you know. Come on in.'

'No. I'd better be getting on.'

'Don't be an idiot. Come inside.'

It occurred to Jo that Lucy's reaction hadn't been anything like she would have anticipated. She had expected the girl to snatch the vibrator out and cover herself up, to remonstrate with her for violating her privacy. Instead she simply lay where she was. It was true she was no longer pumping the vibrator back and forth with the vigour she had displayed when Jo had first seen her, but still she had her legs spread wide and she was working it in and out gently as she stared at her roommate. In fact, Jo realised, it was she who was embarrassed. Lucy seemed as cool as a cucumber.

'Come on,' insisted Lucy, patting the bed beside her. 'Sit down.'

Slowly Jo pushed the door open and stepped into the room, her eyes fixed on her flatmate's vagina.

'What's the matter?' asked Lucy. 'Haven't you ever seen a girl doing this before?'

'No.'

'What, not even at school?'

'We weren't – That is, they wouldn't let us . . .'

'I thought that sort of thing was rampant at convent schools.'

'Not at ours. Look, maybe I'd better leave you to it.'

'I get it. This is embarrassing you, right?'

'No.' Jo shook her head vehemently, unwilling to let Lucy know how taken aback she was by her flatmate's behaviour.

'How did you get on last night?' asked Lucy, her hand still manoeuvring the vibrator in and out of her sex. 'You came home earlier than I'd expected.'

'Oh, it was all right,' said Jo, trying not to watch as the girl frigged herself.

'You didn't go back to his place then?'

'Well yes we did, actually.'

'And?'

'And what?'

'Did you go to bed with him?'

'No. It's not compulsory to have sex on every date you know.'

Lucy placed a hand on Jo's leg. 'Hey, Jo, loosen up,' she chided. 'It's no big deal.'

'Sorry,' said Jo, blushing. 'It's just . . .' She broke off, turning away.

'Just what? Are you having man problems or something, Jo?'

'No. No, it's all right.' The question had been an ironic one, reflected Jo. In order to have man problems, it was necessary first to have a man.

'You can always borrow my little friend here,' said Lucy, indicating the vibrator. 'It's not quite as good as the real thing, but it's better than nothing. I could even do it for you if you like.'

'Do it for me?'

'Sure. It's much more fun when someone's doing it for you.' She pulled the buzzing phallus from her sex and held it out to Jo. 'I'll do it now, if you like.'

'No!' Jo almost shouted the response. She dreaded the idea that she might react to Lucy's touch in the same way as she had her partner's the night before.

'You do it to me, then.'

Jo stared at the sex toy, then at the beautiful naked blonde stretched out across the bed. It was an extraordinary suggestion, yet one that fascinated her. She had never witnessed a woman in a state of arousal before, and Lucy was clearly that, her breasts rising and falling, the wetness gleaming on her sex lips.

'Go on.' Lucy's voice was husky with arousal as she held out the vibrator to Jo.

Jo reached out a shaking hand and took it from her. 'I'm not sure what to do,' she said.

'You've honestly never used one?'

'No.'

It was true. In fact, not only had Lucy never used a vibrator, she'd never even masturbated. At her convent school she had been led to believe that it was evil, and it had put some sort of block into her mind, the same block, she suspected, that had prevented her submitting to the advances of her suitor the night before. She had read about orgasms, heard women talk about them. But the pleasure of a sexual climax was one that had so far eluded her.

Lucy sat up and took hold of her wrist, guiding her hand towards her open crotch.

7

'Just slip it in,' she said. 'It's easy.'

Jo drew back. 'I'm not sure.'

'Of course you are,' chided Lucy. 'It's nothing to be afraid of.'

This time Jo allowed Lucy to pull her hand closer, bringing the bulbous end of the phallus up until it was resting against the entrance to the naked girl's sex.

Once more she held back.

'Push it in,' said Lucy, lying back. 'Give it to me hard, Jo.'

Jo looked down at the vibrator, then up at her friend's face. Everything about the situation was alien to her, yet clearly Lucy was quite relaxed about the whole thing. She closed her eyes momentarily, took a deep breath and pushed. For a second Lucy's flesh resisted the pressure, then the thick object was sliding into her.

'That's great,' gasped Lucy. 'Shove it all the way into me.'

Jo pressed on, instinctively twisting her wrist as she did so. The vibrator was large and long, yet she was surprised to find that she was able to push it home until it was almost completely immersed and her fingers were brushing the soft, moist flesh of Lucy's sex lips.

'Fantastic,' murmured her friend. 'Now frig me, Jo.'

'Frig you?'

'Move it in and out. Like a cock.'

The simile was one that Jo couldn't relate to, but she got the message. She began working the object back and forth. It slipped easily in and out of Lucy's vagina, the sheen of lubrication that coated it easing its passage. Jo concentrated hard on getting a smooth, even rhythm, trying not to think too much about what she was doing.

As she moved it Jo gazed down at Lucy's face. The girl had her head back, grunts of pleasure escaping her open mouth. Her eyes were tightly closed, her hands kneading the soft flesh of her own breasts.

'Mmmm. That's wonderful,' she gasped. 'Oh, yes Jo. Do it harder.'

8

Jo renewed her efforts, watching in fascination as Lucy arched her back, raising her backside and thrusting her crotch up against her fingers, her firm breasts shaking back and forth as she matched Jo's even strokes. Jo had never witnessed anything like it, and had had no idea that such a response could be triggered in a woman. It was as if she was controlling her flatmate, as if the thing inside her vagina was a kind of joystick that drove Lucy's lust. She experimented, moving the end round in a circular motion, then sawing it back and forth, twisting it as she did so. Each new movement brought fresh cries from her partner, and the scent of the girl's arousal began to permeate the room.

'Harder!'

'Are you sure?'

'Of course I'm sure. Do it harder!'

Jo wrapped her fist about the base of the vibrator and began ramming it as hard as she was able into Lucy's vagina. The girl was clearly totally aroused now, her head shaking back and forth as she panted with lust. Jo could feel the way the muscles of her sex were tightening about the vibrator, so that she had to tug hard to move it back and forth.

'God that's good,' gasped Lucy. 'Oh Jo, I think I'm nearly there. Do it harder Jo.'

Jo did as she was asked, pumping the dildo as vigorously as she was able, her mind temporarily blotting out the moral implications of what she was doing as she concentrated on pleasing her friend. She watched the fevered movements of her flatmate, slightly alarmed by the frenzy that seemed to be overtaking her, but determined now to see the thing through

All at once, Lucy's body stiffened and her breath shortened to hoarse grunts. Then she gave a cry, and Jo realised that she was coming.

The orgasm that shook Lucy's body was long and loud. She thrashed about on the bed, her hips jabbing insistently against Jo's hand as she screamed her pleasure. It was all Jo could do to keep hold of the buzzing toy as she watched her companion writhing in ecstasy on the bed.

Lucy came down slowly, the tension in her muscles gradually easing as the urgency of her movements decreased. For her part, Jo clung grimly to the vibrator, continuing to move it in and out until the violent spasms that shook Lucy's body subsided, and at last she lay still, her breasts rising and falling as she regained her breath. Then she stopped, gazing anxiously at her companion.

It was some time before Lucy opened her eyes and gazed dreamily at Jo. 'That was great,' she said quietly. 'Thanks, kid.'

Jo blushed once again, releasing her hold on the phallus and watching as it slipped out of Lucy's sex, still shiny with her juices.

'W-was it that really that good?' she asked quietly.

Lucy sat up and reached for Jo's hand.

'It was the best.'

Jo managed a weak smile. 'I'm glad.' She said. Then she straightened up. 'Well, I'd better be going.'

'Wait!' Lucy tightened her grip on Jo's hand. 'Let me return the compliment,' she said.

'No.' Jo pulled her hand away.

'Come on Jo,' said Lucy, moving closer. Her proximity, naked and still hot from her orgasm, had a strangely unsettling effect on Jo, and when her full breasts brushed against Jo's arm, the touch sent an odd thrill through the girl.

Lucy reached for the knot that held the towel to the younger girl's breasts. She gave it a little tug, and the towel fell away. Jo averted her eyes as Lucy took in the delights of her lovely young body.

'You're gorgeous, Jo,' she breathed.

She reached out and placed a hand on Jo's bare breast. As she did so a shudder ran through the younger girl's slim frame. Jo had never before been touched like that by a woman, especially one who smelt so strongly of sex, and the sensation sparked a raging conflict inside her as she fought down her instinct to remove the hand.

'Come on, Jo, relax,' murmured Lucy. 'You're tense as anything. Lie down on the bed.'

Slowly, her body trembling, Jo allowed Lucy to push her back until she was prostrate, her legs still tightly pressed together. Lucy ran her fingers up the soft flesh of Jo's thighs, sending a new spasm through her young body.

'Open up,' she whispered.

Tentatively Jo relaxed the muscles in her legs, allowing them to part slightly. Lucy slid her fingers upwards and began worming them into Jo's crack.

'No!'

Jo pushed Lucy's hand away, suddenly sitting upright and grabbing for the towel.

'What's the matter?'

'No!' she repeated. 'I can't.'

She climbed off the bed, wrapping the towel about her. Lucy sat looking at her in astonishment, the vibrator still clutched in her hand.

'Hey, take it easy, Jo,' she said. 'It's just a bit of fun.'

'No!' said Jo for the third time. 'I – I don't want to.' She was shaking now, her muscles tense, her entire body rigid. She reached for the doorhandle.

Lucy rose from the bed and crossed to where she stood, placing her hand over Jo's.

'Don't go,' she said. 'We need to talk this over. Is there a problem or something?'

Jo looked at the lovely naked woman, and at the buzzing phallus in her hand. Then she shook her head.

'It's no good, Lucy,' she said. 'I just can't.'

And with that she wrenched the door open and ran off down the corridor, leaving an astonished Lucy staring after her.

Two

Jo stood in the antiques shop staring at the objects in the cabinet in front of her, trying hard to free her mind of the memory of what had happened that morning. She wondered what Lucy must think of her and the hysterical way she had behaved. She thought of the blonde girl, stretched out across the bed, masturbating without inhibition. She recalled the way her lovely young breasts had shaken with every stroke of the vibrator, and the sensation of the girl's arousal as she had worked the toy in and out of her pulsating vagina.

Why was it that she herself was unable to respond the way Lucy did? Why hadn't she been able just lie back and spread her legs? She wanted desperately to liberate herself, to experience the joy and relief of an orgasm and to use her body to satisfy others whilst she was still young and beautiful. What was the mental block that prevented her from doing so?

She moved about the shop as if in a dream. Behind the counter the proprietor was watching her, and she knew it must be obvious to him that she was barely seeing the goods on display. She glanced across at him. He was an old man. In his seventies she guessed, looking almost as moth-eaten and dusty as the goods on sale in his shop.

He caught her glance and cleared his throat.

'Can I be of any assistance?'

She shook her head.

'No. I was just browsing.'

'Was there anything in particular you were looking for? Some furniture perhaps?'

'No. Nothing special.'

She turned away, suddenly embarrassed by his presence. She had better go, she decided. After all, there was nothing for her here. She turned toward the door.

Such was her hurry to leave that she almost missed the book altogether. It was on the top shelf of a bookcase just by the entrance to the shop. Just what it was that attracted her attention she wasn't sure. All she knew was that something about it had caught her eye and she came to a halt, squinting at the title

Secrets of the Whipcord.

The jacket of the book was made of leather, with large ridges down the spine. The lettering was in gold and, despite the book's obvious antiquity, was quite clearly readable. The title meant nothing to Jo, yet something had made her stop and gaze up at the book in fascination, almost as if it held some kind of power over her.

'Interesting, isn't it?'

The sound of the voice just behind her made Jo jump, and she swung round to find the shopkeeper looking over her shoulder. She hadn't heard him move at all, and she suddenly realised that she had been rooted to the spot for some minutes staring up at the bookcase.

'I beg your pardon?'

'The book. That is what you're looking at isn't it?'

'I – er, yes.'

'It's quite old, I think,' the man went on. 'I found it in a house clearance some years ago. The old boy who owned it had a vast collection of erotic art. Most of the other stuff sold pretty quickly, but that's still here. Would you like me to get it down for you?'

'Yes please.'

Jo didn't know why she had said yes. After all, she

13

had no interest in antiquarian books. What could she possibly want with an old tome like that? But there was something about it that drew her to it, and she felt a strange anticipation as she watched the man climb on to a stool, withdraw it and place it on the counter in front of her. He pulled a duster from his pocket and ran it over the cover, then stood back.

Jo reached out a trembling hand and opened the cover. The pages had a silky texture to them and the book fell open at an illustration. Jo leant forward, her eyes taking in the scene depicted.

It showed two figures. The first, a young woman, was quite naked, her breasts and sex lovingly drawn in exquisite detail. She was leaning forward against two vertical posts, and Jo realised with a shock that her wrists were tied to these, and her ankles to stakes in the ground, so that her whole body was spread-eagled and helpless. Behind her stood a man, also naked, his cock erect and jutting out from his groin, each vein carefully picked out by the artist. In his hand he held a whip, and he was in the process of bringing this down across the woman's backside, which already bore a number of stripes.

But it was the expressions on the faces of the two figures that fascinated Jo the most. The man's was cruel, his lips drawn back over his teeth, his eyebrows knitted as he wielded the whip over his helpless captive. The woman's face was convulsed, and at first Jo had taken her expression to be one of pain. Now, though, as she looked closely, she realised she had been wrong. There could be no doubt about it, the woman's look was one of extreme passion, of a sexual pleasure that Jo could only imagine. She thought of Lucy and the way she had reacted to the vibrator that morning. The woman's face was a mirror image of Lucy's.

She began to read the text. It told of the woman's desires. Of how she had given her body to men for her own pleasure, and how the man in the picture had been sent to punish her wantonness. It described in detail how she had been captured, stripped naked, and sentenced to be whipped. Then it told of how the strokes of the whip had aroused her to a sexual peak.

The concept was deeply absorbing to Jo. The very idea of punishing a woman simply for desiring sex was a quite obscene one, but it wasn't that that held her attention. It was the way the book described her response to the pain. How could any woman find enjoyment in being tethered in such a way as to display all her charms to any onlooker? How could the sensation of leather cutting into bare flesh possibly be described as pleasurable? Yet the more she read the words and studied the illustration of the woman's naked body, the more she found herself totally fascinated by the idea.

She turned the page, and gave a sharp intake of breath at what she saw. There was the woman, once again tethered, but now spread-eagled on her back. This time it was the man that held Jo's attention, though. He was kneeling between her legs, his dark, hairy body in stark contrast to her pale, smooth flesh. The whip lay on the ground beside him, discarded for the time being. His onslaught now was of a very different nature. He was thrusting his great penis into her vagina, the cruelty that had previously been in his expression replaced by desire as he rogered his captive. Behind him more men waited their turn, their phalluses jutting proudly upwards. Yet still all that Jo could see on the woman's face was a look of pure pleasure.

Jo read on, turning the pages slowly, totally absorbed in the punishments and the ravishment the woman was subjected to. The language of the book seemed to flow with an extraordinary lucidity. It was as if a voice was speaking in her mind. A voice that commanded all her attention as it told of the woman's pain and pleasure at the hands of her cruel captors.

'You like it?'

Jo gave a start. The shopkeeper's voice seemed to pull her back from a different world. Once again she was aware that she had lost all sense of time, so captivated was she by the book. She shook her head and straightened up.

'Yes. Yes I do. How much is it?'

'Sixty pounds.'

Jo stared down at it again. It was a lot more than she could afford. But there was something about it that drew her to it.

'I – I don't know.'

'Take your time. Feel the quality of the binding.'

Jo closed the book and realised for the first time that, embossed on the cover, was the same picture of the girl being whipped. She reached out and ran her fingers over the leather. Then she gasped.

It felt like no book she had ever touched before. The leather had a strange warmth and softness about it, almost as if it were a living thing. The texture reminded her of the way Lucy's flesh had felt that morning, alive and vibrant. She ran her fingers over the imprint of the woman's body, and the sensation seemed to increase. It was as if she was feeling real flesh. The breasts seemed pliable beneath her touch, although her eyes told her that it was just a picture. Fascinated, she ran her hand down the man's body, her fingers pausing to caress his jutting phallus. Once more there was a curious solidity about it, and she almost imagined she could feel it twitch as she traced its length

All of a sudden, a strange sensation crept through Jo's body. It began at her fingertips, an odd tingling feeling that travelled up her arm and began to envelop her body, transforming into a warmth as it did so. But it wasn't a relaxing warmth. It was more like a heat, and the more she stroked the cover, the stronger it became, permeating her body and filling her with a sudden nameless desire that she did not recognise.

She found her mind filled by the words she had read.

She thought of the cruelty of the men and the desires of the woman; of the descriptions of the whips cutting into her bare flesh and of the men's penises penetrating her so intimately.

And all at once she felt a wetness in her crotch such that she had never felt before, accompanied by an overwhelming desire to touch herself down there.

'See what I mean?' said the shopkeeper. 'Real quality that.'

'Mmmm.'

'Make it fifty then.'

Jo stared at him, barely comprehending his words.

'Pardon?'

'Fifty pounds for the book.'

'Fifty pounds?'

'That's what I said.' He looked at her curiously. 'Are you all right?'

'Yes. Yes I'm fine.' She looked down at the book. Right now she would have paid a hundred. Two hundred even.

'All right.'

'I'll get a bag. Give it here.'

Jo's hands were shaking as she handed the book to him, but he didn't seem to notice and he simply took it from her. She watched him carefully. Did it not have the same effect on him as it had on her? Obviously not, as he placed it in the bag with no apparent ill effects.

He put the bag on the counter. Jo watched as if in a trance, her thoughts filled with the image on the cover, and of the two naked figures so graphically depicted.

'Was there anything else?'

She shook her head slowly. 'No.'

She dropped the money and picked up the bag, backing away from the counter, her eyes still fixed on the man's. It wasn't until she bumped into a cabinet, rattling the china inside that she came to her senses. Then, hugging the bag to her body, she turned and fled from the shop.

Three

By the time she staggered out of the shop, Jo's mind was a whirl, and her body was behaving in a manner totally alien to her. Her sex felt as if it was on fire, and the urge to caress it was almost overwhelming. She couldn't understand what was happening to her. All at once her entire body was alive with desire. A desire she had never imagined before.

She hurried off down the street. She must get home. She was certain people were starting to stare at her flushed face and the way she was breathing so heavily.

She wished she was closer to her flat. The town was more than a mile from home, and as she left its outskirts and turned down the forest track that led across country to the estate where she lived, she was almost running.

She tried to blot out the images that kept filling her brain. Images of naked young men with thick, rigid cocks who pursued her into the wood, laying her down on the grass and tearing her clothes from her before thrusting their manhoods into her. She saw herself tied to one of the trees, like the woman in the picture, a whip laying thin red stripes across her backside. She saw herself stretched naked across Lucy's bed whilst the girl and her lover thrust heavy, buzzing vibrators into her sex and backside. And all the time the desires within her increased until they became almost unbearable.

She came to a halt, leaning against a strong oak, her breasts rising and falling as she panted with desire. It was no good. She'd never last until she got home. She needed to do something now to release the delicious tension inside her that was growing more intense by the second

She glanced about her to reassure herself that she was alone, then plunged off the track into the wood. A narrow game path twisted and turned between the trees and she followed it for a short distance until she reached a small clearing by a river.

She dropped her parcel, then grabbed for the zip on her skirt, almost tearing the garment as she dragged it down over her hips and off. Then she ripped off her panties, tossed them aside and reached for her slit.

'Ah!'

She gave a cry of release as her fingers found her clitoris. It was like she had never felt it before, hard as a nut and protruding between the lips of her sex. As she touched it a spasm ran through her, making her sex lips twitch and releasing a hot, humid feeling within her.

She leant back against a tree and, spreading her legs, thrust a finger deep inside her vagina, whimpering slightly at the delicious sensation it gave her. She inserted a second, moving them back and forth as she struggled to satisfy her lust. She couldn't understand what had come over her, why her desires had been so suddenly and rudely awakened by the book, but she knew she must have relief from the extraordinary craving that welled up inside her.

She thought of the way Lucy had masturbated, and suddenly realised that she needed to caress her breasts. Already she could feel her erect nipples chafing against her bra and she tore at the buttons of her blouse, shrugged it off, then pulled the undergarment over her head, too impatient to undo the catch.

She was naked now, and it felt wonderful. She squeezed and caressed her breasts, rolling the nipples between finger and thumb whilst she continued to masturbate hard with her other hand.

Jo had had no idea that anything could feel so wonderful. She stood, her back arched, her knees bent, her fingers diving in and out of her slit. Now at last she understood what arousal meant, and what it was that had motivated Lucy to try to use the vibrator on her that morning. She thought of the sex toy. If only she had it now. The memory of it made her fingers seem inadequate to achieve the thrill her body suddenly craved, and she began to wonder what else she could use.

Then she saw the man.

He must have been there all along, but she had failed to notice him in the combat-style suit he wore. He was holding a fishing rod, standing beside a tree not twenty yards away, his eyes fixed on Jo's body.

She gave a little cry of surprise, placing an arm across her breasts, her other hand covering her crotch. He remained where he was, still staring at her.

She wondered at the sight she must have made to him, the small, naked girl, her vibrant young flesh contrasting with the gnarled bark of the oak as she leant back against it, her legs spread wide. He must have seen everything, the pinkness of her sex lips, the wetness on her thighs, the long, hard points of her nipples as she caressed them so avidly.

And all at once the image this conjured up sent a renewed spasm of arousal through Jo's young frame. She had been giving him the most wanton display imaginable, discarding her clothes and frigging herself openly in this public place. She should be running away now, hiding her face with shame. But all she could think of was the heat in her sex, and the wonderful feeling her fingers had been giving her.

She stared down at the man's crotch. In his baggy combat gear it was impossible to tell whether he was aroused or not, but the image was enough for her in her present state, and her fingers began to move once more as she thought of his cock hardening to erectness whilst he watched her masturbate. She studied his face. He was about thirty-five, quite good looking, really, with dark hair and deep-set eyes. He was standing completely still, making no secret of his interest in the naked girl.

At that moment Jo's few remaining inhibitions flew away. The desire in her was too great. She didn't know what was happening to her, but she knew she wanted desperately to be fucked, to surrender her virginity to this dark stranger here and now, and to finally experience the pleasure of an orgasm.

She dropped her arm from her breasts, revealing their soft plumpness to him once more. Then, her fingers still deep in her vagina, she began to walk towards him. She moved slowly, still panting with lust as she worked her fingers back and forth, her breasts shaking with every movement. She stopped just in front of him and stared into his eyes. Then she reached out her other hand and closed it over his crotch.

He stepped backwards, twisting away from her, clearly taken aback by her approach.

'Who are you?' he asked.

'My name's Jo,' she replied, her fingers still circling about her love-bud.

'Do you always do this kind of thing, masturbate naked in the woods?'

'No. It's just this thing I bought . . .' Jo wanted to explain about the book, but cut herself short, afraid that he would think her mad or, worse still, would want to take the book from her. 'Don't you like me?' she asked instead.

She took her hand from her crotch and stood, her thighs thrust forward, displaying herself to him.

'You're the sexiest thing I've ever seen,' he said quietly.

'Do you want to have me?'

'Is this some kind of trick?'

'It's no trick. I want you.'

'Right here?'

'Yes.'

His reluctance was making her more impatient than ever. 'You can touch me if you like,' she said. 'Feel my breasts.' She moved closer to him. 'Go on.'

He glanced about, obviously still unable to credit what was happening to him. Then he slowly reached out his hand and placed it over her left breast. She gave a little sigh as she felt his fingers close over her soft flesh. Physical contact had never felt like this before.

He squeezed gently, closing his fingers together and trapping the hardness of her nipple between them. He took the solid teat between finger and thumb, rolling it back and forth and bringing fresh gasps from the youngster. Suddenly her entire being seemed concentrated in that small knob of flesh and she closed her eyes, her body swaying slightly as she savoured his caresses.

But it wasn't enough. There was another fire inside her that needed his attention, and once again she found herself pressing her hips forward.

'Touch me down there,' she pleaded.

He stared at her. She could see the lust in his eyes as he took in her lewd behaviour. But still he seemed reluctant.

'What's the matter?' she asked. 'Don't you want me?'

'Of course I do,' he said. 'You're beautiful and sexy and the most gorgeous woman I've ever seen.'

'Then touch me there.'

He looked into her eyes for a second longer. Then he moved his hand, sliding it off her breast and down her ribcage, running it slowly over her belly and lower towards her dark pubic bush. Jo's body was in a state of delicious tension as she felt his fingers approach the centre of her desires.

'Ah!'

She cried aloud as he found her clitoris, pressing her

hips down against his hand, the glorious sensation of his touch sending a spasm of lust through her trembling body.

'My God you're something,' he breathed.

He turned her and pressed her back against a tree, his finger still toying with her love-bud, each movement sending flashes of pleasure through her. The trunk was hard and unyielding against her soft, tender flesh, but she didn't care now. She simply wanted him to take control of her and to bring her the relief she craved

'Mmmm,' she moaned. 'Is this turning you on as much as me?'

In reply he took hold of her hand and guided it down to his crotch. Beneath the thick material of his trousers she could feel a solid bulge, and a shiver ran through her as she closed her hand over it.

'I want to see you,' she murmured. 'And to feel you.'

He kissed her on the lips. 'Go ahead.'

Her hands shaking, she fumbled with his zip, taking it between finger and thumb and pulling it down.

For a second she hesitated. Then, taking a deep breath, she slid her hand into his fly and delved into his briefs.

Through the thin nylon of his pants his cock felt harder than ever, communicating to her the heat of his passion. Her excitement increasing, she took hold of the waistband of his briefs and pulled them down.

His erection sprang free almost at once, projecting up from his groin, thick and pink. Jo's hand shook as she wrapped her fingers about his shaft. She simply couldn't believe what was happening to her. She had almost come to accept that she would remain a virgin all her life, never experiencing the thrill of a cock inside her. And now here she was, blatantly and outrageously naked, with a man's fingers inside her whilst she stroked a long, hard tool.

She began to work his foreskin back and forth, feeling

his cock twitch as she did so. She ran her other hand underneath and felt for his balls. His scrotum was tight and contracted against the base of his penis and she squeezed it gently, making him moan quietly as she did so.

She looked into his eyes. 'Are we going to do it?' she asked, her face a picture of innocent beauty.

'Do you want to?'

'Yes.'

'Lie down on the grass.'

There was a slight croakiness in the man's voice as he gave the order, and she could see the arousal in his face as she continued to masturbate him. Slowly, uncertainly, she let go of his erection and lowered herself to the grass, stretching out on her back. Then she spread her legs, opening the portals of her sex to him. Staring into his eyes, she began to play with herself once more, her fingers sliding into her vagina.

The man dropped to his knees between her thighs and reached out, brushing her hand from her sex and running his own rough fingers over her slit.

'Oh yes,' she murmured. 'Please take me now.'

The man withdrew his fingers. Then he was lowering himself over her and she caught her breath as she felt the solid, bulbous end of his knob pressing against her sex.

'Oh!'

Another exclamation escaped her lips as he slid into her. She hadn't known what to expect. She had been afraid it would hurt. Instead it was the most gorgeous sensation imaginable and she moaned aloud as he pressed deep within her, forcing the walls of her sex apart and burying himself to the hilt.

Then he began to fuck her.

With a scream she came, the orgasm almost taking her by surprise. Waves of pleasure swept over her body as she at last experienced the exquisite joy of a climax, the muscles of her sex convulsing about his cock as it thrust into her.

'My God you're hot,' he marvelled. 'I've hardly started.'

'Don't stop,' she begged. 'Do it harder. Oh God that's good.'

Even as the intensity of the orgasm began to wane she could feel another building within her. Now that the immediacy of her need was satisfied she was able to savour the treatment she was receiving, pressing her own hips up against his as she matched him stroke for stroke.

He began to caress her breasts, squeezing and kneading the pliant flesh, once more taking the hard buds of her nipples between his fingers and rubbing hard, sending tingles of pleasure through her.

Jo was in heaven, her lovely body shaken by spasms of lust as he drove hard into her body. She had never experienced anything so pleasurable, and she wanted it to go on forever.

All of a sudden she felt the man's muscles go tense and she looked up into his face. His eyes were tight shut, his teeth clenched, the veins in his neck bulging out. Then he gave a shout, and he was coming, spurts of semen suddenly filling Jo's vagina as his cock twitched violently.

Jo gave a hoarse cry as a second orgasm struck her, the sensation of his seed squirting into her making this one even more pleasurable than the first. Her backside banged down against the grass as she crashed her hips against his, her sex muscles tightening about his cock, as if trying to draw the semen from his balls and into her.

Jo seemed to come and come, her body writhing beneath him as he filled her with spunk. It was the most glorious sensation of her life, and she wanted it to go on forever.

Gradually, though, they both began to come down,

the throbbing of his cock becoming less urgent as his seed was spent. Jo felt his movements start to slow, and at the same time her own muscles began gradually to relax, the urgent thrill of the orgasm giving way to a warm satisfied glow as her body finally came back under her control.

His movements became slower and slower. The last dribbles of semen seeped from him, until at last the pair of them were still, both panting for breath as they lay on the soft grass, their bodies still intimately joined.

Jo looked up into his face and smiled at him, a smile of blissful contentment.

'I forgot to ask you your name,' she said.

Four

Jo sat in her armchair, staring across at the white carrier bag that lay in the corner, precisely where she had placed it two weeks before. The room was quite gloomy, the window closed and the curtains drawn, despite the warmth of the lovely summer's day. Through the window the sound of birdsong could be faintly heard, along with the cries of children playing, but here, in the room, there was silence.

Jo sighed the sigh of one who had been wrestling with a problem for so long that she scarcely remembered what the problem was. She rose and walked slowly across the room to the bag. It was made of white plastic, with no markings, and through it she could discern the shape of the book inside and could just make out the title, *Secrets of the Whipcord.* She crouched lower. The picture that adorned the front was just visible, and her stomach knotted as she realised that she was seeing the face of that hapless, naked woman as she stood, still tethered to the post. Jo closed her eyes and turned away, retreating to the far side of the room, fearful of her own emotions. The merest glimpse of the illustration had already begun to stir some of those unfamiliar emotions that had led to the scene with the fisherman beside the river.

She felt her face redden as the memory came back to her. How could she possibly have behaved in such a manner? What could have possessed her to strip off her clothes as she had, and flaunt herself so wantonly? And what must the man have thought of her, panting and gasping like an animal on heat, and shamelessly giving her body to him?

Yet still her eyes were drawn back to the bag in the corner. That book had been at the root of it all. It had to be. There was nothing else that could possibly explain the extraordinary way in which she had behaved. The intimate descriptions of the woman's ordeals, and the explicit pictures showing her submitting to the men's treatment. That was what had started it.

Yet it wasn't just the words. The physical volume itself, the very leather and paper that made it up, seemed to play a part. She recalled the texture of the cover, and the way the depictions on the front had seemed to come to life under her fingers, so that it was as if she was touching real flesh. As real as the flesh of the fisherman's rampant cock that had invaded her so deliciously.

Once again Jo closed her eyes, unable to reconcile the conflicting thoughts that filled her head: on the one hand the shame and humiliation of the way she had behaved, on the other the exquisite pleasure of the orgasms she had experienced at the hands of that man.

During the previous two weeks Jo had, on numerous occasions, resolved to get rid of the book, to take it out and throw it away, and to restore her life to the way it had been before she had entered that infernal bookshop. But she couldn't bring herself to touch even the bag in which it lay, fearful of the effect it might have on her. She had even considered asking Lucy to get rid of it for her, but was afraid of the questions the girl might ask, and even more afraid that she would read the book, and draw the conclusion that Jo was really into that sort of thing.

Since their encounter in Lucy's bedroom, Jo had found herself terribly embarrassed whilst in Lucy's presence, although her flatmate had made no allusion to the incident and seemed quite unaware of any tension that might now exist between the two girls. Once again, Jo was totally unable to understand the topsy-turvy way in which the whole thing had turned out. Surely it was Lucy who should feel embarrassed and ashamed by the incident, and who should be finding it difficult to meet her flatmate's eyes? Instead it was she, Jo, who felt the guilt. Was it really her that was in the wrong? The more she thought about it, the more confused she became.

The other problem was the dreams.

They had begun the night of her encounter by the river, and had continued every night since then. They were like no dreams Jo had ever experienced before. Vivid dreams in which she found herself sharing the dilemma of the women in the book. She would see herself dragged naked through the streets by evil men, who would lash out at her with long, cruel sticks, driving her on to a place of public punishment where a crowd would watch the lash laid across her back. At other times she would be a slave, forced to service both men and women with her body or face further merciless beatings.

She would often awake from these dreams crying aloud, her body bathed in sweat, like a child waking from a nightmare. But these were like no nightmare she had ever experienced. For it wasn't fear that she felt, but a quite different emotion, one that she found much more difficult to comprehend. She would awake with a desire within her that she couldn't recognise. A desire that would make her slide her fingers down to her crotch and find it strangely wet. Sometimes she even dreamt that she had had an orgasm, but could never be certain whether it had been in her mind, or whether her body had genuinely responded physically to the thoughts that were coursing through her brain. Whatever it was, it simply seemed to feed a craving within her, but she couldn't identify what it was she craved. All she knew was that there was something missing from her life, and it needed replacing. Now, as she sat once again contemplating the contents of the bag, she knew she had to do something about it.

In her heart she was aware of what must be done. She must test the book, to see whether it would have the same effect on her again. The problem was, how to do it? She couldn't risk a recurrence of what had happened in the wood. As it turned out, the man had been a normal, hot-blooded male, and the incident had proved mutually pleasurable to the pair of them. But what if he had been some kind of psychopath? Or even a religious nut who was offended by her nudity, and who reported her to the authorities? She didn't fancy having her face splashed across the front pages of the local paper in some kind of sex scandal. Besides, the bank where she worked would never countenance such a thing, and she ran the risk of losing everything. No, if she was to test the power of the book again, it would have to be under controlled conditions. All she needed was a man on whom to test it.

Having finally reached a decision to take action, Jo found herself suddenly more relaxed than she had been for some time. All at once the bag in the corner ceased to be something to fear, but rather an opportunity to change her life for the better. A weight had been lifted from her shoulders, and she found her mind much clearer as she returned to her armchair and began to plan how she would carry out the test.

She would need a man. One that she could trust, and one who, like the man in the wood, would not be shocked or put off by the prospect of casual sex with her.

Casual sex! The very words sent a shiver through her. She could scarcely believe that she was sitting here coolly planning a seduction that would end in bed with a man.

But what if it didn't? What if her experience in the wood was simply a coincidence? After all she had had a most unusual encounter with Lucy that morning. Who was to say that her behaviour hadn't been sparked off by a delayed reaction to the session with the dildo? Perhaps she had been mistaken!

No. She shook her head vigorously. It had been the book that had turned her on. After all she had practically run a mile when Lucy had suggested using the toy on her, yet she had allowed herself to be fucked by the stranger with barely a second thought. It had to be the book. The question was, could it have the same effect again? There was only one way to be certain. She had to go ahead with the test and find out.

So what she needed was a man in the flat. A man who would find her attractive, and would respond positively to any advances made by her. But who?

Then it came to her. Peter! The young man whose advances she had spurned two weeks earlier. The event that had, indirectly, led to her being in the shop, buying the book, and, subsequently, to the encounter in the wood.

The more she thought about it, the more she realised that he was the ideal candidate – young, good looking, and clearly attracted to her. And, should the experiment not prove successful, he would be unlikely to be too disgruntled. After all, after his first rejection, he would hardly be expecting some kind of sex romp.

Jo's mind was made up. She would call Peter up to apologise for her previous behaviour and invite him round for dinner, ostensibly to make up for what had been said. Then, once he was here, she would test the powers of the book. It was perfect.

She checked her diary. It would have to be a night when she had the house to herself. A Tuesday would be ideal, since on those nights Lucy was always out at what she called her club, and always returned late, if at all.

Jo looked across at the bag in which the book lay, and once again she felt her stomach fill with butterflies as she contemplated it. If it really did have the powers she suspected, she was in for quite an experience.

Her hand trembling slightly, she reached for the phone and began punching in Peter's number.

Five

Jo fussed about the dinner table, minutely adjusting the positions of the cutlery and crockery and gazing critically at the wine glasses to assure herself that they were crystal clear. She glanced at the clock. It was five to eight. Peter was due at eight. She went round the table for the umpteenth time to assure herself that everything was perfect.

Having been unable to find any fault with the settings, she slipped into her bedroom to make a final check on her own appearance. She needn't have bothered. Jo looked stunning. She wore a small black evening dress, cut low at the front, the skirt extremely short so that it showed off her long legs perfectly. She had elected for black stockings, held up by a suspender belt, and elegant black high-heeled shoes to complete the outfit. There was no doubt about it, Jo was dressed to kill that night.

Giving her hair a couple of final, and quite unnecessary, pats, Jo went through to the kitchen. She peered anxiously through the glass door of the oven. The casserole was bubbling away merrily, and smelt very good indeed. The seafood cocktails were laid out on the side, and in the fridge a fresh fruit salad was cooling nicely. Nothing to worry about there. She ran her hands down the bottle of red wine that stood on the side, testing the temperature. It felt just right, and a sniff at the cork of the already open bottle told her that it was good.

There was still one more thing to check.

Jo crouched down and opened the kitchen cupboard. There, lying on its side, was the bag containing the book. She had moved it that evening, wearing gloves and carrying the bag between finger and thumb, as if afraid of some kind of infection. It had been the first time she had disturbed the package since she had brought it home, and it was with great relief that she had closed the cupboard with no ill effects whatsoever.

The sound of the doorbell made her jump, and at once a feeling of guilt assailed her, as if she had been caught doing something she shouldn't. She hurriedly slammed the cupboard door and rose to her feet. She suppressed the urge to check herself in the bedroom mirror again and headed for the door.

'Hello.'

Peter stood before her, smiling nervously. He was wearing smart slacks and a white shirt, a bright tie knotted at his collar. He was carrying a bottle of white wine.

'I brought this.'

She smiled back, aware that her own expression was equally uneasy.

'That's kind,' she said. 'I've got a bottle to have with the meal, but we can open this one now if you like.'

She showed him into the living room. He had never visited her at her flat before. In fact this was the first time she had entertained a man at home without others being present, and she found herself momentarily at a loss for what to say.

'I'll get a corkscrew,' she muttered.

Once the wine was opened and both of them had a glass, the atmosphere quickly began to thaw. Jo was soon reminded of what good company Peter had been on their last meeting, and in no time both were laughing as if their previous encounter had never happened.

The meal was perfect, much to her relief – the chicken tender, the spices delicious. Peter was an appreciative guest and she could tell that he genuinely enjoyed her cooking. By the time they both settled down on the sofa with a coffee, they were feeling very mellow.

It wasn't until Peter touched her hand that Jo felt the old, familiar rigidity suddenly return to her limbs as, quite involuntarily, she found herself drawing away from him.

Immediately she felt the atmosphere change as he withdrew his fingers.

'Sorry,' he said. 'I know you don't fancy me that way.'

She shook her head. 'It isn't like that,' she protested. 'I really like you.'

'That's okay,' he said. 'I'll behave from now on.'

'No,' she said. 'I mean yes. I mean . . . I've got to put a couple of dishes into soak. Excuse me.'

She headed for the kitchen.

'Do you want me to go?' he asked.

'No. Please stay. There's some brandy in the cupboard. Pour yourself one. I'll be back in a minute.'

She hurried into the kitchen, closing the door behind her. Once inside she dropped to her knees in front of the cupboard and pulled it open. For a few seconds she stared at the white plastic bag. Then she reached out for it.

Her hand closed about the book, and she pulled it out of the bag. If she had been expecting an immediate effect, she was disappointed. The leather felt soft, but there was no special sensation as she lifted it up and placed it on the table.

For a moment she felt a twinge of concern. Perhaps she was wrong. Perhaps it hadn't been the book at all, but simply some mental aberration that had caused her to behave in such an extraordinary manner that afternoon. Maybe she had made a big mistake in inviting Peter. Then her eyes fell on the extraordinary illustration that adorned the front of the book, and she suddenly felt an odd thrill at the pit of her stomach.

Her fingers trembling, she opened the book at a random page and began to read. Almost at once she found herself totally absorbed by the words. A woman was being strapped to a device in a dungeon by two men. She was quite naked, and the book described in loving detail how the men manacled her hands and feet, leaving her spread-eagled across a wooden bench before tightening the chains that held her. Once again the illustrations were quite explicit and Jo found herself staring in fascination at the detailed drawing, in which the woman's pale and naked flesh made a stark contrast to the heavy leather clad figures of her jailers. As with the cover illustration, the expression on the woman's face was a beautifully depicted mixture of anguish and arousal, and Jo found herself almost hypnotised by her eyes.

She read on, her pulse quickening as the book described how the men teased the woman's nipples to erection before placing cruel, needle sharp clamps over the flesh. Then they began to whip her, leaving thin, stinging weals across her breasts and belly, the pair working in unison whilst the woman's cries echoed about the chamber.

Jo was unable to take her eyes from the text as she felt the unfamiliar stirrings within her. She was panting slightly with excitement as she read on. She picked the book up, cradling it in her fingers, and almost at once it felt soft and warm to the touch, as if it was bare flesh she was feeling rather than dry old leather.

She turned the page and was confronted by a new illustration, this one showing the woman, her body crisscrossed with whip marks, sucking hard at the rampant cock of one of her jailers whilst the other was inserting the handle of his whip into her vagina. The picture made her gasp aloud, and her own crotch suddenly filled with a warm wetness as she contemplated the woman's predicament.

'What's going on? You've been ages.'

The sound of Peter's voice just behind her made Jo start, and she almost dropped the book. She slammed it shut as he came up behind her, her face reddening. She put it down on the table and turned to face him, feeling very flustered indeed.

'Sorry,' she said. 'I got a bit distracted.'

'What were you reading? It didn't look like a Mills and Boon.'

'No, just some old book I found in an antique shop. Let's go back into the living room.'

To her relief, Peter showed no further interest in the book, and happily accompanied her out of the kitchen.

Jo found her hands shaking as she poured them both a brandy, and when she sat down beside Peter, the scent of his aftershave and the closeness of his body sent a shiver of arousal through her. There was no question that the book's effect was the same as before. With every second, Jo felt the heat in her body increase, her nipples chafing against her bra as they stiffened to erection. She thought of the woman in the book, and of the cruel clamps that had bitten into the flesh of her teats and her body was hot with excitement.

'You okay?' asked Peter suddenly. 'You look a bit flushed.'

'It – It must be the brandy,' she stammered. But she knew it wasn't. It was desire that was affecting her so. Pure, wanton desire. Jo was totally aroused now, and as she reached across and took his hand, the contact with his flesh served only to increase that arousal.

She knew that, after her previous rejection of him, it was up to her to take the initiative now. She moved towards him and, wrapping an arm behind his head, pulled his face close to hers. Their lips met, and almost at once she was forcing her tongue into his mouth, drawing him close to her, loving the feel of his strong body pressed against hers.

Peter's initial reaction was one of surprise, and she

felt him tense as she pressed herself closer. But no man could have resisted the pure sexual urge that coursed through the lovely youngster's body, and almost at once she felt him wrap his arms about her and pull her to him.

The kiss went on and on, the two locked together as they licked hungrily at each other's tongues. At the same time, Jo felt Peter slide his hand up her flank and close over her breast, his fingers squeezing the soft flesh through her dress. The contact sent new tremors of excitement through her, and at once she wanted to be naked and to have his hands touch her bare flesh.

She pulled her mouth from his and rose to her feet, He tried to hold on to her but she twisted out of his arms.

'What is it?'

She placed a finger on her lips. Then, standing just in front of him, she reached behind her and pulled down the zipper on her dress.

The dress fell away, and she kicked it aside. Peter's eyes positively bulged as he took her in. Her bra, like the dress, was black, small and low-cut, her erect nipples outlined against the silk. Her matching panties dipped down to a vee, the darkness of her pubic triangle showing through the transparent panels at the front. Her suspender belt, also black, was small and lacy, the stockings it supported leaving a portion of smooth, creamy thigh above.

Jo paused, loving the way Peter was staring at her, aware of how arousing her lovely young body was to him. She wanted to strip slowly, to tantalise him as she gradually laid bare her charms, but there was an urgency in her now, a wanton desire that she couldn't suppress for much longer.

She unhooked the catch on her bra, sliding it down her arms and off. Her breasts felt extraordinarily tender, and she reached up and caressed her nipple, marvelling at the hardness of the flesh and the way it protruded, almost as if it was inviting a pair of lips to close over it, or a tight little clamp to bite into its rubbery texture.

The thought of clamps brought a fresh gasp of lust from the panting girl. She stroked and caressed her lovely, firm mammaries, her eyes fixed on Peter's astonished face.

She let her gaze drop to his crotch, and saw at once the bulge in his pants. She imagined his cock, stiff and hard beneath the thin layer of material and once again her thoughts went back to the woman in the book and the way she had sucked so enthusiastically at her jailer's stiff erection.

Jo dropped her hands to her panties, a new urgency gripping her at the memory of the picture. She slid her thumbs into the waistband and slid them off, over her hips and down her legs, and raising her feet, she kicked them aside. Then she stood, her legs slightly parted, her hands on her hips, staring down at Peter, her heart hammering. She had never felt so sexy, and she knew she looked irresistible, standing there clad in only stockings, suspenders and shoes.

Gradually she slid her right hand down, across her belly and into the short, dark thatch of her pubic triangle. She moved it lower, her fingers feeling for her clitoris. As she touched it she let out a moan of desire. It was hard and moist, and the slightest touch sent spasms of pleasure through her young body. She raised her head and looked directly at Peter.

'Do you like what you see?' she asked, her forefinger describing small circles about her love-bud.

Peter nodded. Small beads of sweat had broken out on his forehead and the bulge in his pants was growing larger by the minute.

'Would you like to touch?'

Once again he nodded.

Jo reached for his wrist with her free hand, guiding it

up to her breast. She placed it over the soft flesh, loving the sensation of having his hand close about her firm globe.

He squeezed her, his hand stroking the puckered flesh of her nipple and bringing another low moan from her lips. She stood, still masturbating as he caressed her there, her body in a state of delicious tension.

Suddenly a strong hand brushed her fingers away from her sex. She let her arm drop to her side as he slipped a finger into her vagina.

The climax hit her suddenly and unexpectedly. One minute she had been standing quietly, holding her body steady as she fought to control her desires, the next she was moaning and gasping, her legs practically giving way as she ground her hips down against his hand, extracting every last ounce of pleasure from his finger, her breasts quivering deliciously as her body rocked back and forth.

Peter seemed taken by surprise by her orgasm, but he kept his finger firmly embedded in her, using his thumb to rub her clitoris to prolong the ecstasy for her.

Jo dropped to her knees, wrapping her arms about his neck and pulling him to her, feeling the rough material of his shirt against her breasts as she held him close. She kissed him again, once more feeling the tingling pleasure of his tongue entwined with her own, but this time with the exquisite sensation of his finger deep in her sex, her body squirming as she pressed herself against him.

When at last she pulled back from the embrace she was still panting from the force of her orgasm. She wanted to curl up in his arms and regain her breath, but she knew that he would have other ideas, and that the evening's pleasure had only just begun.

She ran her hand over his crotch, feeling the hard lump that seemed to strain against the material of his trousers. All at once she had an urgent need to see him, to touch him, to taste him. She fumbled with his fly, yanking at the zipper and delving inside. Her hand closed about something thick and hard and vibrant with life. Carefully she slipped his cock from his pants and it sprang free, standing hard and long from his fly.

Tentatively she slid her fingers down its length, tracing the thick veins, feeling it pulse beneath her touch. She pulled back the foreskin and admired the shiny purple helmet thus revealed. She worked the hood back and forth, pleased with the way it made him groan at the sensation.

Then she could resist it no more and, lowering her head into his lap, she took his hard rod into her mouth. She began to suck, continuing to work her fist up and down his shaft as she did so. Once again he moaned aloud, thrusting his hips upwards and pressing his cock deeper into her mouth so that she was afraid he might make her gag. Still she sucked with vigour, the taste and smell of his manhood awakening primeval instincts within her.

Her hands went to his shirt, almost ripping it apart in her urgency to undo the buttons. She pulled it over his shoulders and off, whilst still keeping her mouth locked on his erection. His trousers and pants followed with equal speed, and soon he too was naked.

She let his cock slip from her mouth, sitting back to admire his body, her hand still working his foreskin back and forth. He had a strong chest, covered with dark hairs. Another line of hair ran down from just below his navel, thickening until it opened into the dark bush of his pubic hair. His penis stood stiff and proud, his large balls compressed by his wrinkled scrotum. She took this tight sac in her palm, kneading it gently and bringing new moans of pleasure from him.

Suddenly Jo was aroused again, and this time she wanted the real thing. She could scarcely credit how rapacious she had become since reading the book. She needed him inside her now and, as she looked up into his eyes she could see her own desire mirrored there.

Slowly, without speaking, she released her hold on his rod and moved backwards, prostrating herself across the floor on her back. Then, gazing up at him, she spread her legs apart, revealing the pink wetness of her love hole.

He dropped to his knees in front of her, his cock rhythmically bobbing up and down as he took in her lovely young body. He slid a hand over her stocking tops, moving it up the smooth skin of her thigh, making her almost scream with frustration as it inched closer to her sex. Then he was there, his thumb slipping into her slit, sliding over the wetness inside as it moved toward her clitoris.

Once again the feel of his thumb against her sensitive little bud sent shudders of desire through her. But she wanted no more foreplay, and she pushed his hand away.

'Do it to me,' she said.

Peter moved his body forward, and she reached out for his cock, guiding it toward the centre of her desire as he lowered himself over her. Such was her state of lubrication, he penetrated her easily, his long penis nuzzling against the entrance to her vagina before slipping inside. She gave a groan of pleasure as he pressed it home, forcing it ever deeper into her until his hips were pressed hard against hers and the two were totally united.

He placed his mouth over her mouth and kissed her again as he began to pump his hips back and forth. At the same time he groped for her breast, grasping it firmly in his hand, his fingers teasing her nipples. He started fucking her hard, driving down against her. Jo responded by wrapping her legs about his body, pulling him down, urging him to probe even deeper into the heat of her love hole and to bring her the satisfaction she craved. She had never felt so totally united to another human being. The tongue that invaded her mouth, the hand that stroked and squeezed her breast and, most of all, the thick cock that pumped in and out of her vagina seemed to join her utterly to this lovely young man. It was as if they were one being, their bodies and their pleasure shared as they conjoined in the most intimate way possible.

Such was her arousal, Jo knew that she couldn't last long, and she sensed that Peter too was already approaching his climax. His thrusts were becoming stronger and stronger, his hips pounding against hers as she matched him stroke for stroke, her bottom coming clear of the carpet as she pressed up at him.

He came with a grunt, his cock suddenly unleashing a gush of sperm into her, then another, then another. His penis seemed to expand as it released his seed, every spurt making it twitch inside her in the most delicious way. Within seconds Jo was coming too, groaning with delight; her previous orgasm was nothing compared to the sheer joy of having a live cock ejaculating deep inside her.

He drove on into her, his semen continuing to fill her, albeit less forcefully now. She clung to him, her mouth still fast against his as she drew the last vestiges of pleasure from him. Only when his thrusts had finally ceased did she break the kiss, throwing her head back and allowing her arms and legs to fall from him, so that she lay spread-eagled and passive beneath his body.

He lifted himself from her, his cock slipping out of her as he rose to his knees. He gazed down at her. She felt a trickle of his spunk escape from her vagina and seep down the crack of her backside. She smiled up at him.

'Shall we go into the bedroom?' she said.

Six

Jo lay on her bed, staring at the ceiling, re-enacting the encounter with Peter for the umpteenth time. She ran her hands over the linen, recalling how the pair of them had slept between those very sheets, and had enjoyed still more orgasms together before he had crept out at the crack of dawn and left her, exhausted and satisfied, to sleep until late.

It had been nearly a week since Peter's visit, but hardly a moment had gone by without Jo recalling some aspect of his lovemaking, and of the pleasure he had given her with his body. For the first time in ages she felt a whole woman, and it was a very good feeling.

She glanced up at the mantelpiece, where the book lay. She had moved it from the kitchen on the morning after her dinner party, being careful not to look inside for fear of arousing herself once more. Now she regarded it with mixed feelings as she lay in the semi-darkness of her room. On the one hand, she knew it had freed her from the block that had for so long prevented her from enjoying the active sex life that she craved. With the help of the book, she knew she need never again freeze up in the presence of a prospective lover. On the other hand, though, she was afraid that the book may become something of a crutch to her, without which she couldn't allow herself to enjoy the sex she desired so intensely.

The book puzzled her. The sex depicted in it was nothing like what she had experienced with Peter, or with the man by the river. It depicted women being tied and beaten, then being taken by rough men who never sought consent, though consent was implicit in the way that the women submitted. It was as if they enjoyed the whipping and the clamps, as if it turned them on and was the foreplay to the final consummation of their desires.

The whole thing didn't seem to make sense. Yet wasn't it true that she herself was equally aroused by the book? That the descriptions and illustrations of the young women being so maltreated were what had originally turned her on? The scenes in which the women were screwed were arousing, certainly. But it was the dimension of pain and servitude that had first held Jo's attention, and that had begun those stirrings of lust that had culminated in the two glorious sex sessions. Now, as she thought back, she realised that, wonderful though the sex itself had been, there was still something missing. Something that she felt would bring her total arousal, and possibly even free her from her reliance on the book.

A sound from outside her bedroom roused Jo from her thoughts. She glanced at her watch. It must be Lucy, she supposed, though she hadn't expected the girl home this early. She was slightly irritated by her flatmate's return. She herself had planned to go to the cinema that evening, but the friend with whom she was going had pulled out, so she had decided on a quiet night at home, alone with her thoughts. Now it looked as if she would have company.

All at once she heard voices. For a moment she thought that Lucy had brought a man home with her, and she felt a tinge of envy. Then, to her surprise, she realised that the other voice was female. She couldn't remember Lucy ever bringing another woman home. She wondered who it could be. A friend from work, possibly, or someone from the mysterious club she attended once a week.

Suddenly overcome by curiosity, Jo rose from the bed and crept towards the door. It was open a crack and she peered through into the living room.

There was Lucy, dressed in jeans and a T-shirt. She was standing by the table opening a bottle of red wine. As Jo watched, the cork popped out and she began pouring the contents into two wine glasses. She held one out to her companion, who was hidden from Jo's sight by the door.

The two exchanged a few words. Jo strained to hear what was being said, but they spoke in low voices, making it impossible. The conversation went on for some minutes, then Lucy crossed the room and headed towards her bedroom.

Jo stayed where she was, her eyes glued to the crack in the door. She heard Lucy's voice again. She was calling from her room, so her words were much clearer.

'Get yourself prepared.'

'Out here?' The girl's voice was high, and Jo wasn't sure whether she detected a note of anxiety in it.

'Don't worry. My flatmate's out. We've got the place to ourselves. Now hurry up.'

'Yes, mistress.'

Jo was puzzled by the exchange. What could they possibly be planning to do that would make the girl concerned as to whether she, Jo, was at home or not? And why had she addressed her flatmate in that strange way?

At that moment the girl moved into Jo's line of vision for the first time. She was small in stature, her brown hair long and wavy. She had a pretty face, with a small mouth and wide blue eyes. Jo's impression that there had been an edge to her voice was strengthened by her expression, which was decidedly nervous, her eyes dancing from side to side. She was wearing a dark coat that came down halfway to her knees. It was loose fitting, obscuring the girl's figure.

'You ready yet?' came Lucy's voice again.

'Not yet, mistress.'

'You'd better hurry, or it'll be the worse for you.'

'Yes, mistress.'

The girl glanced about her once again. For a second, Jo was afraid that she might be detected, but, with the curtains drawn, her room was almost in darkness. Standing where she was, she was virtually invisible. She watched with mounting interest as the girl began undoing the buttons on her coat.

The girl undid the coat all the way to the bottom, then shrugged it off. Jo's jaw dropped as she saw what she wore underneath.

It was a sort of leather bikini, entirely in black. The top was very brief, with no shoulder straps. It was extremely tight, pressing the girl's breasts upwards from beneath, so that the white skin bulged over the top. Her breasts were not large, but were in good proportion to her petite figure, and the tightness of the bra enhanced their shape in a way that fascinated Jo. Below she had on the smallest of briefs, once again very tight and so low across her hips that Jo knew she must have had to shave her pubic hair to prevent it being visible over the top. Apart from these and a pair of shiny high heels, the only other thing the girl had were thin leather bands about her wrists and ankles and a collar that encircled her neck, decorated all the way round with silver studs.

It was the most extraordinary outfit Jo had ever seen, and yet it reminded her of something. She seemed to have seen a girl similarly clad somewhere before. Then she realised. It was in the book. One of the illustrations had shown a girl dressed in an almost identical manner, tied in a dungeon whilst her jailers prepared to punish her. But what could it mean? That sort of thing was pure fantasy, surely?

Jo's thoughts were interrupted by the sound of Lucy's bedroom door opening. The girl's reaction was instant.

Throwing the coat to one side she dropped to her knees on the carpet, her thighs apart, clasping her hands together on top of her head.

If the young stranger's attire had been a cause of surprise to Jo, it was nothing compared to the shock she received when her friend entered the room. Lucy was wearing a one-piece costume in shiny, black PVC. A strap ran round the back of her neck, supporting the bodice, which was cut low, enhancing the blonde girl's cleavage. It was cinched at the waist by a small belt, beneath which, on either side, was bare thigh encased in black fishnet tights. The crotch consisted of a narrow band that ran down from the waist, clinging tightly to her sex, so narrow that, once again, Jo knew that it must have necessitated the shaving of a good deal of pubic hair. On her feet she wore shiny boots that came up almost to her knees, with high heels and clinking spurs. The outfit was completed by a black cap, like an officer's cap, which she wore pulled down slightly over her eyes.

Lucy strode into the room with a genuine swagger, her expression grim. In her hand she held what appeared to be a horse whip, and she slapped it against her boots, making a loud cracking sound.

'Stand up!'

The words were snapped out like an order, and the girl obeyed at once, springing to her feet and standing, her legs apart, her hands still clasped on her head.

Lucy began slowly to walk round the smaller girl, eyeing her up and down, as if carrying out a military inspection. For her part the girl said nothing, but Jo was certain she was trembling slightly. From where Jo stood, the girl was almost sideways on to her, and Lucy came to a halt standing directly in front of the young beauty.

Lucy stretched out the whip, pushing the end under the girl's chin and lifting her face up so that their eyes were forced to meet.

'Why are you here, Patsy?' she asked the girl.

'Because I was sent for, mistress.'

'Who sent for you?'

'You did, mistress.'

'And why do you think I sent for you?'

'To –' the girl's voice trailed away.

Whack!

Jo gave a start as Lucy brought the whip down across the girl's thigh. It was a sharp, spiteful crack that left a thin red stripe down the youngster's leg. Jo saw her bite her lip, but she said nothing.

'Why?' barked Lucy.

'For punishment, mistress.'

'That's better. And why must you be punished?'

'I – I didn't attend the meeting, mistress.'

'That's right. You know that when you are summoned you must attend.'

'I couldn't, mistress. My boyfriend. He wouldn't let me. He made me stay at home with him.'

'Did you fuck?'

The girl dropped her eyes. 'Yes, mistress. He's found out about my . . . About the way I am.'

'He knows you're submissive?'

'Yes mistress. He keeps giving me orders and making me obey him.'

'Nevertheless, you received a summons. You know that is a rare occurrence, and that when it comes it must be obeyed. Yet you chose to ignore it.'

'I couldn't. My boyfriend . . .'

Whack!

Once again the whip descended across the girl's thigh, leaving a second stripe.

'No more excuses, Patsy!' said Lucy.

She began to run the whip down the girl's neck, allowing the end to trace the bulging curves of her breasts.

'Such pretty little titties,' she said, her voice suddenly low and seductive. 'What a shame it would be to lay some stripes across that lovely skin. And what would your boyfriend say if he saw that we'd decorated your breasts with the marks of the whip?'

The girl called Patsy's eyes widened, but she said nothing. For her part, Jo couldn't believe what she was seeing and hearing. There was her flatmate, normally the friendliest of girls, suddenly acting like some kind of dominatrix and actually threatening to whip this girl's breasts. And the girl was offering no resistance, as if she were somehow under Lucy's power.

Lucy moved the whip under the swell of the girl's breasts, alternately pressing the undersides with it whilst the youngster stood silent and passive.

'No, not the breasts this time,' she mused. 'We'll save them for the next time you misbehave. Go and stand by that wall.'

Without a word the girl moved across the room to stand with her back to the wall, still maintaining her passive stance. Lucy followed and, tucking the whip into her belt, took hold of the young submissive's wrists.

There was a snapping sound, and Jo realised that she had joined the two wristbands together by means of small metal rings that were attached to them. Now they acted like handcuffs, linked so close that Patsy had to hold her hands with the palms pressed together, almost like a child at prayer. As Jo watched, Lucy reached up the wall to where a bracket was attached. It was quite a strong fixture, and Jo had always assumed that it had been designed to hold some kind of hanging basket in the past. Now she saw Lucy run a narrow chain through the loop on the bracket, pulling it down and passing it between the cuffs on the girl's wrists. She pulled it tight, dragging the girl's arms above her head, tightening it until her arms were stretched straight above her, the tension showing in her muscles.

Lucy fastened the chain and stood back to admire her handiwork. Patsy was now helpless, standing almost on tiptoe, her body stretched upwards. Yet still she made no protest, although her face was creased into an expression of anguish.

'Right,' said Lucy. 'I think that will stop you misbehaving. Now, let's prepare you for your punishment.'

She reached behind the girl's back, and all at once the bra came undone, dropping to the ground. The girl's breasts were firm and succulent, the mark of the bra leaving a red stripe across them just above the nipples that was almost as bright as the stripes Lucy had placed across her thigh. At the sight of her bared breasts, Jo felt a strange thrill, once again reminded of the women so graphically depicted in the book. The girl's face reddened as Lucy ran a hand over her soft swellings, and Jo was surprised to see how hard her nipples had become under the black-clad dominatrix's fingers.

Only when Lucy reached for the girl's pants did she show any sign of protest, and this was no more than a whimper as Lucy slid her fingers into the waistband. The faint sound was ignored however, and Lucy tugged the tiny briefs down, dragging them over the girl's shoes and off.

Jo's heart pounded in her chest as she took in Patsy's naked body. The pants too had been extremely tight, leaving marks across her belly and around the tops of her thighs. But it wasn't that that caught Jo's attention. She was shaved. Her pubic area was completely devoid of hair, as were the puffy lips of her newly exposed sex. The girl's colour deepened as Lucy stared in undisguised interest at her crotch.

'How long have you been shaved?' she asked.

'About two weeks, mistress' said the girl quietly. 'My boyfriend made me do it.'

Lucy gave a low whistle, sliding a hand down between the girl's legs and bringing a quiet moan from her as her finger penetrated.

'Do you like it like that?'

'It . . . It feels strange.'

Lucy twisted her finger, the lack of hair allowing Jo a perfect view of what she was doing.

'More sensitive?' she asked, her face close to that of her captive.

'Mmmm.'

Lucy brought the palm of her other hand down hard across Patsy's breast, making her yelp with pain and surprise.

'Pardon?'

'Yes, mistress,' the girl stammered.

'That's better. You mustn't forget your place.'

She withdrew her finger and held it up in front of the girl's face. Jo could see that it was shiny with moisture.

'This is exciting you, isn't it?' she said.

'Yes, mistress,' replied the girl quietly.

'Clean my finger.'

Jo watched enthralled as the girl took Lucy's finger into her mouth, and sucked the moisture from it. The gesture seemed to her extraordinarily erotic, and she licked her lips at the thought of tasting her own juices just as the girl was doing.

Lucy pulled the whip from her belt and began to run it over Patsy's naked flesh once more. She flicked at the hard brown flesh of her nipples, making the girl wince as the leather tip snapped down on them. Jo found herself fascinated by Patsy's helplessness, forced to stand there, her body stretched tight as Lucy tormented her.

Lucy moved the whip down between Patsy's legs, sawing it back and forth along her slit. The girl whimpered quietly, and Jo noticed that, far from shying away, she was pressing her hips forward, as if encouraging the intimate contact. Jo imagined the sensation of the rough leather against that most sensitive part of her anatomy and, for the first time, felt a spark of sexual excitement, despite the fact that the book was still resting unopened on the mantelpiece.

Lucy withdrew the whip from the girl's crotch and Jo saw that, like her finger had been, that too was coated with a sheen of love juice. She watched the girl with interest, noting to her surprise that, despite the fact that her tormentor had removed the leather rod, the girl's hips were still moving, her pubis thrusting forward almost imperceptibly in a curious dance of lust.

'Right, little beauty,' said Lucy. 'It's time for your punishment. You will receive ten strokes. Do you understand?'

'Yes, mistress.'

'Turn to face the wall.'

The act of turning was clearly difficult for the girl, shackled and stretched as she was, but she managed to shuffle round until she presented both Lucy and Jo with a view of her plump, pert behind, the cheeks perfectly rounded. Jo, though slightly shocked that such a desire could ever enter her mind, found herself wondering what it would be like to take hold of those cheeks and squeeze them.

Lucy picked up something from the table. It was a stout pole, about a yard long with metal rings fastened to each end. Jo hadn't noticed it before, and assumed her flatmate had brought it into the room when she had got changed. As she watched, Lucy dropped on to one knee and began fiddling with the strap, wrapping it about one of Patsy's ankles. There was a snapping sound, and Jo realised that, like the ones at her wrists, the straps about the girl's ankles had some sort of catch attached. Lucy had used this catch to secure the end of the pole to the girl's ankle. Next she took hold of the other foot and, stretching the girl's legs wide apart, fitted the other strap to the opposite end.

Jo gasped as she realised how totally helpless the young captive now was, her arms stretched above her, her legs forcibly spread so that, such was her proximity to the wall, there was no way she could turn either left or right. Spreading her legs had increased the tension in her slender frame as well, leaving her feet barely touching the ground despite the high heels. Yet still she said nothing, standing naked and passive in her bondage awaiting the pleasure of her mistress.

Lucy ran her hand down over the girl's buttocks, stroking the pale flesh, and once again Jo felt an unaccountable desire to do the same, and to feel the warmth and softness of that young skin. Then Lucy raised the whip.

Jo started as the whip cracked down on the girl's bare flesh. The blow had been extraordinarily hard and, as the weapon dropped away, Jo saw that it had left a thin white stripe across the girl's behind, a stripe that almost immediately began darkening to an angry red.

Almost at once a second blow fell, creating another stripe an inch above the first.

The sound of leather cutting into flesh was extraordinarily loud in the confines of the room, and Jo found herself wincing as the girl's body was thrust forward by the blow, the flesh of her behind quivering slightly under the onslaught.

The blows were falling fast now, with unabated force. Each one found a new area of virgin white flesh across which to lay yet another scarlet weal, making a crisscross pattern on Patsy's behind.

Jo was transfixed by the scene, quite unable to take her eyes off the young girl's naked body. She told herself that she was shocked by what she was witnessing, but deep inside she was aware that another emotion was becoming dominant, that strange, unaccountable feeling that she had experienced on only two occasions before.

Jo was becoming aroused.

The girl's body was in motion now, her torso writhing and twisting under the onslaught. At first Jo thought she was trying to avoid the blows that rained down on her, but as she watched, it became apparent that she was thrusting her hips forward with a steady rhythm. It was almost as if she was screwing, impaled on some invisible lover and working herself back and forth on his erect cock. Jo slid a hand up, under her short dress and ran her fingers over the outside of her panties. Even through the material she could feel the heat of her desire as, moment by moment, her arousal increased.

Jo knew that there was only one more blow to come, now, and she braced herself as Lucy drew back her arm.

The final stroke whipped across Patsy's backside. The flesh was now inflamed all over, the stripes almost lost in the wide expanse of bright red flesh. Jo knew that it must sting terribly, and she listened to the sobs of the punished youngster as she hung there, still moving her hips back and forth in her strange dance of lust.

Lucy tucked the whip back in her belt and stood back. Jo could see that her body was glistening with sweat, and that she was panting slightly. Jo too was panting, but for a different reason, her fingers still stroking back and forth over the furrow of her crotch.

Lucy moved close to the girl once more. She reached out a finger and traced the line of one of the stripes. The girl winced as she did so, but made no sound.

'What a good girl you are, Patsy,' she said. 'So good, that I think you deserve a reward.'

'A reward, mistress?'

'I've brought my little black friend with me.'

'Oh!'

'You'd like that, wouldn't you?'

The girl paused, then said, in a small voice: 'Yes please, mistress.'

Lucy reached up and began loosening the chain that stretched Patsy so tight. Jo's mind reeled as she watched. A little black friend? Had Lucy brought yet another person into the house? And in that case, where were they? What on earth could Lucy mean?

Lucy unfastened the chain from the hook to which it

was attached. As her weight came back on to her feet, the girl staggered slightly, but remained standing. Jo expected Lucy to free her wrists, but instead she used the chain to lead Patsy across to the table. The same table at which she had shared the meal with Peter such a short time before. Progress was slow, since Patsy's legs were still forced wide apart by the pole, but they got there at last, and Lucy turned the girl around, forcing her back against the table.

Patsy prostrated herself across it, her backside projecting over the edge, her shackled legs dangling. Lucy moved across to the other side, yanking the chain so that, once again, the young captive's arms were stretched high over her head. Then she dragged the chain beneath the table and, pulling the two ends apart, attached them to the legs on each side.

For the second time that evening, the naked Patsy was immobilised, but this time her position was even more helpless. Before it had been simply her backside that was unprotected. Now her position was such that her open crotch was perfectly available to anyone who encountered her. Jo rubbed harder at her slit as she contemplated the girl's vulnerability. Lucy had promised that her black friend was present. Jo could scarcely wait to see him appear.

What she saw next shocked Jo more than even she had thought possible. So intent had she been on the naked captive, she hadn't noticed what Lucy was doing. Now, as her flatmate moved back between her and the captive, she had to place a hand across her mouth to suppress her gasp of surprise.

Lucy was still wearing her outfit, but something else had been added. Something that prompted Jo to pull her skirt even higher and plunge her hand into her panties, her fingers finding the soft wetness of her sex.

Standing up from Lucy's groin, for all intents and purposes like a stiff erection, was a huge black dildo.

For a second Jo was unable to credit what she was seeing. Then she realised that the thing was actually strapped to her friend, in order to replicate a man's erection. She had had no idea that such a device even existed. Yet there it was, jutting up from Lucy's crotch. It was only as Lucy approached the prostrate girl that it finally became clear to Jo what her friend had been talking about.

This was Lucy's little black friend.

Jo slipped two fingers into her vagina, suddenly extremely turned on by what she was witnessing as Lucy moved between Patsy's thighs. With Patsy positioned so close to the edge of the table, Jo was still able to see the stripes that covered her behind, yet the girl was apparently oblivious to the pain, lifting her backside up and thrusting her crotch forward as Lucy advanced.

Lucy penetrated the captive without ceremony, simply sliding the thick rod into her. At first Jo thought that the cry that escaped from Patsy's lips was one of pain. Then she saw the desire on the girl's face, and realised that it was something else, and all at once the urgency of her own masturbation increased.

Lucy fucked the helpless young girl hard, and she responded unambiguously, shouting her desire, her backside pumping up and down as she reciprocated her mistress's strokes. It was clear to Jo that the girl was already on the verge of orgasm, and the thought spurred her to increase the force with which she rammed her own fingers into her vagina.

Patsy came suddenly, screaming her desire as Lucy thrust the dildo deep into her. Jo fixed her eyes on the sleek, wet phallus, and suddenly she was coming too, biting her lip to prevent the sound of her lust carrying to the other two women.

She turned from the door and collapsed on to her bed, feeling the wetness leak out on to her hand as she continued to frig herself until her lust abated. When she finally ceased her masturbation, she grinned to herself triumphantly.

Maybe she didn't need the book after all.

Seven

Jo sat at the table in the living room, staring at the bracket on the wall, still trying to come to terms with what she had seen the day before. Somehow she had expected the room to be changed, to bear witness to the extraordinary events that had occurred there, but no clue had been left. It was still the same cosy little room where she spent most of her evenings.

She ran her hand over the table top. It was in this very place that the girl's naked body had been stretched, her sweat staining the surface as she had been so thoroughly rogered by Lucy. Now, though, it was clean and all was as it had been.

Except in Jo's mind.

Jo rose to her feet and, standing on tiptoe, ran her hand over the metal bracket in the wall. Then, almost without realising what she was doing, she placed both hands above her, opening her legs and standing close to the wall, imitating the position that Patsy had been forced to adopt. She closed her eyes, imagining the sensation of the whip slashing across her buttocks. Yet still she was unable to understand her own emotions. Instead of being disgusted or frightened by what had occurred, all she could feel was a sense of excitement. Although she tried hard to deny it to herself, Jo knew that, should Lucy ever try to bind and whip her in such a way, she would find it extremely hard to resist. And the thought of having that great, black dildo rammed into her made her stomach knot up with anticipation.

Jo turned away from the wall, shaking her head. What was happening to her? Why was it that she was becoming obsessed with the idea of punishment? More to the point, why was she making this odd connection in her mind between chastisement and sex? Surely it wasn't natural? And yet, wasn't it true that until very recently she had been quite unable to enjoy any kind of sexual pleasure, that she had been like a locked door that no man had been capable of opening. Now she had experienced the pleasure of orgasms on three occasions, once by her own hand, and in each case it had been the thought of submission and punishment that had been the stimulus.

What still puzzled her, though, was how Lucy had become involved with such things. Up until now she had thought of her flatmate as straight, and the men she had occasionally brought to the flat had seemed to support that theory. Yet last night's events put paid to that idea. Who was Patsy, and how had she dared to walk the streets clad in such a way? It was clear that she had known what was to befall her when she had come home with Lucy. She had been told she was being beaten for not obeying a summons. What kind of summons, though? Who could possibly issue such a command and back it up with so cruel a punishment when it was disobeyed?

Jo placed her face in her hands. There were so many questions ringing in her head she just didn't know where to start. If only she knew more of what had motivated her flatmate to behave as she had. If only she knew the truth of what had gone on.

She raised her head, and realised that she was standing outside Lucy's bedroom door. She hadn't consciously gone down that corridor, yet here she was, and she knew that some of the answers to her questions were inside that room.

Almost without thinking she took hold of the doorhandle and tried it. The door was unlocked. Jo stared about her guiltily. She knew that to enter her flatmate's room was a betrayal of trust. Yet wasn't what had occurred in her own living room only the day before a similar betrayal? After all, most people would have been totally shocked by what she had witnessed. Surely she had the right to investigate what was happening in her own house? She checked her watch. Lucy was not due back for more than an hour yet. She had all the time she needed. Taking a deep breath, she pushed the door open and stepped inside.

On first impressions, Lucy's room was like any other young woman's, the bed carefully made, the dressing table crowded with bottles, jars and tubes, a dressing gown hanging over the back of a chair. The scent was of good, but not over-expensive perfume and what ornaments there were were tasteful. For a moment, Jo was reminded of the last time she had been in the room, and of helping Lucy masturbate. She pulled open the bedside drawer, and there, inside, was the vibrator. She picked it up and remembered pressing it into the girl's vagina, and the evident pleasure it had given her flatmate.

She dropped the object back into the drawer and turned away. That was not what she had come for. In the corner stood a wardrobe and she opened it. The dresses inside were quite normal, of the sort any young girl might be expected to wear. Then she reached through to the back of the wardrobe and felt something cold and smooth. Pulling the dresses apart, she revealed a number of hooks, from which hung very different garments. She recognised the one she had touched as the PVC outfit Lucy had worn the night before. As well as this, there was a similar one in red, and another in leather. There were other odd garments too, in sheer transparent materials and fishnet, designed to cover the body but to hide nothing. At the bottom were boots, from ankle to thigh length, all with extremely high heels.

61

She closed the cupboard and turned to the chest of drawers beside it. Instinctively she opened the bottom drawer first. On top were a pair of jumpers. She tossed them aside impatiently. Beneath were more interesting objects.

She began to pull them out, one at a time. There were leather hoods and masks, a leather bikini like the one Patsy had been wearing, leather gloves, collars and bands. Then there were the restraints: handcuffs; manacles; shackles and chains; the leg restraint she had used on Patsy, as well as a similar one that Jo assumed was for the arms. There were small clamps with needle-like teeth in their jaws, as well as blindfolds and gags.

At the bottom of the drawer were the instruments of punishment. Whips long and short, thick and thin. Wide, flat paddles and long, cruel looking canes that flexed in her hands.

Jo carefully placed all the items back where she had found them, covering them with the jumpers before closing the drawer. There was no doubt that Lucy was into this thing in a big way. But there was still one question unanswered. With whom did she use them? Jo had seen Patsy, of course, but surely she wasn't the only one? Judging from the conversation between the two girls there must be a whole organisation out there somewhere. But who were they?

Jo opened the top drawer of the chest. It seemed to contain only underwear and stockings. Then she spotted a small cardboard file at the bottom. She pulled it out, and opened it. The title at the top of the first page struck her immediately.

'The Whipcord Society'.

Whipcord! The same word as appeared in the title of her book! She began to flick through the pages, looking for something interesting. Her eye fell on a sheet entitled 'The Society', and she read it carefully. It began as follows:

'We, the members of the Whipcord Society, undertake to promote and practice the honourable art of discipline. It is the stated aim of the Society to train young ladies in the pleasure of the whip and other articles of punishment.'

The document went on to outline rules and membership requirements, and Jo flicked on through it, scanning the words. It was clear at once that this was no ordinary society, and she found herself fascinated by its aims. How on earth had Lucy become involved with it, she wondered, and more to the point, how could she find out more?

As if in answer to her question, a slip of paper slid out from between two of the pages and dropped to the floor. As she stooped to pick it up she read the title, which was in bold letters.

'Help us recruit new members!

'The Whipcord Society is always on the lookout for new members, both submissive and dominant. If you know someone who might be interested, why not ask them to come along to one of our introductory evenings? Admission is free, and they will be under no obligation to join afterwards. A demonstration of what we offer will be provided, followed by a talk on the history and aims of the Society.'

An address was given of a venue in East London, along with a phone number and a date. Jo noticed that the date was only two days away. Pulling a piece of paper from her pocket, she scribbled down the address and the number, then placed the folder back where she had found it.

At that moment she heard the sound of a key in the front door. She glanced at her watch. A whole hour had passed since she had entered the room. The sound must be Lucy coming in!

She positively flew from the room, closing the door behind her and heading for her own bedroom. She had barely switched on the light there when Lucy entered the living room. Her mind in a whirl, Jo snatched up the book from the mantelpiece and pretended to read it, though she was careful not to actually take in the text for fear of the effect it would have on her.

Lucy poked a head round the door,

'Hi Jo, what you doing?'

'Nothing,' said Jo, aware that her face was flushed.

'What are you reading?'

'Oh, just a book.'

'It looks pretty ancient to me. What are you doing, casting spells?'

'No. It's nothing, just something I picked up at an antique shop.'

'What's it called?' Lucy squinted at the cover. 'Secrets of the Whipcord?' She stared at Jo. 'Where did you get that?'

'An antique shop. I told you. My father collects books and I thought he might be interested,' she lied.

'It's an interesting title. May I take a look?'

'No!' The word was almost shouted, and Jo blushed as she hugged the volume to her chest. 'I – I mean, it's very old. I wouldn't want it damaged.'

'I'm not going to damage it.'

'No.' Jo crossed to her dressing table and placed the book in one of the drawers. 'I've got to look after it. Sorry.'

Lucy stared at her strangely. 'You can show it to me, you know,' she said. 'I'll understand.'

'There's nothing to understand,' said Jo. 'Let's drop the subject shall we?'

Lucy paused for a moment longer, then shrugged her shoulders. 'If you say so.'

As soon as she was out of the room, Jo collapsed on to the bed, her heart pounding. Perhaps she should have shown the book to Lucy and confessed her desires to her flatmate. After all, it was clear that Lucy's proclivities were in sympathy with her own. But she hadn't been able to do so. It was partly her own embarrassment, and partly guilt at the fact that she had been eavesdropping on Lucy the night before, and then had searched her room. There was no way that she could admit to such subterfuge.

She pulled the piece of paper from her pocket and read the phone number once again.

One thing was for certain. She intended to find out more about the Whipcord Society.

Eight

Jo emerged from the tube station and scanned her map. She glanced up at a building to check the street name, then set off. It was a warm evening, and she had dressed casually in slacks and a blouse. As she passed shop windows she would catch sight of her reflection, and would find herself barely recognising the woman who looked back.

She had on a long blonde wig, with a fringe at the front, which gave a completely different shape to her face. She had made herself up carefully, using rouge and eye liner to alter her features. The final touch had been a pair of glasses with clear lenses. Now she doubted that her best friend would recognise her, and that was exactly how she wanted it.

She had agonised long and hard before finally deciding to go to the introductory evening. It was only behind the mask of her disguise that she had managed to pluck up enough courage. She had tried it out the night before and, when she was finally certain she could attend incognito, she had made the call.

The man on the other end of the telephone had been very well-spoken, and had been patient and understanding with her as she had stammered out her request to be allowed to come to the meeting. He had not asked for her name, simply giving her a password, before assuring her she would be welcome. And now here she was, on her way to the meeting, her stomach full of butterflies as she drew closer to the venue.

The building was a tall, Victorian edifice with a large, imposing door. She paused, her courage almost deserting her as she stared up at it. She glanced about her to ensure that nobody was watching, then reached out a trembling finger and pressed the doorbell.

Almost at once a small oblong vent sprang open, revealing a pair of eyes.

'Yes?'

'I-I've come for the introduction,' she stammered.

'Password?'

'Roissy.'

The vent slammed shut, and moments later the door creaked open. The man who stood behind it was tall and dark, dressed in a black shirt and black trousers. On the pocket of the shirt was a small emblem. It was an embroidered picture of a whip, with a thick handle and a long tail that looped round on itself so that it formed a letter W. He smiled as he admitted Jo, but there was a coldness in his eyes that she didn't much like.

The lobby was bare. Opposite the entrance was another doorway above which was a much larger version of the whip emblem. The man banged the door shut behind Jo and indicated she was to go through. She did so, and found herself in a large reception room. A man was sitting at a table and he beckoned to her. He wore the same outfit as the one who had let her in, complete with the device on his shirt.

'Name?'

'Jane Larwood.' He wrote the name down and indicated that she was to go through yet another door.

This room was more like a hall, hung all around with paintings. There was a waiter just inside the door holding a tray of wine glasses. Jo selected a glass of red, then moved on.

There were about a dozen other people in the room, mostly young women. All the men wore the same black uniform, and the whip emblem was in evidence almost everywhere. Some of the girls were, like her, alone, clutching their wine glasses and looking extremely nervous. One pair was constantly giggling and nudging one another as they sipped their drinks.

Not particularly wanting to speak to anyone, Jo wandered up to the walls and examined the paintings. That was when she had her first shock.

The painting she came to first looked, from a distance, like a classical nude done in oils. As she got close, however, she realised that it was very different. The girl had appeared to be leaning against a tree, but now Jo saw that she was, in fact, tied to it, ropes wrapped round her wrists and ankles and holding her naked body tight against the trunk. The flesh of her back was covered with red stripes and on the grass beside her lay a long, tapering whip.

Jo moved on to the next picture. This showed two barely clad women yoked to a sort of pony cart, their breasts bare, their bodies attached to the cart by straps that ran around their waists and down between their legs. A man was sitting in the cart wielding a whip, and Jo noticed that the artist had caught it in such a position that it described the now familiar W shape as it came down on the hapless pony girls.

The third picture showed a woman bent over a low rail, her backside raised high. A man stood in front of her, and her lips were wrapped about his rampant tool whilst a second man caned her naked buttocks.

Jo examined the paintings with a critical eye. It was true that they were of excellent quality, but they somehow lacked the starkness of the illustrations in her book, and the artists hadn't quite managed to capture the mixture of pain and arousal that the book's illustrator had. Even so, they were very erotic, and she found herself fascinated by them.

'A bit creepy isn't it?'

Jo turned to see that one of the other girls had joined

her. She was small and pretty, with short, dark hair and a trim figure, wearing a long dress with a slit up the side that ran to halfway up her thigh, showing a slender and attractive leg.

'Creepy?'

'Yes. This place. All those guys in black, and that whip emblem everywhere.'

'What do you think of the paintings?'

'They're a bit cruel.'

'Do you think they're erotic?'

'I don't know. I guess so. I'm not sure.'

Jo held out a hand. 'I'm Jane by the way,' she said.

'I'm Diana.'

'Why are you here, Diana?'

The girl hesitated, and Jo wondered whether the question had been a fair one. After all, she wasn't really certain why she had come herself.

'My boyfriend sent me,' said the girl at last.

'Is he into this sort of thing?'

'Yes. He's got lots of mags and things. I wasn't sure about the whole scene, so he suggested I came along.'

'And what do you think?'

'It's weird isn't it? I mean, do you think they really whip the girls?'

'I think that's what we're going to find out.'

'So why are you here? You got a kinky boyfriend too?'

Jo smiled and shook her head. 'No,' she said. 'I'm just curious.'

And a little kinky too, she told herself.

At that moment someone banged down a gavel and the two girls turned to see that one of the men was calling for silence.

'Your attention please, ladies,' he said. 'It's time for the evening to begin properly. First you will see a small demonstration of what the Whipcord Society stands for. That will be followed by a short intermission, at which time you may leave if you wish. Those who wish to see more can stay for a further presentation about the Society. Now, if you'd like to follow me, I'll take you through to our little auditorium.'

He led the way through a pair of double doors. The women followed, some still looking rather nervous. Jo stayed with her new companion, grateful for the company in this rather overwhelming place. They were shown into a small theatre, the seats raised in semi-circular tiers, looking down on to a small stage. The curtains were closed, and across their red velvet surface was embroidered the whipcord motif in gold thread. The two girls took their places about halfway back, near the centre.

'What do you think they're going to do?' whispered Diana in Jo's ear.

'Well it won't be Cinderella, that's for sure,' replied Jo.

As they watched, the curtains opened, revealing a wooden frame in the centre of the stage, from which hung gleaming silver chains. A man was standing beside it, dressed in the now familiar black shirt and pants, and he stepped forward to the front of the stage.

'Good evening, ladies,' he said. 'My name is Lucian, and I am to be your host for this evening. I trust you have been well cared for so far?'

There was a general nodding of heads and another giggle from the pair Jo had noticed earlier. They were now sitting in front of her, occasionally whispering to one another.

'The first part of the evening will be a little demonstration,' continued Lucian. 'We find that this is the best way to sort out those of you who are truly serious about the Society from those who have merely come along through curiosity. After the first part, you are all free to depart and no further attempt will be made to contact you. Now, without further ado, we will bring out our miscreant for tonight, Carla.'

At that moment a curtain to his right swung open and three people entered. Two of them were men, both dressed in tight trousers and long boots, their chests bare apart from leather straps that crossed in the middle. Between them was a blonde girl. She was about twenty years old, Jo reckoned. She wore a dirty, ragged dress, that came down to just below her crotch. There were great rents in the material, through which her pale young skin could be seen. She was tall, with large breasts and a slim waist that was shown off by the tightness of the dress. About her neck was a collar similar to the one that Jo had seen Patsy wearing. On her wrists and ankles she wore the same leather bands. Her hands were secured behind her, and the men were dragging her forward with the use of chains attached to her collar. She seemed reluctant to come out on to the stage, and the men used considerable force to get her to the centre. Here they pushed her down on to her knees in front of Lucian. He looked her over briefly, then turned to the hushed onlookers.

'This is Carla,' he said. 'She had committed an offence against the Society in arriving half an hour late for an encounter with some of the Society's senior members.'

Jo wondered what he meant by the word 'encounter'. She was certain it was no ordinary meeting that had been planned.

'As a consequence,' went on Lucian. 'She is to be punished by the administering of six strokes. Six is a relatively minor punishment. Some offences run to ten, twenty or even thirty strokes, and there are many other ways to inflict pain. But for tonight the six will be sufficient to show that we are serious in what we do, and that we expect you to take it seriously too.'

Another giggle from the seats in front told Jo that at least two of his audience were doing nothing of the kind.

'Stand up!' ordered Lucian.

The girl rose slowly to her feet. Jo could see that her

face was pale, and that the fear in her eyes was genuine. There was something else about her demeanour, though. Something Jo had sensed with Patsy those few nights ago. There was an air of excitement about the youngster that was undeniable, and Jo felt the stirrings of something similar inside herself. At the same moment Diana took hold of her hand and squeezed it hard.

'She's turned on by all this isn't she?' she whispered.

Jo nodded. 'Yes,' she said, and returned the squeeze.

The two warders came forward and picked up Carla's leads once more. She resisted slightly as they turned her to face the wooden frame, but there was an air of resignation about her as she allowed herself to be led forward.

There was a bar across the front of the frame running horizontally about three feet above the ground. The girl was made to stand in front of it whilst its height was adjusted. Then one of the men undid her wrists and pulled her forward, bending her almost double over the bar. At the same time his companion grasped her wrists and attached the bands to catches set in the floor of the stage. Next her legs were forced about three feet apart and similarly shackled.

The men pulled the chains tight, forcing the girl down on to the bar, her backside raised high, the dress riding up her legs until a large expanse of her thighs was uncovered. Jo was breathing heavily now, and she could feel the sweat on the palms of her companion. Even the pair in front had stopped talking, their eyes fixed on the stage.

One of the warders went briefly into the wings, and returned with a thin bamboo cane. He took it straight to Lucian, who bent it back and forth in his hands. It was extraordinarily flexible and, as he took some practice strokes in the air, Jo saw the weapon bend with the resistance. Lucian nodded, apparently satisfied with it, and walked downstage to where the girl was tethered.

72

He held the cane out in front of the girl's face, which was hidden from the audience's view.

'Kiss the instrument of your correction,' he ordered.

Jo could barely discern the motion of the girl's head as she obeyed him.

Lucian turned back to face the crowd and held out the cane to the warder, who took it from him. Then he reached down and took hold of the hem of the girl's dress.

There was an intake of breath about the room as he slowly and carefully lifted the material, uncovering Carla's buttocks. Jo leant forward in her seat, craning for a good view of the scene. Lucian had raised the material to the girl's waist, revealing that she wore nothing beneath, the white flesh stretched tight. So wide were her legs spread that her sex was visible, and Jo contemplated how vulnerable and exposed she was.

Lucian stepped back, and the warder with the cane came forward. He was a young man, with a broad, hairy chest and bulging biceps. He wielded the cane in his strong hands, making a loud whooshing sound as he stroked it back and forth against the empty air. He positioned himself beside the girl and tapped it against her behind. As he did so, Jo felt the Diana's hand tighten on hers once more.

If the onlookers had expected some kind of simulation of a punishment, the first stroke told them they were witnessing the real thing. The cane came down with deadly accuracy, planting a single stripe across the pale white of Carla's buttocks, a stripe that immediately darkened to a blood-red colour. The tethered girl gave a shout of pain that echoed about the room.

The second blow landed about an inch above the first, the stripe lying almost exactly parallel. Jo watched as its colour deepened, once again unaccountably excited by the sight she was witnessing.

Next time the cane laid down a diagonal line, running

from the under side of the left buttock to the top of the right, bringing another squeal from the helpless captive. Jo turned to look at the girl next to her. Diana was leaning forward, an expression of deep concentration on her face. Then Jo's eyes dropped to her lap, and her eyes widened as she realised that the girl's free hand was under her skirt, rubbing up and down her crotch.

Carla's cries were getting louder now, her body writhing about within the small confines she was allowed and, as with Patsy, Jo was struck by the way her hips thrust forward in an overtly sexual way as another dark weal decorated her pretty behind.

Diana was starting to pant now, and Jo stole another look. The slit of her dress had been pulled off her lap, and the leg of her panties pulled aside so that her fingers were actually penetrating her sex, making a soft squelching sound as she thrust them urgently into herself. Jo wasn't certain which was the more erotic sight – this pretty young girl who clutched tightly to her hand whilst she masturbated, or the buttocks, so exquisitely decorated with stripes, on the stage.

The final stroke came down hard on to the girl's behind, bringing a piercing scream from her. At the same moment, Jo felt her companion shudder. Then, with a hoarse cry, she was coming, collapsing against Jo, her fingers tightening on her hand as she gasped out her lust. Jo placed her free arm about the girl, holding her close whilst she came down from her climax, her fingers still working back and forth, but slower now as the tension in her body eased. At last she was silent, and her fingers slipped from inside her. At the same moment the men released the shackles that held Carla's hands and feet and she was helped to straighten up and turn to face the audience.

Jo could see that the tears were coursing down her face, and she knew that the pain was genuine. Yet she could see, too, the arousal on the girl's face, and once again she was reminded of the illustration in the book. When Lucian lifted the front of the girl's skirt and slipped a finger into her sex, the moan was not of pain, but of pleasure, and Jo could see the wetness glistening on the finger when it was withdrawn.

Lucian made Carla turn away once again and raise her skirt to the waist. He indicated the bright red marks that now covered her behind.

'This is the badge of membership to the Whiplash Society,' he said to the audience.

Then he led the girl from the stage, and the lights came up.

Nine

Jo sipped at her glass of wine and looked about her at the rest of the company. They were back in the room with the paintings. There were fewer of them now. The pair who had chatted and giggled earlier in the evening had left in silence, their faces white with shock. One or two others had followed, but Jo was surprised to see that at least half a dozen still remained. Diana, her earlier companion, had excused herself, clearly overcome with embarrassment at her behaviour, but Jo could see her on the far side of the room, ostensibly studying one of the pictures.

There was a different atmosphere in the room now as all the guests contemplated what they had witnessed. There was no doubt that the caning had had a profound effect on everyone who had seen it, and what little conversation there had been had evaporated into a silence that was charged with emotions.

For her part, Jo had been undeniably aroused by the beating, even more so than the one she had seen in her flat, since this had been so public. There was no doubting the effect it had had on her companion, too, and she suspected that all those remaining for the second half of the evening were as fascinated as she was to find out more about the Whipcord Society. These thoughts were confirmed a few minutes later, when they were called back into the auditorium. Jo noted a definite urgency in the girls' steps as they almost crowded one another to get to their seats.

Jo sat where she had before. She hadn't expected her erstwhile companion to join her, but she did, her cheeks still red.

'Sorry about before,' said Diana. 'I don't know what came over me.'

'I do,' said Jo. 'I felt it too. I think we all did. Those who're left, anyhow.'

'It was just so ... So erotic,' said the girl.

'What turned you on, just watching?'

The girl turned away. 'No.'

'You wanted it to be you out there?'

'Yes. That's awful isn't it?'

Jo shook her head. 'I felt the same,' she said.

'Do you think we're perverts?'

Jo laughed. 'If we are, then so are all this lot.'

Diana laughed too.

At that moment Lucian began to speak again.

'Right ladies. I'm glad so many of you chose to stay. The next section of the evening is devoted to telling you a little more about the Society and about its membership.'

As he spoke, the lights dimmed and the beam from a projector speared through the darkness. At the same time a screen dropped down from above, and Jo found herself staring once more at the whiplash emblem.

'The Society was formed more than five hundred years ago,' said Lucian. 'Its original purpose was the correction of recalcitrant ladies from the gentry. Rich landowners would send their wives and even their daughters for periods of retribution if they found them to have misbehaved, particularly in a sexual context. Very few of them ever repeated their misdemeanours. In later years, though, the emphasis changed, so that now all attendance is voluntary, although the methods of the Society have remained largely the same.'

He went on to talk about the history of the Society, illustrating his talk with pictures, some of which Jo recognised from the room in which she had been welcomed on first arrival. He named some of the Society's more illustrious members, and Jo was surprised by how many names she recognised from history.

He then moved on to show pictures of various instruments of torture, including a number of different whips and canes, as well as other artefacts. Jo was reminded of the contents of Lucy's bottom drawer as she studied the pictures.

The talk went on for about forty minutes, and Jo found herself spellbound from beginning to end, particularly by the methods used by the Society to inflict pain. Beside her she could see that her companion, too, was fascinated, her eyes fixed on the screen.

Finally the image of the Whipcord was again projected on to the screen, and Jo sensed the presentation was coming to an end. But then Lucian's tone changed and she realised there was something else to be said.

'The founder of our organisation,' he said, 'was first introduced to the pleasures of the whip by a book. Nobody knows for sure the origin of the book, but it was said to have an extraordinary effect on young women, making even the most chaste young maiden hungry for a taste of the whip, and for the pleasure only a man can give a woman. This book was, for years, in the founder's possession, but was lost at the time of his death. Indeed some members doubt that it ever existed, but we do have a single clue, in this impression of the front cover made by an early member of the Society.'

A new picture flashed up on the screen, and Jo stared at it in disbelief. It was a picture of her book. A rather crude representation, she had to admit, but there was no mistaking the fact that the illustration on the cover was an attempt to copy the one on the book in her bedroom. Then she realised that Lucian was still speaking.

'Naturally the Society will do anything in its power to find the book, and we earnestly request that you look out for it. Meanwhile we must simply hope that one day its whereabouts will be discovered.'

Jo went to raise her hand, then restrained herself. She looked around her at the other women in the room. Just suppose Lucian had the book in his possession. Wouldn't it give him a power over these very women? She thought of the effect it had had on her, and of the desires it had kindled in her. Desires that had brought her to this very place. For the first time, she began to realise its power, and she kept her peace. She would have to think very hard about what he had said, and about the emotions the book could unleash.

The talk ended with a round of applause, and the women filed back into the hall. Some, including Diana, crowded about Lucian, asking questions about membership, but Jo had seen enough. Taking advantage of being left on her own she stole quietly out the door and was soon back on the street, headed for the tube station.

Ten

The first thing Jo did on her return to the flat was to remove the wig and glasses and wash away the make-up. It was quite a relief to be staring at her own face once more as she combed out her hair before the mirror, her mind still preoccupied by what she had seen and heard. She checked the drawer in which she kept the book. It was still there, beneath her clothes. She resolved to find a safer place to put it now that she recognised its significance.

She had intended to have an early night, but her experience with the Society had left her restless and uneasy and she knew she wouldn't be able to sleep for some time. She checked her watch. It was only nine o'clock. Much earlier than she had thought. She wished she had somebody to go out with. She was loath to go to a pub or club on her own. Then she thought of the place where Lucy worked. It was a large, busy pub not far from the flat, and she occasionally dropped in there to chat to her flatmate in the evenings.

She resolved to seek out her friend, although she had no intention of telling her where she had been. She simply felt that she needed some company, and Lucy was the most obvious person. Taking a final glance in the mirror, she grabbed her handbag and headed for the door.

Then she hesitated, and returned to her room. She pulled open the bottom drawer and, lifting a jumper out the way, eyed the book. All of a sudden it had become extremely precious to her, and the thought of the Whipcord Society getting their hands on it was not something she wanted to contemplate. She tucked it back and, taking the key from the inside of the door, locked it carefully before leaving the flat.

The pub was, as usual, crowded with young people, and the music pounded from the juke box over the hubbub of chatter. Jo found herself a spot at the bar and hailed her friend, who served her gin and tonic at once. The two girls made small talk in the intervals between Lucy's dashing up and down the bar to serve the customers. Jo found herself wanting to tell her flatmate where she had been that night, but she knew it wouldn't be a good idea. Instead they discussed the fashions the girls were wearing and the relative attractions of their male companions.

Jo had been in the bar for about half an hour when she became aware of the young man standing next to her. He was tall, about twenty-five years old, with fair hair and the most penetrating eyes Jo had ever seen. Lucy had been serving another customer when he had arrived, but now, as she returned, she hailed him.

'Hi, Hans,' she said. 'How's things? Have you met my friend Jo?'

Jo turned and smiled at the man, who shook her hand. Lucy introduced him as a regular customer and served him a beer.

Hans joined in the conversation with the girls and gradually, as Lucy was continually being called away, he and Jo began chatting together. He was an amusing partner, and before long Jo found herself attracted to him. He spoke with an accent she couldn't quite place, German or Dutch she thought. His droll sense of humour and broad smile were something of a tonic after the seriousness of the early part of the evening and, when he invited her to join him at a table, she went happily, giving a wave to Lucy.

'Lucy's fun, isn't she?' she said as they settled down.

'She is,' he agreed. 'Are you into the kind of stuff she's into?'

Jo looked at him hard. 'What kind of things?'

'Well she has some unusual tastes when it comes to enjoying herself.'

'Unusual?'

'Sure. You mean you don't know?'

Jo hesitated. 'I've got some idea,' she said slowly.

'So you're not in the Society?'

Once again Jo took her time before answering. 'What society would that be?'

He eyed her, for a second. 'Sorry,' he said. 'I spoke out of turn.'

'Does it have something to do with whips and bondage?'

'So you are a member?'

'No. But I have an idea of the kind of thing that's involved.'

'Does that kind of thing turn you on?'

'I don't know. I've never tried it.'

'You mean you'd like to?'

'I'm not sure. It's a bit kinky isn't it?'

'You won't know until you've tried.'

'Is that a proposition?'

He smiled. 'It's whatever you want it to be. I'm not about to put any pressure on.'

Jo paused. This was a most unexpected turn of events. It seemed that everywhere she turned she encountered people wanting to introduce her to the joys, or otherwise, of the chain and the whip. This was, however, her first direct proposition on the subject, and she felt a strange sense of excitement as she contemplated the idea of experimenting with this handsome young man.

'What did you have in mind?' she asked at last.

'Have you ever been tied up?'

'No.'

82

'We could try that if you like. Just for starters.'

'Where?'

'It would have to be your place. My flatmates are all in tonight.'

'I'm not sure.'

'Please yourself. It was just a suggestion.'

'Would you whip me?'

'Not the first time. Not unless you asked me to.'

Jo was silent for a moment. The man's suggestion was an extraordinary one. One that just a couple of weeks ago she would have dismissed out of hand. After her recent experiences, though, she found herself oddly aroused by the whole prospect, and the fact that Hans was a virtual stranger made the idea somehow more rather than less acceptable. After all, there were no preconceived ideas or prejudices to overcome. It was a simple proposition which she was free to take or leave.

'All right,' she said. 'Let's go back to my place and do it.'

He smiled. 'I like a girl with a sense of adventure,' he said.

Throughout the walk back to her flat, Jo's thoughts were in a turmoil. She could scarcely believe what was about to happen, and she kept asking herself again and again why she had agreed. But deep down she knew why. The whole prospect of being made helpless, like Carla and Patsy before her, was one that appealed to her basest desires, and as she turned the key in the door to her flat, her heart was thumping hard.

'Fix me a whisky,' she said, indicating the cabinet. 'I've just got to check something in my room.'

'Find a few pairs of stockings whilst you're in there,' said Hans. 'Preferably old ones.'

'Stockings?'

'Yeah. What else am I going to tie you up with? Unless you've got some rope.'

'No. Stockings it is.'

She unlocked her room, stepped inside and closed the door behind her. At once she dropped to her knees in front of her chest and opened the bottom drawer. She pulled out the book, and opened it.

Actually, she wasn't sure if she needed the stimulus of the book. She was already sensing that the more she was exposed to the reality of sexual pleasure, the more her appetite for it increased. She was fairly certain that her arousal was great enough to enjoy sex without need of the erotic words and pictures of the ancient tome. Nevertheless, she was embarking on a new adventure tonight, and she wanted to be certain that her enjoyment would be total, so she began to read.

The chapter she had chosen was perfect. It told of a young woman captured by a group of men whilst out walking. They dragged her back to their camp, where they stripped her naked, despite her pleas for mercy. Four stakes were banged into the ground and she was tied down to them, her body open and helpless. Jo's hands trembled as she studied the picture of the young girl lying there, staring up at her captors as they prepared to screw her, their thick cocks rampant. Almost at once the now familiar warmth began to fill her crotch, and she felt the dormant desire within her begin to stir.

'Jo? You want this drink or not?'

Once again Jo realised that she had lost all track of time, so absorbed had she been in the words and pictures. It was as if she was physically drawn into the stories they told, as if it was she herself who lay naked on that hard ground waiting to be ravaged by her captors. With an effort, she tore herself away from the text and, tucking the book back into her drawer, rose to her feet.

'Just coming,' she called, her voice husky. She had almost reached the door when she remembered the stockings and hurried back to the chest, pulling out a handful of nylon.

'What the hell were you doing in there?' he asked.

'Nothing,' she replied, though she knew her face was flushed.

She took the whisky from him and gulped it down, her hands shaking.

'You okay?' he asked.

'Yeah. Just a little nervous.'

But she knew that it wasn't nerves that made her shake and caused her face to glow, it was desire, and as she eyed him a shudder of lust ran through her body. She held out the stockings to him.

'These'll do,' he said. 'You want to do it right here?'

She shook her head. 'No, not here. The spare room.'

She couldn't bear the thought of Lucy arriving home and seeing her with Hans. And she didn't want to use her own room. Somehow its cosiness would be out of keeping with the fantasy she was about to live out.

She showed him through to the spare room, which was at the far end of the corridor beside the bathroom. It was a stark little room, the floorboards bare, the only furniture the old brass bed on which was laid a mattress. There was no lampshade, and the brightness of the light bulb made her feel strangely exposed and devoid of cover. She turned to face him.

'What do I do?' she asked quietly.

'Take off the dress.'

She reached behind her and slid down the zipper, allowing the dress to fall to the floor. The floorboards were dusty, but somehow that didn't seem to matter, and she simply kicked the garment aside then stood, facing him, her hands by her sides. Now she wore only white bra and pants, the thin laciness of both exposing the darker shade of her skin beneath.

'Can I leave these on?' she asked.

'I might have to damage them later.'

'It doesn't matter.'

'Lie on the bed.'

She did as she was asked. The mattress was old and hard and the material felt cold against her skin, but she didn't mind, reclining on her back and staring up at him.

He took hold of her hand and began wrapping the nylon stocking about her wrist. He knotted it tightly, though the softness of the material meant that there was no pain. Then he secured the other end to the corner of the bed behind her head. He did the same with the other wrist. Then he moved to her right foot, tying her ankle and dragging her body down the bed, deliberately stretching her as far as he was able before securing it to the bottom corner. The other ankle was swiftly immobilised in the same manner, and he stepped back to take in the sight of his captive.

Jo felt extraordinarily exposed, her body spread-eagled across the old mattress. She tested the bonds at her wrists and ankles. They held fast and she realised with a thrill that she was entirely at Hans's mercy, the tautness in her limbs barely allowing any movement at all.

Her situation was at once arousing and frustrating. The punishment she had witnessed earlier in the evening, coupled with her reading of the book and the feel of Hans's strong hands as he had made her bonds fast had all turned her on more than she could imagine, so that she could feel her sex weeping with warm lubrication. Yet in this position she couldn't even touch herself, much as she longed to caress the protruding bud of her clitoris. She gazed up at Hans, almost panting with desire.

'What next?' she gasped.

'I think I'll have another drink,' he said, smiling.

'Hans!'

But he had left the room, and she could hear him walking down the corridor. Jo tugged at her bonds, but there was nothing she could do but await his return.

He came back a few minutes later, the ice cubes clinking in his glass.

'You could have got me one, you bastard,' she said.

He didn't reply, but sat down next to her on the bed and placed his glass down on her bare flesh.

'Ow!' She tried to squirm away, but couldn't. 'Take that away.'

He smiled. 'How does it feel to be in someone else's power?' he asked.

Jo glared at him and once again struggled against the ties that held her, but in vain. He ran the glass down her stomach, the coldness raising goosebumps on her flesh and leaving a shiny, wet trail behind.

'Stop it!' she shouted.

He took her chin in his hand and pulled her face round to his.

'Quiet, little captive, or I'll have to shut you up myself.'

'Get stuffed, Hans.'

'Right,' he said. 'I think it's time you were gagged.'

'Gagged?' she gasped. It hadn't occurred to her that he might do that. 'No, you mustn't Hans.'

He paid no attention, simply looking about himself for a suitable implement. He picked up the one remaining stocking.

'This will do,' he said. 'But I still need something to put in your mouth.'

He slid his hand down her stomach and paused, fingering the material of her panties.

'These should do.'

'No Hans.' She shook her head back and forth wildly. But he didn't seem to hear her. Instead he slipped his hand down the front of her nether garment and, grasping hold of the material, gave a sharp yank.

The panties ripped at both sides, coming away easily in his hands. Jo could only look on helplessly as the pink flesh of her sex was exposed to his gaze. He held the garment up to the light, and Jo blushed as she saw the wet marks where it had been in contact with her crotch.

Wasting no time, he screwed the panties into a ball and, taking hold of her hair, pressed them against her lips. She tried to resist, but in vain, and soon her head was filled with the taste and scent of her own arousal as he wrapped the stocking about her head.

'Mmmf!' Jo's protests were reduced to a muffled grunt as she stared up at her captor. She couldn't believe what was happening to her, and how she had allowed herself to be made so vulnerable. Yet she knew that she had consented, and that the experience was fast becoming the greatest turn-on of her life. If only her hands were free, she'd be masturbating like mad. As it was, she could only squirm helplessly as Hans grinned down at her spread thighs.

He sat down on the bed beside her, running his fingers lightly over her belly. She groaned with frustration as he stroked his hand downwards, avoiding the heat of her desire as he felt the softness of her thighs.

'Christ you're something, Jo.' He murmured. 'I just gotta get a look at those tits of yours.'

'Mmmf.' Once again Jo's protestations were unintelligible as he reached for her sole remaining garment. She watched wide-eyed as he snapped her bra straps easily, then groped beneath her for the catch.

Jo's breasts were a sight to behold – the nipples like stiff, brown knobs, their erect state further evidence of her almost total arousal. The firmness of her mounds meant that her teats pointed straight upwards, and she raised her head to peer down the valley they formed at the rest of her naked body.

Hans rose to his feet and moved to the foot of the bed. Jo knew he was taking in every inch of her nakedness, and that she was powerless to prevent him. Even the ability to protest had been taken from her. She was entirely under his control, and as she watched him begin to unbutton his shirt, she knew that he was about to take full advantage of the situation.

He discarded his shirt, then kicked off his shoes and socks. His trousers followed, and Jo stared at the bulge that threatened to split his underpants apart. When his cock finally did spring free it was stiff as a flagpole, jutting out proudly from his loins, the circumcised tip purple and swollen.

Hans stood over her, his cock in his hand, his fingers running slowly up and down its length, clearly relishing his power over her. Jo thought back to the picture in the book, and the girl spread naked on the ground awaiting the inevitable screwing she was about to receive, and realised that she was relishing it too. She had had no idea that to be totally in the power of another could be such an extraordinarily thrilling experience. She wondered what it would be like to feel the whip on her bare flesh, and a shudder of anticipation ran through her as the image of Carla's bare behind suddenly filled her mind.

Hans climbed on to the bed, straddling his lovely captive. The contact of his flesh against hers sent new spasms of lust through the naked girl and she stared at the stiff cock that bobbed up and down in front of her face.

'I think we'll have the gag off now,' he said quietly. 'I've got something much better to fill your pretty little mouth with.'

He undid the knot on the stocking and pulled it off her head. She spat the remains of her knickers from her mouth.

'You bastard. . .' she spluttered. But already he was pressing his erection against her lips. She resisted for a moment, but the scent of male arousal was too much for her and she opened her mouth, taking him inside and sucking greedily at his meaty rod. She loved the sensation of having him there in her mouth, and when he began moving his hips back and forth she responded eagerly, licking at his glans as she fellated him. He grinned down at her, his balls slapping against her chin as he took his pleasure, his hands groping for the softness of her breasts.

He went on fucking her face, his tool penetrating so deep that she feared she might gag. She wished she could feel him with her hands, caress his balls, grasp his shaft. But she knew at the same time that that desire was being fed by her situation, and that the bondage itself was the most stimulating part of this extraordinary encounter.

All at once he withdrew, his cock sliding from her mouth. He remained where he was, his tool shiny with her saliva as it hovered temptingly just in front of her face. She craned her neck up, licking at his testicles, making his erection twitch violently as her tongue ran over the surface of his ball sac.

'You're something, Jo,' he said. 'I've just got to get inside you.'

'Mmmm.' There was nothing more that Jo wanted at that moment, and she felt the muscles in her sex contract as he spoke the words.

He moved down her body, once again taking hold of her breasts, leaning forward and placing his mouth over her teats. She moaned softly as he sucked at them, his tongue making circular motions about the nipple which, if anything, was growing even harder by the second.

She felt his hand move down through her pubic hair, and she gasped aloud as he found her clitoris, his touch releasing a new surge of love juice into her burning sex. Then she felt his erection pressing against her and she almost screamed with desire.

When he penetrated her, the sensation was exquisite, triggering a powerful orgasm that coursed through her body, making her scream aloud as the walls of her sex caressed his cock. She bit her lip to still her cries as the wonderful release of climax filled her senses. There was only his cock, nothing else in her whole world but the lovely, stiff ramrod that even now was beginning to pump back and forth inside her.

He fucked her with slow, easy movements, watching her face as, almost immediately, a second climax began to build. Jo struggled in vain with her bonds, her body thrashing up and down beneath him, her limbs stretched and helpless beneath his onslaught. This was sex at its most raw: she a helpless victim; he a merciless ravisher intent only on his own pleasure. And it was what she desperately wanted.

His movements began to quicken, and for the first time she sensed an urgency in him. He began ramming his hips down harder against hers, and she responded as best she could, pressing her pubis up at him, her backside coming clear of the mattress. The smile had gone from his face now, replaced by an intense expression of lust as she felt his limbs begin to stiffen.

Then all at once he gave a grunt, and she felt the delicious sensation of sperm gushing into her vagina, his cock seeming to take on a life of its own as it delivered spurt after spurt of his seed deep inside her. Almost at once she was coming once more, the sensation of his spunk splashing against her womb doubling her pleasure as she thrust her hips upwards, her sex muscles clamping about his jerking rod.

By the time he had spent his seed, Jo too was quiet once more, her breath rasping in her throat as she slumped back on the mattress. He lay over her, his cock still embedded inside her, though already she could sense its stiffness easing as he allowed his body to relax. She nuzzled into his neck, enjoying the smell of his sweat as he slowly began to ease himself from her.

He rose to his feet, his erection still shiny with her lubrication. As he did so she felt a trickle of sperm escape from her on to the mattress. He began to dress slowly, his eyes still fixed on her naked, helpless body as she lay watching him. Once he was decent he sat down beside her and ran his fingers over her flesh once again. Then he got to his feet.

'Aren't you going to release me?' she asked. But he said nothing, simply turning and going out the door. She called after him, but there was no reply. She lay, listening, as he moved about the flat. Then came the unmistakable sound of the front door closing.

Jo could scarcely believe it. He had simply left her, still naked and tied fast to the bed. She yanked furiously at her bonds, but he had tied them too tight, and she was held fast. She went on struggling for some minutes, but to no avail. At last she realised the futility of it and stopped, lying back against the mattress, suddenly aware that there was only one way in which she would get free, and that was with the help of another.

Eleven

It was more than half an hour before the front door opened again. Half an hour in which Jo could do nothing but gaze up at the ceiling whilst she felt his seed slowly trickle from her, leaving a cold, sticky trail down her backside. Now, as she heard Lucy's footsteps come down the corridor, she felt the blood rush to her face as she realised discovery was imminent. She wished there was some other way to free herself, but she knew she had no choice but to call out her friend's name.

'Lucy!'

The footsteps stopped. 'Where are you?'

'In the spare room.'

There was silence for a moment, then the footsteps came closer. Jo watched with apprehension as the door opened.

'What on earth are you doing in here,' said Lucy. 'I thought you were . . .'

She stopped short, her jaw gaping as she stared at the hapless captive.

'Jo!' she gasped. 'What the hell's been going on?'

'Just a bit of fun,' muttered the scarlet-faced girl.

'But who. . .'

'Your mate Hans. He came back with me and, well, I let him tie me up.'

'He's not exactly a mate,' said Lucy. 'I know him from somewhere else. Anyhow it looks as if you and he were getting pretty matey.'

She sat down on the bed and ran her fingers over her friend's stomach. 'I didn't know you were into this sort of thing,' She said, her eyes taking in Jo's lovely young body.

'I'm not,' said Jo defensively. 'At least I wasn't.'

'You mean this is your first time?'

'The first time I've been tied up, yes.'

Lucy moved a hand up and cupped her friend's breast, and to Jo's embarrassment the nipple began to harden at once.

'Ever been whipped?' Lucy asked.

Jo shook her head. 'I told you this was the first time.'

'And did you like it?' Lucy had taken the swollen nipple between her fingers and was rolling it back and forth whilst Jo tried hard not to show the effect her caresses were having.

'It was . . . It was okay I guess,' she said.

'Did you come?'

'Look, Lucy, are you going to let me free or what?'

'All in good time. I'm quite enjoying having you naked like this. And, after all, you let him do it.'

'I still had my bra and pants on when he tied me up.'

'Yeah, but you must have known you wouldn't keep them for long. You still haven't told me if you came.'

'Twice,' she said quietly.

'Twice, eh?' Lucy was massaging both of Jo's breasts now, and the girl had to bite her lip to prevent herself gasping aloud. 'Think you could come again?'

'What?'

'It's just that you did something for me the other day, and I've been meaning to return the compliment.'

'What are you talking about?'

Lucy rose to her feet. 'Don't go away,' she giggled, then slipped from the room.

For the umpteenth time Jo pulled at her bonds, but to no avail. Having placed herself at Hans's mercy, it seemed that she was to suffer the indignity of her helplessness for a while longer yet. She knew she should be angry, kick up a fuss, demand to be released. But she knew too that her helplessness was still extraordinarily thrilling, and the way Lucy had stared at her, along with the soft caressing of her breasts, had been extremely arousing. Now as she lay, her legs spread, the most intimate parts of her anatomy on open display, a shiver of excitement ran through her tethered body at the prospect of what was to come.

When Lucy returned, she had discarded her dress, leaving her clad in black bra and panties. Not for the first time, Jo was struck by the size and shape of the blonde girl's breasts. They were lifted by the bra, which barely covered her nipples, leaving small half-moons of brown flesh showing just above the black lace. The panties were very brief indeed, and Jo could discern her friend's pubic bush through a transparent panel at the front.

But her eyes didn't linger long on Lucy's underwear, as she caught sight of what her friend was holding. It was the vibrator, the one that she herself had used on Lucy that morning in her bedroom. It all seemed so long ago now, and she wondered at the change in herself since that occasion. Then she had been scared of the smallest touch from another person. Now, the sight of the long, rubbery phallus sent a spasm of pleasure through her.

Lucy sat down beside her once more.

'Now, my pretty little captive,' she said. 'We're going to see what you're like when you come.'

'No,' said Jo. 'You mustn't Lucy. It's not right.'

Lucy smiled. 'You've given me that line before,' she said. 'But this time you can't run away.' She stroked the end of the dildo over Jo's breasts, smiling at the obvious pleasure this gave the girl. 'Besides,' she went on. 'I think I detect a change in you, Jo. Last time you were scared of this thing. This time you're practically panting for it.'

95

Jo's colour deepened. She was aware of the way her body was reacting, the way her nipples had puckered to tight brown knots and her hips were moving back and forth in a manner she simply couldn't control. When Lucy pressed the switch at the base of the phallus, the very sound of the machine brought back the sweet memory of Jo's lovely flatmate lying naked on her bed masturbating, and Jo moaned quietly as the girl began to rub the tip of the toy about her nipples, sending darts of rapture through her body.

Lucy manipulated the vibrator expertly, seeking out erogenous zones in parts of her body where Jo had never dreamed that any existed. She moved with a slow deliberateness, experimenting with various places and testing Jo's reaction. For Jo's part, she was getting more and more turned on by the second. She had already come twice, yet her arousal was as strong as ever now, and once again she longed to be able to caress herself whilst still savouring the pure eroticism of her bondage.

At last Jo could take no more.

'Oh God, Lucy,' she gasped. Please do it to me. That thing is driving me crazy.'

'Do what to you?' asked Lucy, an evil smile on her face.

'Do what I did to you. Make me come. You said you wanted to see me come.'

Lucy leant forward and kissed Jo on the lips. 'All right, little slave,' she said.

The words had an odd effect on Jo. Little slave. She thought of the women in the book, and the way the men treated them. Why was it that she found the idea such a turn on? What was it about submitting totally to the will of another that seemed so exciting?

'Oh!'

She cried aloud as the bulbous tip of the vibrator found her clitoris, her hips jabbing forward against the rubbery device. Lucy began circling, sending shocks of delight through her young body as it rubbed against the very centre of her desires. Then she moved it to the entrance to Jo's vagina and began to press and twist against the soft, delicate flesh.

The dildo slipped easily into Jo's love hole. Hans's spunk and her own copious juices had left her well lubricated, and her muscles contracted to caress the thick object as it plunged deep into her. Jo bit her lip to prevent herself shouting aloud as she felt herself so completely and deliciously filled by the throbbing phallus.

Lucy began working it back and forth inside her, watching her flatmate's face as she frigged her. Jo's eyes were tight shut, her head back, her fists clenched as she savoured the wonderful sensation of being stimulated thus. Her breasts felt as if they were swollen to twice their size, and when she felt Lucy's lips close over her nipples and begin to suck she could control herself no longer.

The orgasm was long and glorious, her behind hammering against the mattress as she thrust her hips forward against the vibrator, her head shaking from side to side. A strange mewing sound came from her lips as Lucy continued to work the vibrator in and out with vigour, at the same time sucking hard at Jo's teats, clearly delighted at the effect she was having on her friend. No sooner had the intenseness of her orgasm begun to abate than a second racked Jo's body, followed by a third. Only then did she begin to come down, exhaustion finally getting the better of her as Lucy's motions began to slow.

By the time Lucy slipped the vibrator from inside her, Jo was spent, her body limp as she slowly regained her breath. She scarcely noticed as Lucy began to undo the bonds that held her hands and ankles, and it was fully ten minutes before she opened her eyes.

Lucy took her hands and helped her to her feet. Her

limbs felt stiff after their prolonged immobilisation and she stretched; her lithe young body arched back as she enjoyed the luxury of freedom of movement once more.

Lucy put her arms about her friend and kissed her on the lips. 'That was a bit different from the last time I tried to give you an orgasm.'

Jo dropped her eyes. 'I'm sorry about that,' she said. 'That was before . . .'

'Before what?'

'Before something happened to change things.'

'What happened?'

'It was the book.'

'*Secrets of the Whipcord?*'

'How did you know?'

'I knew the book existed. There are people who have been searching for it for years. Tell me how you found it.'

Jo recounted the whole story, not omitting the encounter with the fisherman or her experiment with Peter.

'And the book really had this effect?' asked Lucy incredulously.

Jo nodded. 'That's why I was worried when I heard that the Whipcord Society knew about it.'

Lucy's eyes widened still further.

'You know about the Whipcord Society? But how?'

Jo went on to recount how she had witnessed Patsy's punishment, and her visit earlier that evening to the Society.

'So you know my little secret,' said Lucy. 'Are you going to join?'

'I don't know. I'm not sure I'd want them to know about the book.'

'Why not?'

'It's too powerful. I'm afraid they might use it to ensnare women who weren't really suited to that kind of thing.'

'Do you really think it could do that?'

Jo nodded. 'You have no idea what it does Lucy. That's why the Whipcord Society mustn't find it.'

'Oh.' Lucy flushed and a look of dismay crossed her face.

'What's the matter?' asked Jo.

'I'm sorry, Lucy,' she said. 'They already know.'

'What?'

'I saw you with it in your room the other night. You tried to hide it, but I recognised it at once. I went back and told the Society. I assumed they'd offer you a good price for it. I thought I was doing you a favour.'

'No,' Jo shook her head. 'They mustn't get hold of it. I can't let them.'

'All right,' said Lucy. 'I'll go back and say I was mistaken. I'll convince them.'

'You must,' said Jo. 'We can't risk letting them get their hands on it.'

'May I see it?' asked Lucy.

Jo gazed at her doubtfully, then nodded. 'I suppose so. But be warned, the effect it has is very powerful. Come on.'

The naked girl led the way out of the room, with Lucy following. She pushed open the door of her own bedroom, then stopped short.

'Oh no!'

'What is it?' Lucy pushed past her.

The room was a mess. All the drawers and cupboards were open and clothes were strewn all over the floor. But Jo scarcely paid them any attention. She went straight to the bottom drawer of her chest and looked inside. Then she turned to face Lucy, her features pale.

'The book's gone,' she said.

Twelve

'But just who the hell was Hans?' asked Jo.

'I really don't know. I was introduced to him only the night before at the Society. They told me he was visiting from Holland for a couple of days. He was a member of the Society over there. We have branches in quite a few European countries you know.'

'So you'd only met him the once?'

'Yes. If I'd known he was going to do this I'd have warned you. You know that, don't you?'

Jo studied her friend's face. She certainly seemed to be sincere. It was difficult to believe she could have had anything to do with the theft of the book.

The two girls were sitting in the living room, both wrapped in dressing gowns and sipping at cups of coffee. Now that the initial shock of losing the book was wearing off, Jo's dismay was beginning to turn to anger as she contemplated how the deed had been done.

'To think that I let the bastard into the house myself and allowed him to tie me up,' she said. 'I couldn't have made it easier for him if I'd tried.'

'It wasn't your fault,' said Lucy. 'You weren't to know he was from the Society. I'm just angry at myself for not realising what was going on. I should have guessed the moment he turned up at the pub last night that something was up.'

'But how could he have known I would be there? I only decided myself at the last minute.'

'I don't think he did know. I suspect he was just sussing out who I was and where I live. Then, when you turned up, he grabbed the opportunity.'

'That bastard,' said Jo again. 'If only I'd suspected.'

'Well you didn't, and that's that,' said Lucy. 'The point is, what do we do now?'

'I've got to get that book back,' said Jo decisively. 'Where do you suppose it is?'

'It's probably half way to the Lodge by now,' said Lucy.

'The Lodge? What's that?'

'It's where the Society keeps its most precious artefacts. The Society has a number of buildings all over the country, but the Lodge is the most secret. Its whereabouts are kept confidential except to the most senior members of the Society.'

'You mean even you don't know?'

Lucy shook her head. 'I'm not fully initiated, you see. It takes a couple of years.'

'Two years?'

'That's right. You have to pass five ordeals to be accepted. It's pretty tough.'

'But why two years?'

'Believe me, you need to leave a long time between each ordeal, if only for the marks on your behind to heal.'

'But it's not a strict timetable? You could do it in less time?'

'I suppose so. Nobody ever has, though.'

'Well I'll be the first.'

Lucy sat upright in her chair.

'Surely you're not going to join?'

'I have to. Can you think of any other way of getting the book back?'

'But you don't know what you're letting yourself in for.'

'I've got a pretty good idea.'

'No. You mustn't. Listen, I'll do some snooping around the Society. Maybe I can come up with some information.'

Jo shook her head. 'No, Lucy. You'd be too obvious. After all, they know you're my flatmate, and that you're bound to want to help me.'

'But you don't know how dangerous these people can be.'

'In which case I'll have to find out. Anyhow, if they are dangerous that's all the more reason why you should keep out of this. All I want from you is some moral support. First thing tomorrow, I'm going to call the Whipcord Society and apply for membership.'

And so it was that, three days later, Jo found herself making her way up to the door of that mysterious building in London for a second time. Once again she wore the false spectacles, but this time she had actually bleached her hair to the blonde colour of the wig. It would raise a few eyebrows at work, she knew, but that was small price to pay.

It was little enough disguise, but she hoped it would be enough to throw them off the scent. After all, if any of them had heard a description of Lucy's flatmate they were unlikely to recognise her as the girl. Besides, her first visit to the Society had been as a blonde, so that was how they would remember her. The only danger was that she might run into Hans, but Lucy had come home the previous evening with the news that, his job completed, he had returned to Holland, so she felt pretty safe on that score.

She had rung the Society two days before. At first the man on the other end had been cautious with her, but on hearing that she had attended the introductory evening he had relaxed somewhat. Now she was on her way to an appointment to discuss initiation into the Society, a notion that filled her with both fear and excitement.

She rang the doorbell and the flap opened. She gave the password and the doorman admitted her. This time, however, she was made to wait in the entrance hall whilst someone was sent to escort her. He was a large, ugly man in his late thirties, dressed in the now familiar black uniform. He had thick, ape-like features, and his gait too was decidedly simian. Jo wondered whether his knuckles ever scraped on the ground as he lumbered toward her.

'Name?' he asked in a deep, gravelly voice.

'Jane Larwood.'

'Follow me.'

The man loped off with Jo close behind him.

They passed the door to the auditorium where she had been introduced to the Society, and climbed a wide staircase. At the top, the man turned to her.

'Stand still and let me take a look at you.'

Jo stood where she was as he walked round her. She was wearing a short skirt and a simple blouse that showed off the shape of her breasts to good effect. The man inspected her carefully, brushing a stray hair from her shoulder with one of his great, hairy hands. When, at last, he was apparently satisfied with her appearance, he set off again, beckoning for her to follow.

They came to a heavy oak door, and he halted outside it. Then he raised his hand and knocked twice.

'Come!'

He pushed open the door and indicated that Jo was to enter. She stepped through and he followed her in, closing it behind her.

Jo found herself in a large room. It was almost devoid of furniture apart from a large oak desk at the far end and a low couch and two armchairs set about a coffee table by the window. The windows were obscured by heavy drapes and the walls were lined with oak panelling. A thick burgundy carpet covered the floor, giving the whole place an unmistakable air of luxury.

Sitting behind the desk was a man in a dark-grey suit. Jo's companion urged her forward and she crossed to where the man was sitting.

He was about forty-five years old, though his hair was still dark, with flecks of silver at the temples. He had thick, bushy eyebrows that seemed permanently creased in a frown, and a neat goatee beard. His eyes were brown, set deep, and Jo immediately felt uncomfortable under his gaze. She stopped just in front of the desk, her hands hanging at her side, and waited for him to speak.

'Miss Larwood I believe.' His voice was low-pitched, with an odd sense of menace to it.

'Yes, sir.' The 'sir' came automatically. This was the sort of man you called sir.

'Why are you here Miss Larwood?'

'I explained on the phone, sir.'

'Explain again. To me.'

'I came the other night. To the introduction.'

'And?'

'And I wanted to learn more.'

'How do you mean?'

'I want to join the Society.'

'You understand what we require of our female members?'

'I think so.'

'Tell me.'

'You tie them and whip them.'

'The key word, Miss Larwood, is obedience. Complete and unquestioning obedience. No matter what.'

'Yes, sir.'

'It isn't easy to gain entrance to our ranks. There are a number of tests. Many fail.'

'I won't fail.'

'Take off your clothes.'

Jo stared at him. 'I'm sorry?'

'It was a simple enough order. I want you to strip naked.'

Jo stared round at the gorilla-like figure behind her. 'Right here?' she asked.

Bang! The man's fist came down hard on the table.

'A few seconds ago you told me you wouldn't fail,' he barked. 'Yet you are already disobeying your first order. Now get out. You are of no use to the Whipcord Society.'

Jo was stunned. The whole thing was so unexpected. The order, his anger, and now her apparent dismissal. Her mind was a whirl. Every instinct told her she should do as he said. Leave this hateful place and forget all about the Whipcord Society. Then she thought of the book, and of the danger it represented in the hands of such people, and she knew she couldn't.

'I'm sorry, sir,' she said quietly. 'I wasn't thinking. It won't happen again.'

She reached up and began unbuttoning her blouse.

Jo was aware of the man's eyes upon her, as well as those of her escort, but she tried not to think of them. Instead, concentrating solely on what she was doing, she opened her blouse and shrugged it from her shoulders. There was nowhere to hang it, so she simply dropped it to the floor. She reached behind her and unzipped her skirt. It was a tight fit, and she eased it down over her hips and off. Her underwear was, as always, brief, and already she was a sight to bring stiffness to any man's cock as she stood before the two men.

The bra fastened at the front, and she slipped the catch undone with a flick. The cups fell apart, revealing her plump, luscious breasts as she allowed the garment to fall to the floor behind her. Now she wore only panties, shoes and a pair of black hold-up stockings that came up to about four inches below her crotch. She hesitated for a second, reluctant to lose the last vestige of her modesty. She looked across at the man, but he was stony faced. Slowly, reluctantly, she hooked her thumbs into the waistband of the panties and slipped them off.

'Leave the stockings. Place your hands behind your head and spread your legs.'

She obeyed, widening her stance and flattening her palms against the back of her head. She stared straight ahead of her, her cheeks glowing as she thought of the sight she must make, her breasts jutting forward, the nipples hard, her bare crotch open due to the stance she had been forced to adopt.

'I see your hair colour is not natural,' he said.

Jo's face reddened still further at the remark. She had considered bleaching her pubic hair as well, but had not thought it necessary on this first occasion. Now she wished she had.

'You will restore your hair to its normal colour as soon as possible,' ordered the man. 'Use a dye until it has grown back.'

'Yes sir.' Jo was relieved at the order. Keeping her hair bleached would have been a problem, and the initial blondeness had served its purpose in helping to conceal her real identity.

The man had pulled a piece of paper from a drawer and was writing on it. He folded it and held it out to Jo.

'Take this to the man at the front door,' he ordered.

For a second Jo was uncertain that she had heard him right. Surely he couldn't be asking her to go out of the room in this state? She glanced down at her clothes then back at him. His face was expressionless.

Slowly she reached out a hand and took the note. She opened her mouth to speak, then thought the better of it. Instead she gritted her teeth and, turning away from him, headed for the door.

She stepped out into the passage feeling very conspicuous indeed. She glanced right and left, but there was nobody about. She made her way back down the corridor. At the end was a full length mirror, and she found her eyes drawn to her own reflection. She studied her body, her eyes taking in the firm breasts that shook deliciously as she walked, then dropping to the neat black triangle of her pubic hair and the thick, pink lips of her sex.

She descended the staircase, her eyes still glancing guiltily about her, fearful that at any moment she would encounter someone. She retraced her steps past the auditorium and on towards the entrance hall. Her hand dropped to the doorknob and she paused momentarily, bracing herself for the encounter. Then she turned the handle and pushed.

The man was standing beside the door. As his eyes fell on her his face broke into a grin. She said nothing, keeping her eyes lowered as she entered the room. She handed the piece of paper to him and he read it.

'New recruit eh? What's your name?'

'Jane.'

'Jane, sir!'

'Jane, sir.'

'Well, Jane, just come in here with me.'

He moved across to small door off to the right of the entrance hall, opening it and indicating that she should enter. She went through with the man close behind her.

She found herself in a room that reminded her of a stable tack room All about the walls were hooks from which hung a variety of straps and chains, as well as whips, canes and other similar objects. There was a strong smell of leather. Jo turned to look at the man.

'Stand where you are, hands behind your head.'

Jo obeyed, placing her legs apart. The man moved across to the wall, where the objects were hanging, and for a moment she feared that she was to be whipped then and there. The man ignored the articles of punishment, however, turning instead to the straps. He selected a number of thin leather bands, each with a silver ring attached, along with a thicker studded collar, similar to the one she had seen Patsy wearing in the living room of the flat. He laid them out on a bench, then beckoned to her to approach.

He started with her wrists, wrapping the bands round and buckling them so that they fitted snugly against her skin. Then he made her stand on the bench whilst he fitted similar straps to her ankles. Jo stood silent as he fitted them, trying not to think about the perfect view he had of her sex as he looked up at her.

Once he was satisfied with the bands he ordered her down to the floor again and turned her round. Then he attached the collar to her neck. He fiddled with it a little, then gave a grunt.

'This'll need a bit of adjustment,' he said, undoing it once more.

At that moment the doorbell rang.

'Get that would you?'

Jo simply stared at him, certain that she couldn't have heard him correctly.

'What's the matter? I told you to get the door. I'm busy adjusting this damned thing.'

'But I'm . . .' she broke off, unwilling to state the obvious.

'You're what?'

'I'm . . . I'm not sure what to do, sir.'

'You know the fucking password. Just check that, then let whoever it is in. Get a move on, for God's sake.'

Jo hesitated a moment longer. Then, realising that he was perfectly serious, made her way out of the room. As she did so the doorbell rang again.

The flap was fastened by a simple bolt, which she undid, sliding the cover back. Outside was a young man with a girl in tow. Both were exquisitely dressed, he in an evening suit, she in a long and expensive looking dress, her neck and arms bedecked with sparkling jewellery. The man frowned.

'Why were you so long?'

'I'm sorry, sir. May I have the password?'

'Roissy,' he snapped.

Jo closed the flap, bolting it carefully. Then she unlatched the door and opened it, keeping her body behind it. She waited for a moment but nobody entered. She peered round the door to see that the man was still standing on the step.

'Have you no manners girl?' he said. 'Stand in the doorway, where I can see you.'

Jo gritted her teeth. Then she moved out of the protection of the door and stood beside it. The pair stayed where they were, their eyes roving up and down her naked form. Jo began to wish that she hadn't worn the hold-up stockings. Somehow they seemed to draw attention to her nudity – the contrast of the black nylon with the creamy whiteness of her flesh having an extremely erotic effect.

Still the man did not move. Behind him she could see people staring in her direction and pointing at the girl who stood so shamelessly in full view of the street. She felt the colour rising in her cheeks once more, but still she dared not move.

At last the man took his companion's arm and led her through the doorway. With relief, Jo was able to close the door, only too aware of the catcalls and wolf whistles coming from those outside. As the couple passed into the house she heard the girl giggle loudly.

She latched the door and went back to where the doorman awaited her. He said nothing, simply moving in behind her and placing the collar about her neck. This time it fitted perfectly, and he buckled it so that it was snug against her neck.

'Put your hands behind your head.'

She obeyed.

With a shock she realised that he was attaching the rings on her wrist bands to a catch at the back of her collar, which held them fast and completely incapacitated her arms. He checked the security of the catch, then moved his hands down, closing them over her breasts. She gave a sharp intake of breath as he caressed

109

her succulent mammaries, his fingers kneading the soft flesh.

'Right, Jane,' he whispered in her ear. 'Go back where you came from. You're done here.'

He removed his hands from her breasts and gave her a little push in the small of her back. She stepped out the door, aware of the way her nipples had stiffened under his caresses and praying that she wouldn't encounter anyone.

Her luck was out. As she approached the auditorium she heard voices, and she rounded the corner to discover the couple she had admitted, along with about a dozen others, standing outside the room with drinks in their hands. All talk stopped as she approached and made her way between them, her eyes cast down. Once again she heard their giggles and lewd comments. She was glad when she was past, and able to climb the stairs away from them. She was acutely aware of them staring at her firm, pert behind as she climbed the stairs.

When she entered the room again, she found a third man there, dressed in the customary black shirt and trousers. He was about forty years old, strikingly good looking, with a firm chin and deep blue eyes. There was no doubting the approval in his expression when he saw Jo enter, her hands still trapped behind her neck so that she was forced to thrust her breasts forward in order to hold her head up. Her clothes were nowhere to be seen.

The man behind the desk rose and began to walk about Jo, his fingers testing the fit of the bands and collar. She stood stock-still as he did so. He began making the most personal comments about her to the new arrival, discussing the size and shape of her breasts, the stiffness of her nipples and the damp sheen that now covered her sex lips. It was almost as if she was an animal at a cattle auction being assessed for her sale price.

Yet the emotion that was beginning to dominate Jo's mind was not shame or humiliation, but a creeping sense of sexual arousal. There was something about the way these men treated her, about the enforced nudity, the bondage and the servility, that appealed to an instinct that she was only now beginning to come to terms with. Now, as she stood, her naked body being so intimately examined, she could feel the heat and dampness in her crotch increase with every moment. It was an enormous relief to her when he finally he completed his examination and returned behind his desk.

'Well, Miss Larwood,' he said. 'You seem to be serious in your intentions. Are you prepared to go on to the next stage?'

'Yes, sir.'

'This gentleman is called Lander. He is to be your personal tutor and mentor. When in this building you will obey his commands at all times. Do you understand?'

'Yes, sir.'

She stole a glance at the man, but he was stony faced. She wondered if the sight of her nudity turned him on.

'Do you have any questions you wish to ask?'

'Yes, sir. How long will my initiation last?'

'There are five tasks to be performed, each of which is progressively more difficult. You must undergo all these ordeals before you can become a member of the Society. It normally takes two years.'

'Must it take that long, sir?'

'What do you mean?'

'Couldn't a girl do it in less time?'

He looked into her eyes. 'There is no time limit whatsoever. It usually takes a girl some time to gain the courage to progress to the next step.'

'I believe I could do it in two months, sir.'

He smiled. 'Nobody has ever done it in less than six.'

'Nevertheless I'd like to try, sir.' Jo's heart was hammering in her chest as she spoke. She wasn't even certain she could survive the first ordeal. But she knew she must act fast to recover the book before the wrong use was made of it.

The man behind the desk turned to Lander. 'It seems your new charge is ambitious,' he said. Perhaps you should start tonight.'

A shiver ran down Jo's spine at the words. Tonight! She wasn't at all sure she could take any more tonight. The whole evening had already been an ordeal. But she said nothing.

'There is a reception downstairs,' said Lander. 'I'm sure we could find someone willing to break her in.' It was the first time she had heard him speak. He had a deep and sonorous voice that seemed to dominate the room. The kind of voice that was accustomed to giving orders.

'All right,' said the man. 'Take her out. Miss Larwood is about to discover the pleasures of pain.'

Thirteen

Jo shivered slightly, and small goosebumps appeared on her bare flesh. The room wasn't cold, though. It was more a shiver of anticipation as she waited to see what would happen next. She was standing in a small, stark room with white walls and ceiling. Her back was to the wall, her hands still locked behind her head, but now she was further disabled by their being attached to a stud in the wall, so that she couldn't move from where she stood. On the opposite wall was a mirror, clearly placed there with the deliberate purpose of allowing captives to see themselves in bondage.

She ran her eyes up and down her own body. There was no doubt that she looked extremely sexy: her pert breasts pushed forward; the nipples pointing upward, the tips slightly swollen. Her eyes dropped to her flat belly and the neat, dark triangle below. Lander had ordered her to stand with her feet placed apart, and this left her sex lips visible. She was still extremely turned on, and she could feel the wetness seeping from within her and see the sheen of dampness down there that betrayed her state of arousal. She looked lower, to her long, slender legs, still enticingly encased in black nylon, the black high-heeled shoes making them appear even shapelier. Not for the first time she wished that her hands were free, and that she could caress her body and reduce the aching urge within her. She imagined her fingers sliding into the warmth of her sex, and a faint moan of frustration escaped her.

She wondered how long she had been in this room. At least half an hour, she was sure. Lander had led her down here immediately after her interview, securing her and leaving her alone with scarcely a backward glance. Since then she had had only the figure in the mirror for company.

She shuffled her feet. She wasn't sure if the waiting wasn't the worst part of the ordeal. Left alone with her thoughts, she found herself unable to rid her mind of erotic imaginings, the illustrations from the book seeming to fill her head. Jo could scarcely believe the change that the book had brought about in her. She knew now that it had completely cured her of her inhibitions and that, in truth she had no more need of it. Her own sexuality was confirmed, and her mind was freed to allow her to enjoy her lovely young body. Yet still she feared for any girl exposed to the book against her will, and it was for that reason she was standing in this featureless room, awaiting whatever fate was about to befall her.

All at once she heard footsteps in the corridor outside. She stiffened, holding up her head and staring straight in front of her. There was the sound of a key turning in the lock, and then Lander was beside her, his eyes cold and uncommunicative.

She wanted to speak to him. To ask him about what was to happen to her, but she dared not. Instead she merely stood passively whilst he released her from the wall.

Once she was free, he undid her hands from the collar. All at once Jo realised how stiff her arms had become, and she stretched them luxuriously above her head, then moved her shoulders round in circles, easing the dormant muscles. She wasn't free for long, though. No sooner had she dropped her arms than Lander had taken hold of them, pulling them behind her back and fastening them at the wrists. Then he withdrew a chain from his pocket about the length and thickness of a dog's lead. There was a ring at the front of her collar, as well as the back, and it was to this that he attached it. Jo realised at once that it was, indeed a lead, and when he tugged at it she followed him obediently from the room.

The cell was in the bowels of the building, and Jo was led along narrow corridors and up a pair of small staircases back into the part of the building with which she was more familiar. They approached the auditorium and, for a brief moment, she feared that she might be the entertainment for the evening, but they passed it and went on to another room close by. Lander paused at the door and knocked, then he opened it and pushed the girl inside. He did not follow her, but closed the door behind her leaving her confused and apprehensive.

The room was dark, the only illumination small wall lights that glowed dimly. Jo paused, trying to orientate herself. The furniture was low and comfortable looking, giving an overall impression of an expensive cocktail bar in a first-class hotel. From somewhere came the sound of piped music. Jo blinked into the gloom, trying to make sense of where she was. For a moment she thought she was alone. Then she began to discern the shadowy figures that sat about the room, all dressed in dark clothing and talking together, their voices barely audible above the music.

Slowly, as Jo's eyes accustomed herself to the darkness, she realised that the people in the room were the ones she had encountered earlier, outside the auditorium. They were sitting about low tables, sipping their drinks, the occasional peal of laughter punctuating their conversation. Jo gazed about her, uncertain what was expected of her. She felt pale and isolated, standing naked amongst these people, all of whom were resplendent in evening dress. The fact that her hands were trapped behind her only served to increase her sense of vulnerability. When no orders were forthcoming from

115

the group, she resolved to remain where she was, her legs planted apart, gazing straight in front of her.

She remained like that for a full ten minutes, with barely a glance being thrown in her direction. The whole situation seemed oddly anticlimactic to the girl. They had brought her to a high state of passion by stripping her and taking away the use of her hands. Now they seemed indifferent to the presence of the naked and aroused young woman who stood in their midst, aching to be touched. She began to wonder if she was in the right place, or if it was she who was expected to take the initiative, yet she dared not move for fear of the consequences.

Another five minutes passed. Then, at last, one of the men rose to his feet. She recognised him as the one she had admitted to the building earlier in the evening, and she averted her eyes as he walked over to her.

'My, my. We don't seem to be able to get away from one another this evening,' he said, coming to a halt in front of her, his eyes wandering frankly over her bare charms. 'Do you always go about like that?'

'No, sir.'

'What's your name?'

'Jane, sir.'

'Well, Jane. Come over and meet some of my friends.'

He took hold of the lead that Lander had left dangling between her breasts, and led her across to where he had been sitting. There were three more couples at the table, as well as the man's own companion, who grinned at the sight of the naked and helpless Jo.

'This is Jane,' the man said. 'Turn the light up and let's see her properly.'

One of the men reached up and flicked a switch on the wall. All at once a bright spotlight came on, its beam shining directly on Jo. She screwed up her eyes as the powerful light illuminated her body. It was as if she had been stripped naked all over again, and she blushed hotly at the sight she knew she must make, her breasts and sex starkly displayed to those watching.

'She's a pretty little thing, isn't she?' said the man holding the lead. He placed a hand over Jo's breast, smiling as he saw her sharp intake of breath. 'Yes, very pretty,' he mused, his hand squeezing her soft flesh. 'Such a pity she's not quite fully trained for her role of obedience. Still, I think we can start putting that right this evening, don't you?'

Jo couldn't see his companions through the brightness of the light, but she could hear their murmur of approval.

The man's hand left her breast and took hold of her chin, pulling her head round to face his.

'You didn't do a very good job of letting us in this evening, did you?' he said. 'First of all you took so long I had to ring twice, then you tried to hide that pretty little body of yours from us. That wasn't a very friendly way to behave, was it?'

'No, sir.'

'No,' he repeated, stroking her cheek. 'You must learn that here tardiness is taken as disobedience, and a reluctance to show off your body when you have been stripped for precisely that purpose is a serious misdemeanour. Do you understand?'

'Yes, sir.' Jo understood all right. She understood that the man was playing a game in which anything she had done would be considered a transgression. He was simply finding an excuse for what she knew must follow.

Punishment.

The word sent a shiver through her. She thought of the punishment that Patsy had received in the flat, and of Carla on the stage. She thought of the sound of the whip descending and of the red marks on their behinds. She shivered again, a shiver of excitement.

'Because we know that it's your first offence, we will be lenient,' said the man. 'Ten strokes with the paddle across my knee will be sufficient to teach you some manners, I think.'

As he spoke, Jo heard a sound and looked back to see that a chair had been placed immediately behind her in the full glare of the spotlight. Then she felt another tug at her lead.

'Over on the wall there is a rack, holding a set of paddles,' said the man. 'Choose one and bring it to me.'

Jo blinked in the direction he was pointing. The brightness of the light had left her bereft of any night vision, but as she stumbled off in the direction he had indicated, the residual beam lit up a series of narrow shelves on the wall. As she came closer she recognised that on each one was a wooden implement. They were each about fifteen inches long, rectangular in shape, but tapering to a handle at one end. They were of even length and thickness, but varied in width. Jo studied them, aware that whichever one she picked would soon be cracking down on to her bare flesh.

It was an almost impossible decision. If she picked one of the very thin ones she knew that it would sting her flesh unbearably. On the other hand, choosing one of the wider paddles might incur the wrath of her punisher and cause him to increase her punishment. Eventually she decided on a compromise, choosing a paddle about an inch and a half across.

It was only then that it occurred to her that she couldn't take it back to him in her hands. The rack was far too high up the wall for her to be able to reach, even if she turned round. For a moment she just stood, staring at the rack in confusion. Then she realised that she would have to use her mouth.

Leaning forward she rested her chin on the paddle and eased it to the edge of the shelf so that it partially overhung. Then she took it between her teeth. She turned and made her way back to where the man was standing.

He took it from her mouth and examined it. 'A good choice,' he said at last. 'This should serve my purpose adequately.'

He sat down in the chair and motioned her to approach him.

'Turn around,' he said.

Jo turned, facing into the light once more. She felt him fiddle with her wrists, then her hands were free. But once again her freedom was short-lived, as her hands were brought up behind her neck and locked in place once more. Clearly the move had only been to make her backside more accessible, and to prevent her covering it with her hands.

'Over my lap,' he ordered.

Tentatively Jo lowered her body over his lap, so that her pubis pressed against the top of his legs and her breasts hung down on the other side. The material of his suit felt smooth and warm against her bare flesh, and the sensation of contact with his strong body sent new spasms of excitement through her.

He ran a hand over her buttocks. His touch was light and sensuous and she gave a gasp as he squeezed the soft flesh of her behind.

'Spread your legs.'

Jo obeyed, trying not to imagine the sight she made. Through the glare of the light she could see the man's companions leaning forward in their chairs, whilst other couples had left their seats to stand and watch the show.

'Oh!'

Jo gave an exclamation as she felt him lightly trace the lips of her vagina, his fingers barely touching her clitoris as he made an intimate exploration of her most private place. She knew that the others all had their eyes fixed on her, and that they could see the dampness of the soft flesh and the way her sex muscles contracted. She knew that some of the women were laughing at her wantonness, but she knew too that many of the men were as aroused as she was, and even in the glare of the light she could see the bulge in their pants. She could feel one too, a hard lump that twitched every so often, pressing against her belly and she licked her lips as she imagined the proximity of his stiff cock to her burning sex.

He withdrew his hand, and she felt him wipe the wetness from his fingers on to her bare behind. Then she felt something else – the cool, hard surface of the paddle as he tapped it against her bottom.

Jo gritted her teeth. How many times since she had first read the book had she fantasised about being beaten, and had imagined the whip cutting into her flesh? And now here she was, on the verge of experiencing the pain of a thrashing for the first time, her naked body positioned like that of a schoolgirl about to be spanked.

The paddle came down on to her upturned behind with terrible force. The blow stung abominably, and it was all she could do not to cry out.

Down it came again, cracking into her flesh and causing the tears to well up in her eyes as the searing pain of the blow shot through her.

Never had Jo dreamed that the simple little wooden paddle could hurt so much. She found herself desparately struggling to release her bonds so that she could cover her behind with her hands.

Every time the paddle fell, Jo told herself that the pain couldn't possibly get worse, and every time she was proved wrong. For the first time she began to doubt that she could go on to face the other ordeals that had been promised to her. If a mere paddle had this effect on her what would a whip be like? She simply couldn't imagine.

The blows rained down relentlessly on the hapless girl, who writhed and moaned with pain.

But all at once she realised that something else was happening to her. Gradually, with each stroke that fell, Jo was becoming aware of a change in her emotions and of a feeling she would never have imagined could accompany such a severe beating. Every blow from the paddle, as well as setting her behind on fire, was accompanied by a surge of excitement inside her.

As the punishment continued, Jo found herself suddenly obsessed by the image of the illustration on the book's cover, and the expression on the woman's face. At the same time, she realised with a shock that her own expression must be the mirror image of that very picture. It was truly a revelation. At that moment, she was finally convinced that, whether she liked it or not, she was the perfect candidate for membership of the Whipcord Society.

Jo thrust her pubis down against the man's legs, her swollen clitoris rubbing deliciously against the material of his trousers. Her movements were overtly sexual now as the new passion built inside her. She knew there was one more blow to come, but the pain was receding from her mind as her thoughts were overwhelmed by a desire for an orgasm.

The final blow came down with extraordinary force, the paddle crashing into her red and stinging behind. Jo screamed aloud, jabbing her hips forward against him, grinding her love-bud against his thigh.

Then his fingers touched her vagina and she knew she had to come. The tension, the public display of her nudity and finally the bittersweet experience of the beating had taken her to the very edge, and she had to go all the way.

Suddenly careless of the onlookers, and of the exhibition she was making of herself, she half rose from his lap. Spreading her legs wide, she forced her open sex down against his knee and began to masturbate in the only way she knew possible at that moment, her bright red backside pumping back and forth with a terrible urgency, gasping as she drove her swollen clitoris down against him

The man watched her as she brought herself off on him, her breasts bouncing up and down before his eyes. Jo bit her lip, every jab of her hips bringing a new surge of lustful pleasure as she fought to satisfy her desires.

All at once orgasm racked her body, a low keening wail coming from her lips, her breasts shaking back and forth as she forced herself down against his knee, a dark wet patch appearing on the material. He did nothing. He simply sat back and watched her as she rode out her naked passion in the most wanton manner possible, extracting every ounce of pleasure she could from him until exhaustion overcame her and she fell back over his lap, gasping for breath.

A hand grasped her lead and pulled her to her feet. She turned to see the man's companion grinning at her, and her face turned the colour of her backside as she realised what a spectacle she had made. The man who had administered her punishment rose too, reaching out and caressing her breast.

'I can see you're going to be a real asset to the Society,' he said quietly.

Fourteen

Lucy inspected her appearance in her bedroom mirror. She was wearing the same clothes she had worn on the night she had beaten Patsy in the living room, except that this time she also wore the wrist and ankle bands that identified her as a slave. She checked every detail of her appearance, adjusting her stockings and brushing a speck of imaginary dust from her shoulder. She placed the cap on her head and checked the angle, then turned and gazed back over her shoulder at herself, examining every inch of her outfit.

At last she was satisfied. Her masters at the Whipcord Society would find no grounds for criticism tonight. She crossed to the bed, picked up her long overcoat and pulled it on before removing her cap and stuffing it into her handbag. She checked her watch. It was time to go.

It was quite unusual to get a summons from the Society at such short notice. She had been at work when she was called to the phone. The voice on the other end had been terse. 'The Society demands your presence in one hour. Don't be late.' Then had come the click and buzz of the line being disconnected. At once she had made an excuse and hurried home to get changed. And now here she was, ready to face her masters.

Lucy wasn't sure why, but she felt oddly nervous as she checked the windows in the flat. She wished she had had time to talk to Jo before going out. The two girls were becoming very firm friends now, and she had been at home when Jo had returned from her first ordeal, able to offer her sympathetic words and to rub a cooling ointment into her stinging behind.

Tonight, she knew, was the night of Jo's second ordeal, and she had hoped to be in the flat when her friend returned. She felt very guilty about what Jo was putting herself through, aware that it was her own fault that the book had fallen into the hands of the Society. In fact she had tried to find out where the book was herself, and had asked a few discreet questions of other Society members, but without success.

If truth be told, though, Jo was standing up to the ordeals handed out so far extremely well. In fact she had confided to Lucy the oddly erotic effect that the paddling had had on her, and had showed surprisingly little apprehension about the second stage of her initiation. Perhaps, after all, Jo was naturally suited to the ways of the Whipcord Society.

Lucy caught a cab to the Society, unwilling to ride the tube in her outfit despite the protection of the coat. She rang the bell and was soon inside, divesting herself of her outer garment and putting the cap back on her head. She wondered what they had in store for her. A summons such as this normally meant that she would be required to mete out a punishment to some unfortunate slave. The Society had, some time before, recognised her qualities as a dominant party and she was quite often called upon to beat young girls and even men for the members' enjoyment.

This time, however, she was led upstairs to the office of the overlord. It was unusual, to say the least, to be summoned by the leader of the Society. In fact it was the first time she had been to his office since, like Jo, she had been taken there on her first evening.

The ape-like man who she knew to be Bruno, the overlord's assistant, led her upstairs and knocked on the office door. He pushed her inside but did not follow.

Lucy felt very nervous in the presence of the man, and she hurried across to his desk, taking up her submissive stance with her hands behind her head and her legs apart.

The overlord didn't look up at first. He was intent on something on his desk. As Lucy glanced down at it, her eyes widened in surprise.

He was reading the book!

There, open on his desk, was *Secrets of the Whipcord*. She recognised the leather binding and the slight yellowing of the pages. She felt her heart leap with excitement. So it hadn't been taken out of London after all, and there was still a chance to get it back! For a second Lucy completely forgot about the reasons for her summons to the overlord's office, her attention fixed on the heavy tome that lay on his desk.

At that moment he looked up and she dropped her eyes, hoping he hadn't noticed her interest in the book.

'Ah yes,' he said quietly. 'Miss Stone. How are you progressing with the Society, Miss Stone?'

'I . . . er, fine sir,' stammered the flustered girl.

'Good.' He said. 'And are you happy with your situation?'

'Y-yes sir.' Lucy was confused. Surely he hadn't dragged her down here just to be asked these trivial questions?

'And when do you undergo your final ordeal?'

'In about a month sir.'

'Good.'

At that moment the telephone on the desk rang and the overlord picked it up. He spoke a few terse words into the instrument, then replaced it.

'Apparently Bruno and I are called away,' he said. 'You are to remain here until we return in about twenty minutes. Do you understand?'

'Yes, sir.'

Lucy watched as the two men departed. The door closed behind them and she was left alone in the room.

For Lucy the temptation to read the book was overwhelming. She gazed down at it, still standing where she was, trying to discern some of the writing on the page. But the combination of the distance, along with the fact that it was upside down made it virtually impossible. She glanced about herself. She was alone in the room, and the overlord had said he would be at least twenty minutes. Slowly she edged closer to the desk and skirted round it until she could make out the words on the page.

She began to read. The page bore an account of a young woman waiting naked and shackled in a dungeon. As she awaited her captors, she considered the possibilities for her impending punishment. Lucy read the account with increasing fascination as the woman recalled graphic descriptions of tortures she had witnessed, each one more painful and more erotic than the last. Lucy's fingers dropped to her crotch as she read, and she began to rub herself through the leather, her arousal increasing with every word she read.

She turned the page to be confronted by an illustration of the woman hanging in her chains in the dark, damp dungeon. Lucy studied the picture, totally transfixed by every inch of the woman's naked form which was picked out in perfect detail. She began to moan softly as she continued to move her fingers back and forth over her slit.

Suddenly she looked about herself and remembered where she was. She shook her head as if trying to shake the words she had been reading from her mind. She recalled Jo's description of how the book had the power to dominate one's consciousness to the exclusion of all else. She was beginning to understand what her friend meant. She had been totally absorbed in what she had been reading, her arousal was extraordinary and the temptation to masturbate was almost overwhelming.

It was at that moment that she knew what she must

do. Jo had been right. No book with the powers of *Secrets of the Whipcord* should be allowed to fall into the possession of unscrupulous men. And there was no doubt that the leadership of the Whipcord Society had very few scruples indeed. In their hands the book could be the undoing of many an innocent young girl. It was imperative, therefore, that the book be returned to Jo.

Once again Lucy looked about the room. She was still completely alone. This was the perfect opportunity to reclaim the book. Once it had been taken to the Lodge, she may never get another chance. But did she dare do it? The consequences if she was caught were unthinkable. Even if she got away with it, she knew she could never return to the Society. The thought dismayed her. The Society was part of her life, and she knew of no other place where she could receive such sexual gratification. Yet the theft of the book had been her own fault, and she must make amends to her friend.

Slowly, her hand shaking, she reached out and picked up the book. At once she experienced the sensations that Jo had described. The book felt warm and soft beneath her hands, as if she was touching a living thing. She felt an overwhelming desire to caress herself, but she knew there was no time.

She closed the book, averting her eyes from the picture on the cover, then tucked it under her arm. She made for the door, her heart pounding as much with fear as with the sensation of feeling the book's unique powers. She opened the door and glanced out. The corridor was deserted. She crept out and headed for the stairs.

At the foot of the staircase was a cloakroom. She slipped inside and picked up her coat. She put it on quickly, tucking the book underneath. Then she made for the front door.

The doorman eyed her idly. She knew him well. Indeed he had whipped her and fucked her on more than one occasion. She smiled at him.

'I'm finished for the night, sir,' she said.

He nodded, his eyes still fixed on her, and for a moment she feared that he would want something from her. Then she heard a moan from the next room and saw the naked young beauty hanging in chains on the wall, her back striped with the marks of the whip, and she knew he was otherwise occupied. She stood quietly whilst he unbolted the door, then stepped out gratefully.

Straight into the arms of the waiting Bruno.

She tried to struggle as he pulled her back in, but she knew it was in vain. He simply took her two wrists in one massive hand and, gagging her with the other, dragged her over the threshold, where the doorman was waiting to close the door.

Bruno stripped her unceremoniously, ripping the leather outfit apart as if it was made of cotton. In no time it was a heap of rags lying at her feet as she stood, red-faced and naked, still clutching the book.

He hitched a lead to her collar and, with a jerk that threatened to detach her head from her shoulders, dragged her off. The whole thing had taken less than half a minute, and she had barely had time to cry out as he pulled her back towards the overlord's office.

The overlord sat grim faced behind his desk as Lucy was brought in. Bruno took her right up to the great desk and brought her to a halt. Lucy stood, staring at the ground as the Society's leader cast a cold eye over her.

'Put the book down,' he said in a low voice.

Lucy stepped forward and placed the book carefully on his desk top. Then she straightened.

'Tie her.'

Once again Bruno moved with surprising speed for one so heavily built. He grabbed hold of Lucy's wrists, pulled them behind her and attached the bands together. Then she felt the cold steel of cuffs being placed round her arms just above her elbows, dragging them together and completely incapacitating her arms. The bonds had the effect of thrusting her shoulders back, making her plump, white breasts even more prominent as her chest was forced forward.

'Now, Miss Stone,' said the overlord, 'what have you to say for yourself?'

Lucy said nothing, simply staring at the carpet in front of his desk.

'You didn't expect to get away with it, did you?' he asked. 'From the moment you started asking questions about the whereabouts of the book we began to suspect your motives. That's why you were summoned here to-night.'

Lucy knew there was no point arguing. The whole thing had clearly been a trap from the start – a test of her loyalty to the Society. There was no doubt that they had expected all along that she would attempt to steal the book. She cursed her own stupidity. She should have known that they would never have made it that easy. And now she was in deep trouble, and further than ever from recovering her friend's property.

'Tell me, Miss Stone. Did you read any of the book?' asked the overlord.

'Yes, sir.'

'And is it true the effect that it has on women?'

In the excitement of the past few minutes, Lucy had all but forgotten the feelings the book had aroused in her. Now, though, as he reminded her, she realised that her nipples were still stiff and protruding, and that the muscles of her sex were pulsating, threatening to force the wetness within her into the open. Despite everything, she was still extraordinarily turned on. And all because she had read a few lines and glimpsed an illustration.

'Miss Stone?'

'It's true, sir,' she muttered.

He smiled. 'Good.' He said. 'And now, Miss Stone, there's the question of what we must do with you.'

Lucy said nothing. She knew that no amount of pleading or cajoling on her part would make any difference. These people were masters at sadistic practice, and to show weakness to them was precisely what they wanted.

'I think you should be put away for a period,' said the overlord slowly. 'We have just the place we need in the north of the country. A few months naked in a cell with regular beatings might bring you back into our fold. Otherwise we'll have to think of a more permanent way of disposing of you, perhaps in the Far Eastern slave markets. They'll pay a good price for a succulent young Westerner like you. It's up to you, really, Miss Stone.'

Lucy stared at him, unable to believe what she was hearing.

'But you can't . . .'

'We can, and will,' he replied. 'We have ways of covering up your disappearance. Nobody will suspect. You'll simply be called to the sick bed of an ageing relative, then won't return. Take the traitorous little bitch away.'

'No!'

But, once again, resistance to the powerful Bruno was useless, and the naked, captive girl found herself being dragged off towards the door.

'Oh, one other thing,' called out the overlord. Bruno stopped, still gripping Lucy's lead.

'That book seems to have had a remarkable effect on the young lady,' he said. 'See to it that she is not allowed any sexual contact for a week. Not even masturbation.'

Then he returned his attention to the books on his desk, without bothering to look up as Lucy was dragged from the room.

Fifteen

Jo stood in the street, staring up at the high Victorian edifice before her. It was certainly a large house. Four stories of tall, forbidding windows, with a further level below ground, presumably for the servants.

She pulled the piece of paper from her pocket and checked it again. This was the address all right. The letter from the Society had been delivered to her at work that very morning. She had chosen to use her work address for fear that some alert member of the Society would spot the fact that she and Lucy shared a flat. Lucy had assured her that it was not an uncommon practice to use a work address. Many of the girls had husbands or boyfriends from whom they wished to conceal their bizarre nocturnal recreation, and the Society was very discreet when making contact. The envelope had been delivered by a courier, who had insisted on handing it to her personally.

She had read it in the ladies' room, her fingers trembling as she tore it open and unfolded the sheet of paper inside. The note was short, terse even:

'The Poplars, 71 Grove Road. 8pm. Wear only what the Society has supplied.'

That last sentence had caused her a good deal of consternation. All she had received from the Society was her wrist and ankle bands and her collar. She had sat for ages staring at them, wondering what was really required of her. In the end she had decided to take it literally, and straps and collar were all she wore beneath her coat as she stood, staring up at The Poplars.

She checked her watch. It was a minute past eight. She dared not delay any longer. Slowly, reluctantly, she made her way up towards the front door and pressed a trembling finger against the bell-push.

She waited in silence for a short time, then heard the sound of footsteps approaching. The bolts on the door were drawn back and the door opened.

The man standing in the doorway was clearly the butler, and once again she was reminded of the master-servant relationship that the house had originally brought to mind. He wore a dark coat and trousers, with a bow tie. He had snowy white hair, and she guessed he was at least seventy.

'Yes?' His voice was cold, as was the look he gave her.

'I was sent for. My name is Jane Larwood.'

'Yes, Miss Larwood. You are expected.'

He stepped aside for her to enter. The interior decorations of the house matched the exterior. It was like stepping back a hundred years in time. None of the furniture or fittings would have looked out of place in a museum, and there was an air of dustiness and decay that seemed to hang over everything.

'This way.'

He led her past a loudly ticking grandfather clock and down a corridor, from the walls of which portraits of long-dead men and women glared down at her. At the end was a door that led through to a narrow staircase. This was clearly the entrance to the servants' quarters, the walls being bare and painted white, the wooden stairs without a carpet.

At the bottom of the stairs, a maid in a black uniform with a white apron was waiting for them. The butler stopped at the top and waited until Jo reached her, then turned and went back into the main part of the house.

The maid was young, no more than twenty-five years

old, Jo guessed, but her demeanour was that of one much older. The hair tied severely up in a bun under her cap, accompanied by the heavy rimmed glasses, gave her a slightly forbidding air. She eyed Jo with disdain, then turned away.

'Follow me.'

Jo was led through a large kitchen, where a much older woman was working. Lounging in a chair in the corner was a young man in footman's livery, and once again Jo was struck by the impression of having stepped back in time.

The girl took her into a room off the kitchen.

'Close the door,' she ordered.

Jo did as she was told, then turned to face the maid.

'Take off the coat.'

Jo had known the command was coming, but still she hesitated. What if she had misunderstood the note? What if this girl had no idea why she was here? How would she react when she saw that Jo wore nothing underneath?

'The coat,' repeated the maid.

Jo began undoing the buttons one by one, holding the coat closed at first, suddenly dreadfully embarrassed by her situation. When, at last, all the fastenings were undone she continued to hug the garment to her.

The maid held out a hand, and Jo knew she could delay no longer.

She let the coat fall open and shrugged it from her shoulders, her face reddening as she revealed her nakedness. The maid raised an eyebrow at the sight before her, but said nothing, taking the garment from her and placing it on a hanger.

'Come over here.'

She beckoned Jo across to a dressing table. As she did so she flicked a switch. At once an array of light bulbs lit up around the mirror. It reminded Jo of a theatrical make-up table, and the various items of cosmetics that lay on the surface reinforced that impression.

'Sit down.'

Gingerly, Jo lowered herself on to the stool that stood in front of the table. It was upholstered in a silky material that felt smooth and cool beneath her bare backside. The bruises from the paddling had just about cleared now, but there was still a slight ache, and she pondered apprehensively about what awaited her in this mysterious abode.

At once the maid set about making up Jo's face. She worked quickly and expertly, applying mascara and eye liner, then a bright lipstick. The image she produced was verging on the tarty, and Jo began scarcely to recognise her own features as she worked on. It seemed strange to be sitting there naked in front of this girl. She eyed the swell of her breasts in the mirror, the nipples brown and succulent. She felt an urge to caress them. The situation she was in was beginning to make her feel sexy, and, for the first time that evening, she began to feel the first awakenings of arousal deep within her.

The girl put some finishing touches to Jo's face. Jo had to admit that she had an extraordinary touch. There was something about the dark eyeliner and the scarlet lipstick that seemed to speak of her own wantonness.

What happened next took Jo by surprise. The woman closed her palms over Jo's breasts, making her gasp as she began to squeeze and caress them. At once the nipples responded, hardening into solid points as the caresses began to have their effect. The maid went on toying with them until they tingled with excitement. Then she picked up a small pot of rouge and a paintbrush.

She began to apply the rouge to Jo's nipples, the brush rubbing gently over the puckered skin and bringing fresh gasps from Jo. She was astounded. The idea of painting her nipples had never occurred to her before, and she watched with fascination as the young woman highlighted her swollen teats.

Once she was finished, the maid stood back to admire her handiwork.

'On your feet and over to that table,' she said suddenly.

Jo obeyed at once, hurrying over to where the woman pointed as fast as her high heels would allow. The table was large and solid, and would have looked perfectly at home in the Victorian kitchen outside.

'Sit on the edge,' ordered the maid. 'Then lie back and spread your legs.'

Jo was beyond surprise now. She simply turned her back to the table and levered herself into a sitting position, then prostrated herself, her breasts falling apart slightly as her back came into contact with the hard wood of the table top. Once prone she began slowly to spread her legs, only too aware of the view she was giving the maid of the soft petals of her sex lips.

The young woman crouched down and peered between Jo's legs. It was the most intimate of examinations, and the naked girl wondered what she could possibly be looking at. Her question was quickly answered, though, when the maid opened a drawer and withdrew a razor and a can of shaving foam.

Jo shivered as the foam was squirted on to her sex, then gasped as the maid began to rub it into the areas about her sex lips. It was an extraordinary sensation, at once sensuous and arousing as her fingers slid easily over the sensitive flesh, working it in with a smooth, rotating movement.

The girl opened the razor and ran it up and down a leather strap that hung down from the side of the table. Then she approached Jo once more.

A shiver ran through Jo's body as the cold steel of the razor came into contact with her flesh. She held herself as still as she was able whilst the woman set about her business. She worked slowly and methodically, scraping the blade along in small movements, collecting a mixture of foam and wiry hairs as she did so, pausing every now and again to wipe them on to a cloth.

It took no more than a few minutes for her to denude Jo's sex of all traces of hair. Jo had expected her to remove the dark bush that covered her pubis as well, but she shaved only to just above her slit, contenting herself merely to trimming what was left to a neat triangle and cutting the hairs to less than half an inch in length.

When, at last, she had finished, she wiped the area off with a warm flannel. Then she pulled Jo to her feet and led her across to a full-length mirror by the door.

Jo surveyed her body critically. The combination of her make-up and the red paint on her nipples made her appear oddly licentious. She looked down at her crotch, remarking on how visible her sex was, the dark triangle pointing like an arrowhead to the pink slit that was now so obvious, seeming almost to making a tacit statement about her sexual desires. Before, her nakedness had made her appear simply available. With her sex shaved, though, she seemed to be advertising her need to be looked at, and ultimately to be fucked. No woman could possibly depillate herself in such a way and not want her body to be admired. It was as if she was openly admitting her desire to give her body to a man, or men.

The maid picked up a hairbrush and ran it through Jo's hair. She had dyed it as instructed, and was glad to have it back to what was almost its natural colour. A further inspection followed, during which the girl removed the odd stray hair, then she nodded her satisfaction.

She pulled Jo's wrists behind her, and the now familiar click told Jo that the wrist bands were securely fastened. Then she picked up what appeared to be a black velvet bag from the table. She moved behind the naked girl, and placed the bag on her head, pulling it down over her eyes. Jo realised at once that it was a blindfold, an extremely efficient one that ran all the way down to cover the bridge of her nose. The maid adjusted it, then tightened a strap at the back of Jo's head, pulling it snugly against her face and removing all possibility of sight. Jo was suddenly enveloped in total blackness.

She felt a hand at her collar, and a metallic clink told her that a lead had been attached. Then she heard the door open, and the tug on the lead told her to follow.

She stepped uneasily into the kitchen, and a muffled snigger confirmed to her that the footman was still in his seat. She felt her cheeks colour as she stumbled along in her heels, her naked breasts thrust forward.

She followed the maid back to the stairs and up towards the main part of the house. Her instincts screamed at her to hang back. Being naked and tethered in the servants' quarters was bad enough. Somehow, the thought of joining those upstairs in her current state seemed twice as bad. But there was no escaping her fate now, and an impatient tug at her neck told her that the maid was having none of it.

She heard the door at the top of the stairs open, then felt the softness of the carpets beneath her shoes. The maid led her back to the entrance hall.

'Wait here,' she said. Then Jo felt another slight tug on her lead, followed by the sound of retreating footsteps.

She moved back slightly and felt the tension in her lead. It had clearly been tethered to something, leaving her unable to move more than a few inches in either direction. There was nothing for her to do but wait.

Jo had no idea how long she stood there, alone in the hallway, unable to move or to see anything, the only sound the ticking of the great clock beside her. As she waited she contemplated her fate, and not for the first time wondered what on earth she was doing, standing naked and cuffed in an unknown hallway awaiting a punishment she had done nothing to deserve. In any normal circumstances she would be at home now, curled up with a book or watching television in the comfort of her own sitting room. Yet the excitement she felt now was such that she already knew her life could never be the same again, and that the desires awakened in her by the book and by the Society would come to dominate her life from now on.

All at once she heard a step on the stairs and she froze. Somebody was coming down, and she trembled slightly as she imagined the sight she must make.

The footsteps stopped just in front of her, and she heard the sound of heavy breathing. She gave a start as she felt a hand touch her shoulder. It was an old, rough hand, and she guessed that it was the butler who stood before her, taking in her naked charms.

The hand moved lower, slipping down over the soft swelling of her breast and pausing to run a finger round the hard knob of her nipple. It went lower still, down her ribcage, over her belly and on through her pubic hair until it found the bare lips of her sex. She gritted her teeth as it sought out the hard little button of her clitoris, barely able to suppress a gasp as it probed her in her most private place. Jo knew she should be disgusted by the thought of this old man caressing her so intimately, but such was her arousal that the sensation of his fingers felt delicious, and she wished only that he would go further, drive his fingers deep into her and bring her the relief she craved.

She almost cried out with disappointment when he withdrew his fingers, and she felt the lips of her sex convulse. Then he was undoing her lead from whatever it had been attached to and she knew that the next part of her ordeal was approaching.

He led her up the stairs. Unlike the narrow passage that led down to the kitchen, she could tell that this stairway was much wider and richly carpeted. At the top was another corridor, and she followed the butler along it. Ahead of her she could hear voices, and a knot began to form in her stomach as she contemplated what was to come.

They came to a halt, and she heard the butler knock on a door. Then it was opened and the sound of the voices became suddenly much clearer. She felt another tug on the lead and she was inside the room.

At once the voices fell silent, then a woman gave a little shriek of delight.

'But my dear she's gorgeous. Where did you find her?'

'She came to us,' replied a man's voice.

Suddenly there were voices all around Jo. She couldn't tell how many, but she estimated at least ten people had watched her enter and were now chatting excitedly. Their accents were very different from those she had heard downstairs. Clearly she was among the aristocracy here.

All at once the chatter died away, and a single voice reached her ears.

'What is your name girl?'

'Jane, sir.'

'Why are you here, Jane?'

'The Society sent for me, sir.'

'All right Feathers, you may go,' said the voice, clearly addressing the butler.

'Will there be anything else, sir?'

'Yes. I shall require a cane. Make sure it's good and whippy.'

'Very good, sir.'

Jo felt her lead released. It hung down between her breasts, the metal feeling cold against her bare skin. Then the door closed behind her.

'Where are your clothes?' said the voice again.

'I didn't wear any, sir. Just my straps and a coat.'

'You came to my house naked?'

'Yes, sir.'

'Don't you think that is the act of a wanton woman?'

'It was what I was told to do, sir.'

'And are you in the habit of obeying such outrageous orders?'

'I must obey the Society, sir.'

'Society or not, you have deeply offended my guests by displaying your body in so depraved a manner. For that you must be punished.'

'Yes, sir.'

The words sent a new shiver of excitement through Jo's small, curvaceous frame. Already she was extremely aroused. Her nudity and the way the butler had touched her up had seen to that. She thought of the man's words. Was she really wanton and depraved? She knew he was simply playing the game, giving himself an excuse for the punishment that must inevitably follow, yet he had spoken the truth. Her actions that evening could only be described as both wanton and depraved, and the description triggered a new surge of wetness inside her.

The door opened again and Feathers returned. Jo heard him cross to where the voice had been coming from, and master and servant exchanged a few words in a low tone. Then she heard a swishing sound, like someone wielding a cane, and once again her stomach tightened.

'Prepare the girl for her punishment,' ordered the voice.

Jo felt the butler take hold of her lead and pull her forward. She stepped carefully, disoriented by the apparent size of the room. She was brought to a halt, then a pair of hands on her shoulders urged her forward a little more and she felt the edge of what appeared to be a table top suddenly press against her body at about the level of her pubis. Hands fumbled with the catches at her wrists, and all at once her arms were free. Then she felt hands on her shoulders once more, forcing her to bend forward over the table.

The wooden surface felt cold and hard against her

140

bare skin as she prostrated herself across it, her breasts pressed flat as he urged her down. Then the butler was undoing her lead and she heard a click as some new device was attached to her collar. She tried to move and realised at once that the ring in the collar had been attached to some sort of fitting in the middle of the table top, making it impossible for her to straighten up. As she was contemplating this new restriction she felt her hands grabbed and fastened to similar devices at the top of the table, stretching them above her head.

Jo was now trapped: her arms pulled tight; her body forced down on the wooden surface so that her cheek was hard against the table. She felt Feathers's fingers check her bonds, then he was behind her, his hands on her knees, forcing her legs apart until he was finally satisfied with her position.

Jo lay in her darkness, wondering at the sight she must make: her pale, naked body held fast; her backside projecting over the edge; the skin stretched tight. She knew too that, with her legs spread so wide, the occupants of the room would have an unrestricted view of her sex and anus, made even more visible by her recent depillation. It was a perfect position for a caning, she mused, then her stomach gave another lurch as she realised it was also a perfect position to be fucked in. Should any of her captors desire to take her, in her current situation there was nothing she could do about it.

The touch of a hard cane against her rear told her that, at present anyway, the occupants of the room were intent on her punishment. The tip of the weapon traced her spine up to her neck, then back down again, running through the crack of her behind and making her shiver as it paused against the tight hole of her anus.

'Now, young lady.' The voice was so close to her ear that it made her jump. It was that of the man who had spoken when she had first been brought in, and it had an undertone of menace that Jo found extremely unnerving.

'For your wanton behaviour in daring to present yourself to my guests in such an indecent state, you will receive ten strokes of the cane. Do you understand?'

'Yes, sir,' she said quietly.

'Kiss the instrument of your correction.'

Jo felt the end of the cane close to her face, and she kissed it lightly. Then it was withdrawn and she felt it tap her backside once more.

The first stroke almost took her by surprise as it came down hard across her backside. For a second there was only numbness, then the fire of the pain hit her and she bit her lip to avoid crying out.

Almost before she had registered the first stroke, the cane struck her again, cutting into the tender flesh of her backside with extraordinary force. The paddle paled to insignificance compared with the dreadful pain inflicted by this cruel instrument. It was as if the thin wood was slicing into her very skin and she felt the tears welling up behind her mask as the agony of the beating overwhelmed her.

Jo's hands curled into fists as the onslaught continued. Every stroke of the cane seemed to find a new area of skin to lay a fresh, red stripe across. Jo's backside was afire with pain now, yet the punishment had only begun.

Then, all at once, Jo realised that, along with the agony, the cane was arousing quite another emotion within her. She had thought it impossible that anything could distract her from the appalling sting of the weapon. Yet once again she was shocked to feel the surge of sexual excitement that it was bringing, and she felt her nipples pucker into tight knots.

This time she was quite unable to suppress a yelp of pain as the thin instrument of her punishment began finding areas that had already received a lash, doubling the agony as it lashed anew on to her soft behind. Yet still her mind was filled with images of eroticism and she found herself thrusting her hips forward against the edge of the table in a vain attempt to generate some friction against her swollen clitoris.

Jo screamed still louder as the cane descended like the stinging of a thousand wasps. She was tugging at her bonds now, desperate to cover her behind and protect it from the dreadful force of the beating. But her struggles were in vain, and she tensed herself for the ultimate stroke.

The final blow landed right in the most tender part of her punished behind. Then the room was silent, apart from Jo's stifled sobs.

They left her there for another five minutes, until her breath was restored and the tears had ceased to flow. Then she felt her wrists and collar freed and she was able to stand once more. Jo's pain was excruciating, as if her behind was on fire, yet it was the heat in her sex that dominated her thoughts, and she could feel the muscles contracting down there, something that she knew must be visible to all those in the room. She ached to touch herself, but dared not, simply standing with her arms by her sides.

A hand touched her backside, making her wince with the pain, but she made no sound.

'I trust this punishment has taught you a lesson,' said the man's voice.

'Yes, sir.' It had taught her a lesson all right. It had taught her of the appalling pain that a cane could inflict, and of her ability to take that pain. It had taught her also of her own extraordinary response to this kind of treatment. Nothing she had read in the book had ever turned her on as much as now, and she found herself longing for the attentions of a man. Even Lucy's vibrator would have been a relief.

'I see the pain brings out certain desires in you, young lady,' the man went on. Jo cursed the recalcitrance of her body, and the way her sex continued to pulsate with

143

desire. She knew that her sex lips would be coated with a thin sheen of lubrication now, and that this must be obvious to those watching.

'If I were a more lenient master,' he continued. 'I might grant you release from your yearning. But I prefer to leave you with your frustration, and allow you instead to relieve my own tensions. After all, this is supposed to be a punishment. Now, get on your knees.'

A few weeks before such an order would have led to a blaze of indignation from Jo. Now, however, she was quick to obey, dropping to a kneeling position at once. She sensed the man moving closer, then he took her hand and guided it to his crotch.

Jo gasped as her fingers closed around a large, thick cock. It felt hot to the touch, and every now and again it would twitch under her fingers, revealing the man's own state of arousal. She reached up with her other hand, running it down his shaft and sliding it underneath to cup his balls, caressing them gently.

'Suck me.'

Once again there was no hesitation. She leant forward until her nostrils were filled by the scent of his excitement, then opened her lips and took him into her mouth.

His cock tasted salty, and she ran her tongue back and forth over the small hole at the end, bringing a sharp intake of breath from her punisher. Then she moved her head forward, taking almost the entire length into her mouth and beginning to suck at him.

For the moment the fire in her own belly and behind was forgotten as she concentrated on pleasing her master. She grasped his cock with one hand, working the foreskin back and forth as she bobbed her head up and down. Once again she wondered at the sight she must make, naked and blindfold, her backside crisscrossed with angry stripes whilst she sucked hungrily at the very man who had put them there. She could feel her breasts bounce with the rhythm of her movements, and she knew the rest of the people would be watching them. Yet somehow she didn't care. At this moment she was no longer Jo, the shy young clerk; she was Jane Larwood, slave and mistress, and the man she was sucking at so greedily was her master, the man she must serve.

She began to move her head faster, and was rewarded with renewed gasps from the man. He was thrusting his hips forward now, grasping her hair and forcing his rampant penis ever deeper into her mouth. Then he stiffened, and she braced herself to receive his seed.

He came with a spurt of semen that splashed against the back of Jo's throat, threatening to make her gag. Barely was she able to gulp down this first helping than a second load of spunk shot from his rod, then a third. Jo fought to swallow every drop of the warm, viscous fluid that seemed to be coming in an endless stream now. She could feel it escaping from the corners of her mouth and dribbling down her neck on to her breasts, and still she bobbed her head up and down, milking him of every drop until at last he gave a sigh and slipped from within her. Jo remained where she was, kneeling before her audience, feeling the trickle of sperm run over her breast and drip from the tip of her nipple onto the carpet. Her backside hurt, her cheeks glowed with embarrassment at her behaviour and her sex burned with desire. Yet she allowed a small smile of triumph to cross her face.

She had survived her second ordeal.

Sixteen

Jo woke early the following morning. She rolled over on to her back and winced as she was suddenly reminded of her caning. She reached tentatively down and stroked the tender skin of her behind. Her fingers were able to trace thin ridges that marked where the cane had fallen, and even after a night's sleep the marks still stung dreadfully.

She eased herself on to her stomach and slid out of bed. Her foot caught something on the floor and she bent down to pick the object up. It was Lucy's dildo, and she smiled at the sight of it. It had been lying on her pillow when she had come home and she had used it eagerly, enjoying four orgasms in quick succession after the frustrations and eroticism of her ordeal.

The people at the house had dismissed her soon after she had brought her punisher to orgasm. The butler had led her down to be collected by the maid and taken into the servants' quarters again. Once more the footman was treated to the sight of her naked body, this time with her behind decorated with weals and her breasts and neck still sporting evidence of her master's orgasm. He had made a lewd comment as she was led through the kitchen, but she had ignored it, and before long was out of the building and headed back to her flat.

There had been no sign of Lucy on her arrival, and she had been unwilling to try to wake her friend. Besides, the discovery of the dildo had been a welcome one and she had stripped off her coat at once, not even pausing to remove her straps before crouching on all fours on the bed and sliding the whirring phallus into her sex. It had taken some time to finally satisfy her extraordinary desires, but at last she had dropped the vibrator on the floor and fallen almost at once into a deep sleep.

She moved across to the mirror and examined her reflection, turning her back to the glass and craning round. Her backside was quite a sight – the normally pale, soft skin covered in bright-red stripes, some of them stretching right round to the front of her thighs, evidence of the extreme whippiness of the cane. She was beginning to get some kind of inkling as to why the initiation into the Society took so long. Lucy had told her that it had taken months of lesser beatings to bring herself to a point when she could withstand ten strokes of the cane on her bare behind, and she herself had done it in less than a fortnight. For the first time she began to doubt her ability to gain initiation to the Society in such a short time. Perhaps she was being a little over-ambitious, she told herself. Certainly she would be unable to wear any knickers for a few days, and she hoped she would not be required to sit down for too long when she got to work.

She pulled on a thin, transparent robe that hung by the door and stepped out into the living room. She would wake Lucy and recount her experiences of the previous evening. Besides, she knew that her friend had an ointment that was particularly effective against the marks that had been left by her beating, and she could do with a little relief from the throbbing pain in her rear.

The first thing she noticed on entering Lucy's room was that the bed had not been slept in. This surprised her, since normally her flatmate was careful to tell her if she was staying out all night. Besides, they had already agreed to exchange experiences this morning, before Jo left for work. It really was most unlike Lucy to break such an agreement.

Suddenly it struck Jo how tidy the room was. Normally there would be clothes discarded on the floor and a mass of bottles and jars on the dressing table. Today there was no sign of any of these. Jo went to the wardrobe and opened it, then gave a cry of surprise. It was empty. Where before Lucy's great collection of outfits had filled it, now there was no more than a row of hangers that clanged together as she pulled the door wide.

Jo turned to the chest of drawers, pulling each one open in turn and checking inside. Once again there was nothing.

It was then that she spotted the piece of paper on the table beside the bed. It was a purple notepaper that she knew was of a type used by Lucy. As she came closer, she saw that her own name was scrawled across it.

Jo picked it up. It was folded in two, and she opened it. There were just a few words, and she read them carefully.

'Jo. Had a call from my mother. My aunt's been taken ill, so I'm going up to help look after her. Sorry about the short notice. Rent's in the drawer. See you sometime. Lucy.'

Jo read and re-read the sheet, her mind scarcely able to take in the words. She pulled open the drawer and there, indeed, was a bundle of twenty-pound notes. She counted them. There was more than enough to cover rent and other bills.

Jo shook her head. How could Lucy have deserted her so suddenly, without even waiting to say goodbye? Certainly an ailing relative was something of an emergency, but surely she hadn't needed to leave quite so suddenly? And not even a forwarding address where she could be reached. It really was too bad of Lucy to leave her in the lurch like this. In fact it was completely out of character. Lucy was normally so reliable.

Jo studied the note once more. She wasn't familiar with her friend's handwriting, but the style was so unlike the girl. Normally there would have been some kind of more personal comment. And then there was the dildo. Leaving that for her was typical of Lucy's sense of fun. To have done that, then left this terse note just didn't make sense.

All at once, Jo was convinced. Lucy hadn't written the note. It just didn't seem to be in character with the girl she had shared a flat with for so long. On an impulse she picked up the phone and dialled the number of the pub where Lucy worked. It rang for a while, then a sleepy voice sounded on the other line.

'Yeah?'

'Hello, sorry to wake you. I wanted to know if Lucy was in last night?'

'Lucy who?'

'The barmaid. Did she work last night?'

'Who is this?'

'It's her flatmate. Only she didn't come home last night.'

'No. She wouldn't. I got a call to say she won't be coming back. Sick aunt or something. Bloody nuisance.'

'Did she call you herself?'

'What do you mean?'

'I mean did she make the call in person?'

'I can't remember. Wait a minute ... No. It was a man. Said he was her boyfriend. Listen what's the problem?'

'Nothing. You've been helpful. Thanks.'

Jo placed the receiver slowly back in its cradle. Something very strange was going on. Lucy's disappearance just didn't make sense. At once Jo's imagination began to run wild. Perhaps some kind of psychopath had got hold of Lucy and she was lying dead in a ditch somewhere. Maybe she should call the police and report her missing.

But even as the thought entered her mind she dismissed it. This was no psychopath. What kind of psychopath would come back and clear her flat, then write notes and telephone her employer. Then there was the money. What sort of nutter would leave a wad of notes behind? And neither was it likely to have come from Lucy. She was always complaining how hard up she was. How could she suddenly find so much cash? But something extraordinary had certainly happened. This whole thing bore the hallmarks of some kind of trickery. Someone had removed Lucy from the scene, and had cleared her things. But who?

Jo knew at once that there was only one possible answer. Only one group had the facilities and the organisation to carry out such a deed.

The Whipcord Society.

Once again she considered ringing the police, but then shook her head. How could she explain the Society, and her own involvement with it, as well as Lucy's? Besides, Lucy had confided to her that the Society had members from all walks of life, including the police, the judiciary and the government. She was more likely to end up in precisely the same position as Lucy.

But what if her friend was in danger of her life? Jo considered the possibilities carefully. Lucy was a beautiful young woman, with a propensity for both giving and accepting punishment. As such she was a valuable asset to the Society. Lucy had told her of institutions where girls were held for the purpose of giving pleasure to Society members. She herself had confided that she wasn't certain whether some of the girls went willingly. If it were true, then it was almost certain that Lucy was being held in such a place.

Jo's resolve returned. The only way to find out what had happened to her friend was to penetrate the Society. She had to go ahead with the other three ordeals now, and as soon as possible. What had started out as a quest to retrieve her book had now become a far more important task. She had to find Lucy, and find her as soon as possible.

Seventeen

It was a week later when Jo contacted the Society head-quarters to arrange her fourth ordeal. During that week she had waited hopefully for news of her friend, but none came – the absence of news simply confirming her belief that her friend was a prisoner of the Society.

The marks of her caning had taken a long time to fade so that even after a week her behind was still dark with bruises. Yet her determination to gain full membership was as strong as ever as she punched in the Society's number.

The phone was answered by a male voice, and she asked at once to speak to Lander. When he came on the line his voice seemed distant and non-committal.

'Yes?'

'This is Jane Larwood, sir.'

'What is it?'

'I want to take the third ordeal.'

'It's too early. Call again in a month.'

'No!'

'I beg your pardon?' His tone was cold.

'I'm sorry, sir. But I can't wait.'

'It's only been a week since your last encounter. You need more training.'

'I can do it. Please let me, sir.'

'Nobody has ever gone to the third stage so soon.'

'I'm not anybody. Let me try, sir. I can only fail.'

'If you fail you will be required to wait a year before trying again.'

'I understand, sir.'

There was a long pause. Then:

'Meet me the day after tomorrow. I'll tell you where.'

And the phone went dead.

Jo replaced the receiver and sat down. She was trembling slightly, but she wasn't sure whether it was with fear or excitement.

Her instructions, when they came through, were to meet Lander in a wine bar in a back street near Covent Garden. When Jo arrived he was waiting at the bar and, as soon as he saw her, ordered a bottle of red wine and led her to a cubicle in the corner of the room. As with all matters concerning the Society, Jo was consulted on neither the venue nor what they would drink, but she had become used to their ways and was happy to comply with Lander's wishes, as well as to wear the wrist bands and collar, despite the fact that it was a public encounter.

She sat down opposite him in the booth, sipping her wine and enjoying the warm feeling it brought to her stomach. At first he did not speak, and she remained silent herself, easily adopting the subservient role the Society required of her. When, at last, he did speak, he took her quite by surprise.

'How's your backside?' The question was asked so casually that he might have been enquiring after the health of a relative.

'It's okay, sir,' she replied.

'Let me see.'

The order took her completely unawares, and she simply stared at him.

'I want to see your marks,' he insisted. 'Are you wearing any panties?'

'Yes, sir.'

'Take them off.'

Jo stared about her. There were other customers in the wine bar, but none was looking in her direction, and the cubicle in which they were sitting was fairly secluded. Even so, the request was certainly an odd one.

'Come on young lady,' he snapped impatiently. 'I told you to take them off.'

Jo knew she had no choice. It was all part of their game with her, and her role was to obey. She was wearing a very short black dress, and now wished she'd worn a longer one. Glancing about one final time, she raised her backside from the seat and reached under her dress, hitching it up as she did so. She slipped the panties off in a single movement, pulling them over her shoes and smoothing down her dress once more. It was only when she had finished that she realised that a waiter was standing near the bar and must have witnessed everything. She blushed and lowered her eyes when she saw him watching her.

'Put them on the table.'

Slowly Jo brought up her hand from underneath the table and placed the brief white garment down in front of Lander.

'Now, come round here and show me your backside.'

Jo could barely believe that he was serious. But she dared not hesitate again, so she slid out of her seat and went round to stand beside him.

'Turn round.'

She obeyed, and found herself facing the waiter once more. She felt Lander lift the back of her dress, and once again her face reddened as she saw the waiter's eyes on her.

Lander took his time, running his fingers over her bare behind and tracing the marks of the cane. Every now and again he would press hard on a particularly sensitive spot, and Jo would wince with the pain.

At last the inspection was over, and he lowered her dress.

'Sit down.'

She obeyed, grateful to be in a less conspicuous position.

'You still have marks, and they still cause you pain.'

'Yes, sir.'

'And yet you're willing to move to the next test?'

'Yes, sir.'

'Most girls take months, slowly learning to deal with the pain. You realise that next time it will be the whip?'

'Yes, sir.' In fact Jo hadn't been certain what to expect, but she had guessed that the whip would be a logical escalation.

'And you know you won't be allowed simply to satisfy your punishers with your mouth?'

'No, sir.' The words sent an odd tremor through Jo's body.

'Your marks still hurt?'

'They're not so bad now, sir.'

'Nevertheless, if you insist on going ahead it'll be in less than a week's time.'

'I'm ready, sir.'

'Very well then, you will report next Thursday at seven in the evening. You may wear what you like, but be certain to have on your straps.'

'Yes, sir.'

Thursday. Only five days away. Jo wondered if she would really be ready.

Eighteen

Thursday dawned wet, and the rain persisted into the evening. Jo headed down the street in the direction of the Society's headquarters, dodging the puddles and the other pedestrians huddled under their umbrellas. Under her coat she wore a simple blouse and miniskirt, along, of course, with the mandatory straps. She shivered as she hurried along, her head bowed into the rain, her heels clicking loudly on the pavement.

As usual, the sight of the building sent a tremor through her, and she absent-mindedly ran a hand over her bottom. The bruises were completely faded now, though she still felt a slight twinge whenever she sat down. And now she was going to start it all over again, she thought to herself.

She went through the normal formalities for gaining admission and, having handed over her coat, was shown to a small room in the basement, where she was ordered to wait.

The room was without any furniture at all. Jo stood in the centre, her hands behind her head and her legs apart. She had not been told to do this, but had taken up the submissive stance on her own initiative. In the ceiling was a small video camera and she watched it warily as it stared down at her, occasionally emitting a whirring sound as it tracked back and forth.

The wait was a long one, but she had come to expect that. Keeping the girls waiting was clearly a tactic employed by the Society to ensure that they suffered maximum anxiety whilst contemplating what was to come.

At last the door opened, and Lander came in. His face was, as always, expressionless, but Jo was glad to see that he expressed no disapproval of the way she was dressed. He walked around her, his eyes constantly fixed on her figure, his expression so intense that it seemed to burn into her. At last he spoke.

'Take off the skirt and blouse.'

Jo was too experienced with the Society's ways to register any surprise at this order. She reached at once for the buttons on her blouse and began to undo them. She pulled the garment off and dropped it on the floor. The skirt swiftly followed and soon she was standing in a white lacy bra that lifted her breasts beautifully and a matching pair of panties that were so brief as to be little more than a G-string.

Once again, Lander could find no fault. He moved behind her and, taking hold of her wrists, snapped her straps together, pinning her arms behind her. Then, to her surprise, he produced another set of straps and proceeded to attach them to her arms just above the elbow. These too he joined together.

The addition of these straps brought a new dimension to Jo's bondage. Not only did they totally disable her arms, but they also had the effect of thrusting her chest forward, making her firm breasts even more prominent. Lander ran a finger down from her shoulders over the skin of her arm, making the tiny, downy hairs stand on end.

'In future you will wear these straps too when you are summoned here,' he said.

'Yes, sir.'

'Now,' he went on, 'tonight's ordeal will be a long and arduous one. There were no Society members available at such short notice, so we have found substitutes. The two men you will be entertaining have paid well for

156

the use of you, so you will have to try doubly hard to please them, is that clear?'

'Yes, sir.'

'These men have paid for the use of your body, and they are free to use it in any way they wish short of actually damaging you. You understand the implications of what I'm saying?'

'Yes, sir.'

Jo knew precisely upon what terms she had presented herself that evening, but hearing them voiced so clearly made her stomach tighten into a knot. She glanced down at her scantily clad body, and shivered with anticipation.

Lander attached a lead to her collar, then they were off down the winding corridors of the building once more. She had expected to be taken upstairs to one of the suites, but instead Lander halted outside a heavy oak door. He knocked once, then pushed it open, leading her inside.

The room was dimly lit, and it took a few seconds for Jo to accustom her eyes to the gloom. In one corner was a table laid for dinner, with a lighted candlestick in the centre. Two men were seated at the table, eating. As Lander brought Jo in they looked up. He pushed her forward until she was standing close to the table, her legs apart as she knew he would insist.

She eyed the two men who had paid for her company that night. Both were in their late forties, one balding and somewhat overweight, the other slimmer with short silver hair and glasses. Neither was exactly what she'd call attractive, but still she felt a thrill as their eyes took in her barely clad body.

'This is Mr Green,' said Lander, pointing to the balding man. 'And this is Mr Brown.'

'Good evening, sirs,' said Jo, wondering briefly what their real names were.

'Jane here is yours for the evening,' Lander went on. 'She will obey your every command.'

'Good,' grunted the man referred to as Green. 'Undo her arms for a second.'

Lander snapped the catches on Jo's wrists and elbows undone, and she immediately placed her hands behind her head. The action had almost become instinctive now, and she even had difficulty preventing herself taking up the stance at work when confronted by a senior.

The men both put down their knives and forks.

'Take off your bra,' said Brown.

Once again Jo obeyed straight away, unhooking the straps and letting the garment slip down her arms and off. She dropped it to the floor and placed her hands back behind her head, her cheeks reddening as she saw how hard her nipples were.

'Turn around,' said Brown.

She did so, averting her eyes from Lander's as she faced him. She stood, almost feeling their eyes as they took in the curves of her lovely young body.

'Face us.'

Again she turned.

'Mmm. Very nice, Mr Lander. Very nice indeed. Such succulent tits. I think we'll be well pleased with her. Now shackle her whilst we finish our meal.'

Lander took Jo across to the wall beside the table. Hanging from the ceiling were two chains with manacles attached to the ends. He took her hands and closed the manacles about her wrists, tightening them until they were a snug fit. Then he hauled on another chain and she found her hands dragged high above her head. He continued to pull until her body was stretched taut, her breasts pulled almost oval such was the tension in her. Then he undid her lead and slipped it into his pocket.

'Will you be requiring me any longer, gentlemen?' he asked.

'No,' said Green. 'It all seems to be in order.'

Lander gave a little bow, then headed for the door,

closing it behind him. The two men, with barely a glance at Jo, continued their meal.

Without Lander, Jo felt strangely abandoned. It wasn't as if he showed her any sign of friendship or sympathy, but he was, at least, a face she knew, and she felt most uncomfortable alone with these two men. There was a mirror on the wall opposite her in which she could clearly see her reflection. This was a feature of the Society that she was becoming used to. It was clear that these mirrors were deliberately placed where the young captives would be able to see themselves as their punishments were meted out, and it was a device that, in her case at least, never failed to increase her arousal. This time was no exception, and as her eyes took in her stretched body, the breasts firm, the nipples pointing upwards, she felt her lust begin to increase.

The men seemed in no hurry to enjoy their sensuous acquisition, however. They ate without any sign of haste, sipping at their wine glasses and talking in low voices, only occasionally glancing across at the lovely young girl, so deliciously bared and shackled by their table.

When, at last, they had finished what was before them, Brown picked up a small brass bell from the table and rang it. Almost at once the door opened and in came two young women, each not much more than sixteen years of age, and both dressed in waitresses outfits, with short skirts and aprons. Jo was shocked that girls so young could be being used by the Society, but when they caught sight of her they froze, staring openmouthed, and she realised that they must simply be working for whatever catering company was supplying the meal.

'Come on, clear the table,' ordered Brown.

The girls looked at one another, then back to Jo, and giggled, clutching their hands to their mouths. Then they began clearing the plates and dishes.

If Jo thought her wait was over, however, she had another thing coming. The waitresses returned with a sweet trolley from which both men partook, followed by cheese and biscuits, coffee, brandy and cigars. An hour later, Jo was still hanging where Lander had placed her, her body stiff and aching from the constant tension. Yet still the fire burned within her, and even the mocking looks of the two girls failed to dampen her ardour – their giggles, on the contrary, making her feel even more aroused as she contrasted her bare breasts with their safely covered ones.

At last the waitresses cleared the table and wheeled the trolley away. Then they returned to stand by the table. Green regarded them both.

'You have been told there are extra duties for you tonight?' he said.

'Yes, sir,' chorused the pair.

'And you are aware that anything you see or hear within this room is totally secret?'

'Yes, sir.'

'I hope so. You are both being very well paid to assist tonight, and if you do as you are told there may be other occasions. Now release the slave.'

The girls turned to each other with questioning looks in their eyes, then Brown indicated Jo with a nod of his head.

The two girls approached Jo on either side. They had clearly been tutored in the workings of her chains, and in no time had loosened them and removed the manacles. For Jo the relief from the stretching of her limbs was wonderful, and she longed to windmill her arms to try and relieve the ache. Instead she clasped her hands behind her head and stepped forward, rather unsteadily, to stand beside the table.

'The lights,' said Green.

One of the pair pressed a switch on the wall, and all at once a number of spotlights lit up on the opposite side of the room. They were trained away from the dining table and on to a large wooden frame that stood on its own. In the darkness it had been almost invisible, but now Jo saw that it was a rectangular lattice, almost like one that might be seen in a garden, though made of much thicker wood. It was supported by two upright posts that were attached at the centre of each side, so that it was able to pivot round them. At each corner, chains glittered in the brightness of the spotlights.

'Remove her pants.'

'Sir?' The two waitresses stared at him once again.

'The slave. I want her quite naked. Remove her pants please.

The youngsters exchanged glances.

'Come on!'

The pair hesitated a moment longer, then one of them stepped forward

Jo made no move, simply staring straight ahead as the waitress approached her. The girl dropped to one knee in front of her then, hooking a finger into each side of the waistband, dragged the skimpy panties down her legs. Jo raised her feet to allow them to be pulled off. She knew that, from her low perspective, the girl would be able to see how the hair was shaved away from her sex. She suspected too that, standing as she was with her legs akimbo, the wetness that had been seeping into her sex for the last hour would be visible.

The girl handed Jo's knickers to Green, who tossed them aside. 'Secure her to the whipping frame,' he ordered.

This time the waitresses seemed to know what was required, once again fuelling Jo's suspicions that they had had some degree of training in the use of the equipment. They each took hold of one of Jo's arms and led her across the room towards the frame. As she drew close, Jo saw that it was a very sturdy construction indeed, the lattice running diagonally with holes about five inches across. She was made to stand close up to it, so that her protruding nipples brushed against the hard, wooden surface. Then her hands were pulled up above her head, and once again she felt the cold steel of manacles closing about her wrists, attaching them to the top corners of the frame.

When these were in place, the pair went to either side of the frame and, moving back a small lever, began to rotate it on its pivot, rocking Jo's body forward until she was lying horizontally on her face across the wooden square.

The two girls took hold of Jo's wrists once more, urging her further up the frame and pulling in the chains that held her wrists. Then they slipped off her shoes and dragged her ankles apart, fastening them to the bottom corners, once again tightening the chains until Jo's body was in tension. Having checked the security of her bonds, they then rotated the frame back until it was about twenty degrees from the vertical.

Jo's situation was extraordinary. She was completely clear of the ground, pinned to the frame like some biological specimen, her body forming an X. Through the hole in front of her face she found herself staring at the inevitable mirror opposite. A single spotlight had been placed on the other side of the frame shining straight up at her, and she couldn't help noticing how her breasts protruded through the lattice holes, the brown nipples still stiff.

She heard a footfall behind her and strained round to see that the two youngsters had stood back whilst Green and Brown came forward to inspect their captive. She had never felt so helpless, her limbs totally immobilised, leaving her completely at the mercy of these two strangers.

Green moved round the frame so that he was facing her. In her current position she was able to look down on his balding head as his eyes took in her body. He reached out a hand and ran it over the surface of her breast, his fingers squeezing the nipple. Then she gasped as, behind her, another hand ran down over her backside, tracing the crack of her behind and probing gently at her sex.

'She's wet,' said Brown's voice. 'That's good. We were told she was a slut.'

'Only a slut would have let herself be put in this position,' agreed Green.

Jo listened in silence. Perhaps they were right. Perhaps she was a slut. All she knew was that the pain of the manacles that pulled at her wrists was as nothing compared to the intense sexual excitement that the bondage was bringing her. Then she wondered: surely a slut was a loose, slovenly woman who didn't care what happened or who had her? Jo was none of those. She cared deeply about penetrating the Society. She was undergoing these ordeals in order to save her friend and retrieve her book, wasn't she? And yet she couldn't deny the extreme perverse pleasure she was getting from allowing herself to be stripped and abused in this way.

The hands left her body, and Jo saw Green beckon to the waitresses. The pair moved round in front of Jo, and she realised that they were carrying something. Each of them held a whip in her hand. The whips were at least four feet long and made of leather. The handles were the thickness of a broom handle, and tapered down until, at the end, they were no thicker than a piece of string. The tip of each was tied into a tight little knot about the size of a pea. As Jo watched, the girls approached the two men and offered each of them one of the cruel looking implements.

Brown had moved round to beside Green, and it was clear to Jo that she was intended to see the instruments of her torture being handed over. Both men took the whips in their hands and Jo was able to see how flexible they were, bending over almost double at the centre as the men held them up.

163

The men flicked them deftly, the sound of the cracks echoing about the small chamber and sending a cold feeling into Jo's gut.

Each man moved round beside Jo and offered his whip in front of her face. Once again she was forced to go through the strange ritual of kissing the very weapons that would soon be used on her. Then they stood back on either side of her. Jo gritted her teeth.

The blows fell in quick succession, one slicing into her back, the other catching her just below the cheeks of her behind. In both cases the knot at the end wrapped about her body and struck her flank like a hot needle penetrating her flesh. The pain hit her like a thunderbolt, driving the breath from her body as she was thrust hard against the frame.

Down came the whips again, one high, one low, biting agonisingly into her tender flesh. Jo couldn't believe how they stung, and it was all she could do to prevent herself screaming aloud.

Blows rained down on her shoulders and the backs of her legs, the knots once again bringing what was literally a sting in the tail as they wrapped about her, the upper one catching the side of her breast.

The lashes kept coming down. All at once Jo realised that they had not set a limit on the number of strokes she was to receive, and the thought appalled her. For all she knew the punishment might go on all night.

The blows seemed to merge into one single wall of pain as the two lashes worked their way over her legs and back. She was dimly aware that, up until now, her bottom had been left untouched, the men being content to flog the rest of her lovely young body, which was now aflame with the agony of the whips.

Yet once again it wasn't simply pain that the beautiful young girl was experiencing. As they lashed her bare flesh, every blow brought a new surge of arousal to her. Strapped, naked and helpless whilst her body was mercilessly flogged, all she could think of was the picture she must make, her soft flesh decorated with a wicker-work of bright-red marks, her sex shining with moisture as she gasped with lust. She pressed her pubis down hard against the unyielding wood of the frame, trying in vain to obtain some sort of friction against its surface and satisfy the desires within her. Jo knew that the men and their assistants would see this wanton dance and would understand its meaning, but she didn't care. The sexual excitement in her was almost overriding the suffering of her body.

She didn't know how long they had been whipping her. Her mind was a cacophony of pain and arousal, above which she could barely discern a voice that was screaming with pain and uttering the most extreme profanities. Then she realised that the voice was her own, and that she was begging for mercy, offering the men whatever they wanted if only they would stop.

The blows rained down relentlessly.

Then, suddenly, there were no more, though in her fuddled state Jo failed even to notice at first. It took a full minute before she became aware that the men had stopped, and two more for her to bring herself under control and to cease her cries for mercy. Her body was wet with perspiration, and she could feel a steady trickle of sweat running down her back and into the crack of her backside.

She became dimly aware that someone was saying something to her, and she opened her eyes to see Lander standing in front of the frame. She hadn't heard him enter the room, and had no idea for how long he had been speaking. She shook her head and struggled to concentrate on what he was saying.

'. . . your last chance, do you understand?'

'I . . . I didn't hear . . .'

'I said, this is your last chance. Speak now and I will release you. This need go no further tonight.'

She stared at him, then shook her head.

'No,' she gasped. 'I'll see it through.'

Lander stood, eyeing her for a moment, then turned away without another word. Almost at once the whips began to fall again, this time across her backside.

Jo lost all sense of time from then on. She may even have entered an altered state of consciousness on one occasion, she wasn't sure. The men lashed her in relay now, one resting whilst the other wielded the terrible whips. She became detached from what was happening, almost as if someone else were up on the frame, their body being so cruelly abused. When finally they stopped and released her bonds she simply slumped onto the floor, her back, behind and legs a mass of sensitive flesh.

They let her lie for some time whilst they returned to their table and drank another glass of wine. Then Green barked an order and Jo was pulled to her feet.

The waitresses, now pale-faced, led her across to the table. Her legs felt weak, but she was determined to walk by herself, her tear-stained face held up proudly. The pair took her to Green's table, where she stood, her aching arms barely able to hold her hands behind her head.

Green reached up and placed his hand on her breast. Despite her state, Jo was amazed at how the touch affected her, sending a tremor of pure lust through her. All at once she realised how turned on she was, and how much she wanted to fuck. When he moved his hand lower, brushing through her pubic hair and sliding a finger over her crack she almost came then and there, her hips thrusting forward against his hand.

He smiled and turned to Brown.

'Lander wasn't exaggerating about this young woman,' he said, holding aloft a finger shiny with her juices. 'I think it's time we found out what else she has to offer.'

He nodded to the waitresses who, taking hold of Jo's wrists, pulled her forward across the table, forcing her down so that her sweat-soaked body was pressed against its cold, hard surface. Behind her, Jo heard the sound of a zip being pulled down, then she felt something thick and hard brush against her backside.

The man reached down to her sex, prising the lips apart with his fingers. Then she felt the hot, bulbous end of his cock begin to press against her love hole.

With a gasp of relief she spread her legs wider, pressing her bottom back, oblivious to the pain as his hands took hold of her burning cheeks. Then he was inside her, ramming his penis deep into her vagina, bringing cries of lust from her lips as he began to fuck her.

He screwed her hard, his hips thrusting against her backside, banging her pubis against the table edge as he took her. Jo couldn't believe her own reaction, her body consumed with desire. It was as if her cunt was made for his cock, and that her body's sole purpose was to be punished and then to satisfy the carnal desires of men. All thoughts of pain were forgotten, her entire being concentrated on the stiff, meaty erection that was ramming into her with such gusto.

At the first spurt of his semen she came, her cries loud and long as he filled her with his seed, the hot, sticky fluid invading her totally and bringing wave after wave of extraordinary pleasure surging through her. By the time he had finished she was spent, flat out across the table, her body rising and falling as she gasped for breath.

When they pulled her to her feet she left a perfect imprint on the table top, her breasts and belly outlined in a pattern of sweat. She glanced across at the mirror, and was shocked to see how dishevelled she looked, the tracks of her tears and sweat streaking her body, a trickle of semen running down the inside of her thigh. The glance was a short one, however, as she was pulled down on to her back. She felt her legs dragged apart, then looked up to see Brown advancing on her, his stiff cock grasped in his hand as he guided it towards her sex.

Nineteen

Lucy lay on her narrow bunk staring up at the light that was beginning to filter through the small, barred window above her head. She shifted her position, trying to find comfort, but it wasn't easy with her hands shackled above her head. She wondered what time it was. It seemed to have been daylight for ages, yet nobody had visited the small, featureless cell in which she lay.

She raised her head and gazed down at herself. She was naked apart from the mandatory straps and collar, as she had been since Bruno had stripped her of her outfit nearly three weeks before. She had been brought to this place under cover of darkness and had been soundly whipped by Bruno on her arrival. Apart from that she had spent the entire three weeks in the vicinity of this dingy cell, being allowed out only for exercise, for her meals and for beatings. She had been visited by nobody in that time except her jailer, a large man in the customary black uniform of the Society, who would tie her to her bunk and cane her severely every day. In all that time she had heard no more than a dozen words from his lips.

She knew that the purpose of the campaign was to wear her down, and it was certainly beginning to have its effect. She longed for company and for someone to tell her what was happening outside this dull institution. She longed, too, for some sexual relief. When they had first shackled her to her bunk, she had still been alive with the arousal the book had instilled in her. For fully two days she had writhed about, longing for the simple relief of her own fingers, but even that was denied her. Her desires had abated somewhat with time, but even so, in her bondage and enforced nudity, the words and illustrations of the book were never far from her mind.

She wondered what Jo must be thinking. She knew they would leave some kind of false trail when they took her, but would Jo have swallowed the story? And if not, what would she do? She guessed that her friend had more sense than to contact the authorities, but what she feared most was that the girl would try to rescue her. The last thing she wanted was for both of them to be incarcerated in this place.

All at once she heard footsteps outside the door and the clank of a key in the door to her cell. She looked up just as Haddow, her jailer, entered. He was about thirty years old, tall with a broad chest and muscular arms. Now, as his eyes ran down from her breasts to her crotch, her legs forced open by the shackles on her feet, she felt, not for the first time, a surge of desire inside her. The knowledge that she was helpless, and quite unable to prevent him should he decide to take her, only served to increase her ardour as she stared up at his strong body.

But, as always, he did no more than look, before starting to undo her bonds. Soon she was standing beside the low bed, stretching her limbs and enjoying the luxury of her freedom. The normal morning ritual followed. First her shower and toilet, during which time she had to endure Haddow's eyes on her constantly, followed by breakfast alone in a large dining room. This, like all her meals, was served by a sour-faced woman who, as always, eyed her naked charge with disdain as she brought the food. Then Haddow fastened her hands behind her and fitted her lead.

Lucy set off immediately in the direction of the exercise

yard, but was surprised to find Haddow pulling her in a different direction. They walked down a narrow corridor flanked with cells. Most of them appeared to be empty. Lucy had yet to encounter another full-time inmate of the prison in which they kept her, though she was aware that girls were occasionally locked up there for a night. She had often heard the sound of the whip coming from adjoining cubicles, as well as the cries of desire as the men enjoyed their captives' bodies. By the next day, though, her fellow prisoners had usually departed.

They climbed a flight of stairs and came up to a heavy oak door with no handle on it. Haddow rapped on the door and barked out a few words. Moments later it was opened by another guard.

As she stepped through, Lucy was immediately struck by the contrast with the part of the house she had just vacated. That had been a dingy place with long corridors lit by harsh strip lights and stone floors. Here she was standing on a deep carpet staring round at panelled walls hung with expensive-looking oil paintings.

She was given little time to admire her surroundings, however. Haddow tugged at her lead and she set off after him. The house was obviously huge, with dozens of rooms and high, ornate ceilings. Here and there they would pass a maid or manservant at work, who would pause to stare at the beautiful, naked blonde being led past. Lucy avoided their eyes, staring straight ahead, unwilling to meet their gazes, her face glowing with embarrassment. Somehow she had almost become accustomed to her nudity in the cell block, whose clinical lack of decoration seemed to reflect her own naked state. Here, though, amid all this finery, she suddenly felt very conspicuous, and she longed for some means of restoring her modesty.

Haddow took her to the end of one of the corridors and into a large room. There were double doors on either side, and in the centre was a tall pillar on which was placed a glass case. Lucy gave a sharp intake of breath as she saw what was inside.

It was the book.

She stared at it in wonder. All at once the memory of what she had read in it seemed to come back to her in a flash of recall, and, try as she might, she couldn't prevent the passion beginning to rise in her once more. She looked away, staring instead at Haddow, who stood beside her. She wondered if he could sense the arousal that she felt, and if he knew how willingly she would give herself to him if she had the opportunity.

'Ah, Miss Stone. I trust you are appreciating your stay?'

Lucy recognised the voice at once as being that of the overlord, but she could see no sign of him. It was impossible to tell just where the voice was coming from. It seemed to emanate from all around her, and she guessed that the room was rigged with an elaborate speaker system.

Suddenly the pair of double doors on the other side of the room opened, and in walked the overlord, the ubiquitous Bruno at his side. Lucy froze, her eyes fixed in front of her as he strode across to where she was standing. In her peripheral vision, she saw that Haddow had retreated to a spot against the wall, from which he was watching proceedings.

'I see you have found the book,' continued the overlord. 'Well out of harm's way, though. I don't think you'll be getting your hands on it again.'

'How long are you going to hold me here?' she asked.

Bruno slapped her backside with the flat of his hand.

'Remember your manners,' he growled.

'And you remember yours,' shouted Lucy. 'This is bloody kidnapping, you know. It's not a game any longer.'

Bruno raised his hand to slap her once more, but the overlord shook his head.

'No,' he said. 'The young lady's quite right. We can't hold her here indefinitely. Let's just say this is a little career move.'

'Career move?'

'Certainly. What were you earning per week in your job, Miss Stone?'

'About two hundred.'

'Since you arrived here you have been on a salary of a thousand pounds a week, and that will continue until we release you.'

Lucy was taken aback, and unable to reply for a moment. A thousand a week was a lot of money for doing nothing.

'I see you weren't expecting that,' he said.

'Wait a minute,' said Jo, remembering her indignation. 'I don't recall signing any contract.'

'Nevertheless you have been officially in my employ for three weeks. It's all quite legal.'

'Legal?' Lucy indicated the bonds that held her hands. 'These hardly constitute working clothes.'

'I agree that the terms of your employment are hardly conventional,' he acquiesced. 'But then again, the Society is not a particularly conventional organisation.'

'This talk of employment is all very well,' went on Lucy, switching her tactics. 'But when will you release me?'

'That rather depends on you,' he replied.

'I don't understand.'

'We are planning a rather unorthodox recruitment drive, with the help of the book. Girls who apply to join us will be treated to some extracts from the text, and be allowed to see some of those extraordinary illustrations. It is to be hoped that this will encourage them to join our numbers.'

She stared at him. 'You mean you'll use the book to get them aroused?'

'Merely as an aid,' said the overlord.

'But that's outrageous. No woman with any kind of sexual drive could resist that book.'

'Precisely. Naturally all the candidates will be warned. This is merely a method of ensuring that those with the right proclivities are not scared off. And that's why we need your help.'

'Mine?'

'Certainly. You see, we want some extracts from the book read on to tape so that they can be played to the new recruits. And we feel that you would be ideal for the purpose.'

'You want me to read the book?'

'Exactly.'

'But it'll make me . . .'

'We are aware of the effect it will have, but you have, at least, had some exposure to the volume. Besides, you will be provided with all the toys you need to relieve any effects you might experience. And failing that, there's always Haddow here.'

Lucy glanced across at her jailer, who remained stony faced.

'And what if I refuse?'

'Then your stay here will be a prolonged one, whereas, if you co-operate, and the initial experimental run is a success, any request to leave will be looked upon with favour.'

'What's the experimental run about?'

'We shall be inviting some of our more experienced members to an evening, during which we will test the effects of the book. If that works well, your case will be considered with a good deal of sympathy.'

'And how do I know you're serious about the salary?'

'I have here a contract and an account book into which three thousand pounds have already been deposited. You have only to sign, and we can get started. Release her hands, Bruno.'

At once the overlord's burly assistant stepped forward

and undid the catches that were binding Lucy's wrists. Then an envelope was thrust into her hands.

She examined the contents. The first was an account book in her name, which, indeed, showed a credit of three thousand pounds. With it was a contract, and she read it through carefully. It was an agreement that she was not being held against her will, but was a salaried member of staff, and that she agreed to co-operate with the Society in any venture they put forward.

'What if I sign this, and you decide not to release me?' she asked.

'The only thing that will prevent us from letting you go is non-co-operation,' replied the overlord. 'Behave yourself and I promise your stay here will not be a long one.'

'And if I refuse?'

'Then I can't say, although I have to tell you that your salary will be reviewed on a monthly basis, and that it can go down as well as up. And then there are those slave markets we were talking about.'

Lucy looked from the overlord to Bruno, then back to the overlord. She didn't believe for a moment his claim that any new recruit exposed to the book would be warned beforehand. There was no doubt in her mind that they would use subterfuge to lure the girls to the Lodge. Unfortunately, though, she really had no choice but to fall in with his scheme, and she knew it. At the moment her only hope lay in Jo, and she knew full well what a difficult task she herself had had in penetrating the Society. At least signing the paper gave her some control over her own destiny.

'Do you have a pen?' she asked.

The overlord looked at Bruno, who pulled one from his pocket. Lucy hesitated only for a moment, then she took it from him and scrawled her signature across the bottom of the document.

Twenty

Jo stood before the mirror, examining her appearance critically. This really was the strangest garment she had ever been asked to wear, and her stomach knotted at the thought of anyone seeing her in it. The costume consisted of a sort of ragged bikini, the top supported by a single strap, the holed and tattered material barely covering her breasts so that the lower parts were on view and the slightest movement caused the cloth to lift and reveal half moons of her areolae. The skirt was no better, being little more than a piece of rag wrapped about her hips and tied on one side, so that her backside and crotch were in imminent danger of exposure. Together with her collar and the leather straps at her wrists, elbows and ankles, the effect was that of a savage slave girl captured from some wild tribe, and it wasn't difficult to guess that this, or something very like it, would be her role for the evening.

Once again it seemed no time at all since she had last presented herself to the Society in order to undergo one of the five ordeals that she hoped would soon lead to her acceptance as a full member. The marks from her previous encounter had barely faded, and her breasts still bore small red spots at the side where the knots of the whip had lashed her. Lander had told her afterwards that it had been one of the most thorough and systematic whippings he had witnessed in all his time with the Society. He had been surprised at her stoicism in being able to satisfy the desires of the two men so thoroughly afterwards. Indeed both men had taken her twice after the whipping and she had achieved orgasm on each occasion.

The more Jo experimented with the cult of sadism and masochism, however, the more she realised her own propensity for it. It wasn't simply that the book had aroused these secret desires within her. It was clear to her and to Lander that she was something special. Now, as she prepared for her penultimate challenge, the thrill that she felt was undeniable.

The door opened and in came Lander. He was stony faced, as he always was before her ordeals, and he eyed her up and down before making her turn around and fastening her wrists and elbows. As on the previous occasion, he had been opposed to her taking yet another step towards membership so soon after the last, but his protestations had, like before, fallen on deaf ears. Jo hadn't even taken a day off work after her whipping at the hands of the two diners, though she had been in considerable pain for some days and had been unable to wear underwear for a week. Even now she felt the occasional twinge in her legs and back, yet here she was, about to face the Society once more.

Lander hooked the lead to her collar and she followed him from the room. She had prepared for the evening in the basement of the building, but this time she was led upstairs. The room he took her into was quite large and empty of people. Alongside one wall was a long table, laid out with food under plastic covers and rows of wine glasses, rather as if a cocktail party were planned. At the end was a dais, about three feet high, and it was to this that she was taken. On one side was a wide table, and on the other a frame, not unlike the one she had encountered on her previous visit. In the centre two metal rings had been set into the floor about three feet apart and about the same distance from the wall. Here she was made to stand, facing the room, whilst Lander attached her ankles to the rings, pinning her into place, legs akimbo. Once her legs were trapped, he took the lead from her collar, and pulled a long, much thinner chain from his pocket and attached it to the front of her collar. He went round behind her, pulling the chain through between her legs and passing it through a ring set about four feet up in the wall. Then he began pulling it tight.

Jo could barely suppress a cry as the cold metal came into contact with her bare sex. Lander adjusted the tension so that it ran precisely between her cunt lips, biting into the soft flesh and producing a delicious friction against her clitoris. Jo's position was a remarkably arousing one: her arms trapped; her legs forcibly spread; the delights of her young body barely concealed by her skimpy outfit. But it was the chain on which her mind was concentrated. There was absolutely no escape from its intrusion, and every slight movement caused it to rub against that most sensitive of spots, bringing a surge of arousal to the brazen youngster. It was all she could do to keep her hips still as she stood there, displayed like some life-sized erotic ornament.

Lander made a final check of her bonds, then stood back. He appeared to be about to speak, possibly even to wish her good luck. Despite his cold exterior, Jo felt that his interest in her was more than simply academic, and she sometimes sensed a degree of admiration in his voice as he witnessed her endurance at the hands of her torturers. However, on this occasion he said nothing. He simply grunted his approval and turned away, leaving her alone with her thoughts.

As always the wait was a long one, the apprehension being almost as much a torture as what was to follow. Jo found it hard enough to concentrate on such occasions at the best of times. Now, with the intrusion of the rough chain into her most private place, she found it well nigh impossible, and the temptation to satisfy her desires against its hard surface was almost overwhelming. Above her, though, was the cold eye of a video camera, and she knew she was being watched. So she fought down the desires within her, standing as still as she was able and trying to keep her mind off what was to come.

At last the door opened and two young men entered. They wore waiters' outfits, and paused only briefly to admire the barely-clad beauty on display before setting about taking the covers off the food and pouring wine into the glasses. Soon afterwards the guests began to arrive.

They were all relatively young, mostly in their twenties and dressed formally, the men in black tie, the women in long, elegant gowns and glittering jewellery. As they entered and accepted their drinks they wandered across to admire the lovely young girl on the rostrum.

Jo felt extraordinarily conspicuous, being, as she was, nearly naked before these beautiful people. To make things worse, as they took in her form, they made loud comments, speaking as if she wasn't there or was unable to understand what they were saying.

'My God, look at her, like something out of the jungle.'

'She's been whipped recently. Look at those marks on her side.'

'Serve her right, brazen little hussy.'

'Do you think she's wearing any knickers? That chain must go right through her cunt.'

'She looks an arrogant little slut. We'll have to knock that out of her.'

Jo stared straight ahead of her, avoiding their eyes, unwilling to disclose her own emotions. She felt ashamed and embarrassed at the display she was being forced to make, yet at the same time, the situation was arousing an exhibitionist tendency within her which made her stand up proudly as their eyes took in her beauty.

The room filled up rapidly. Soon Jo estimated that there were at least thirty people in there eating, drinking and chatting, or simply standing and looking at her. For some time nothing else happened, but soon the plates were being stacked empty on the tables and attention was beginning to turn to the small stage where the lone figure stood. Finally a man mounted the platform and stood beside Jo. He was about twenty-five, with short, dark hair. He clapped his hands twice, and a silence descended over the gathering.

'Good evening ladies and gentlemen,' the man said. 'You all know who I am, of course.'

'Yes, Peter,' someone said. 'Get on with it.'

The man smiled. 'I trust you all enjoyed the meal and are ready for the entertainment?'

There was a general nodding of heads around the room.

'This is Jane,' he went on. 'She is here to provide an amusing diversion. Tonight will form part of her initiation into the Society so I hope you will all assist in making it a true ordeal for her. Now, may I have the first suggestion as to how we can help her to fulfil her wish?'

There was quiet for a moment, then a young woman stepped forward.

'I have a pretty little adornment she might wish to try,' she said, reaching into her handbag.

She pulled something out, and held it up. It was a fine gold chain at the two ends of which hung identical shining objects that looked, at first glance, like a pair of silver clips.

A ripple of applause ran through the audience, and the man called Peter invited the girl up on to the stage. Jo eyed her nervously, still unsure of the purpose of the device she held.

'Ah, Clarissa,' said the man. 'Trust you to have an idea. Show her what you've got for her.'

The girl they called Clarissa moved closer to where Jo was standing. She was lovely looking, with a slim, shapely body and the greenest eyes Jo had ever seen. She fluttered her long eyelashes and dangled the objects under Jo's gaze.

At each end of the chain was a clamp, held closed by a strong-looking spring. The jaws of the clamps were lined with tiny needle points, like rows of silver teeth which curved inwards. She pressed the levers behind the jaws, making them open and close, all the time smiling an evil smile at the young captive. Jo stared at the objects, her heart beating hard. They were clearly designed to cause pain, but how would they use them?

She didn't have to wait long to find out.

'Go on, Clarissa, put them on her,' shouted a voice.

'Yes. Let's see them on her,' called another.

Clarissa looked questioningly at Peter, and he nodded.

She stepped forward and, taking hold of the rag that served as a bra for Jo, pulled hard at it. It ripped apart easily, and she tossed it aside. Jo was taken by surprise by the move, and her face glowed as her pale, plump breasts were suddenly revealed to the crowd, jutting forward, their prominence enhanced by the way her elbows were pinned back behind her. A murmur of assent went up from those watching as they pressed forward for a better look.

The girl reached out and traced the line of red marks that ran down the side of Jo's breast, the remaining signs of her whipping.

'So pretty, these,' she said. 'I like to see the mark of the whip on a girl's body.'

She hung the chain about Jo's neck, so the two clamps dangled down on either side. Then she placed both palms over the captive's nipples and began to rotate them. Jo let out a little gasp as she felt the flesh come erect, her large brown nipples suddenly engorged with blood. Clarissa took these knobs of flesh between finger and thumb, rolling them back and forth and sending tingles of pleasure through Jo's body.

'So sensitive,' she murmured as she watched the expression on Jo's face. Jo tried desperately not to betray her emotions, but she knew her arousal must be showing and she fought hard against the overwhelming urge to drive her hips down against the rough metal of the chain between her legs.

Clarissa caressed Jo's breasts for a full minute, then reached for the clamps once more. Jo glanced down at her nipples. They were rock hard, protruding proudly from her soft, white mounds. Then she saw the girl open one of the clamps, and her eyes widened as she realised what was about to happen.

The girl positioned the clamp over Jo's right nipple, then slowly allowed the jaws to close. Jo gritted her teeth as the vicious little needle points bit into her flesh, tighter and tighter until the tears welled up in her eyes. By the time the girl released the clamp, the stinging of the points was almost unbearable, and the flesh was squashed and distorted. Still smiling, the girl lifted the second clamp and proceeded to close it over the captive's left teat.

Jo bit her lip, tears of pain rolling down her cheeks as the pain of the clamps almost overcame her. The stinging of the devices was indescribable, and it was all she could do to remain silent. There was worse to come, however, as Clarissa took hold of the chain and began to pull it, stretching Jo's breasts forward into an almost conical shape, the jaws biting even deeper as the curved teeth were driven into her skin. Jo found herself leaning forward in a vain effort to reduce the tension, but Clarissa simply pulled all the harder, much to the appreciation of those watching. The movement caused the chain between Jo's legs to dig even deeper into her sex, and the mixture of extreme pain and exquisite pleasure was almost more than the hapless girl could stand.

The torture went on for a further five minutes, with Clarissa clearly enjoying the expressions of pain pass across the captive's face as she tugged at the clamps. The audience watched the spectacle with enthusiasm, cheering her on and shouting yet more lewd remarks as they watched. At last, Clarissa turned to face those watching and raised her eyebrows.

'What next?' she called.

'Let's see her cunt,' someone shouted.

'Yes, get that skirt off her, Clarissa.'

'Show us where that chain's going.'

Clarissa moved her face close to Jo's.

'What do you think, my love?' she asked. 'Should we show them the rest?'

Jo made no answer, her eyes fixed on Clarissa's

'Ow!' The sudden sharp tug on the clamps had been unexpected, and for the first time Jo cried out.

'Answer me,' said Clarissa. 'Do you want to show these men your cunt?'

'If you wish, mistress,' said Jo.

The girl smiled. 'She's agreed,' she called to the assembly.

A cheer went up.

Clarissa moved round to stand beside Jo, and her hands went to the knot on the girl's hip. Like the top, the skirt was made of no more than an old rag, and when she pulled at it, it came away easily, simply ripping apart. Once again Jo felt the blood rush to her cheeks as the last vestige of her modesty was torn from her. This time there was no mirror, but she could imagine the sight she made: her breasts thrust forward; the nipples distorted by the terrible clamps; her thighs forced apart to reveal the pink gash of her sex to the onlookers, the silver chain disappearing between the soft folds of skin.

For a moment the audience was silent, then a voice sounded.

'Too much hair.'

Clarissa turned. 'Was that Tom?' she asked. 'He always preferred his women shaved. Or so I'm told. Come to the front, Tom.'

A ripple of laughter ran round the room as the man pushed his way through the crowd. Like most of those present he was in his mid-twenties, with streaked blond hair swept back across his head. His face was tanned and, when he smiled, he showed a perfect row of white teeth. To her surprise, Jo found herself attracted to him at once and, as his deep blue eyes took in her nudity, she gave a little shiver of excitement.

'What do you think, chaps?' asked Clarissa. 'You reckon she'd look better bald down there?'

Once again the crowd's assent was clear, and Clarissa nodded her head. She turned to the waiters, who had been watching passively since the show had started.

'Get some shaving things.'

The short time it took the young man to reappear with a mug of soapy water and a small leather pouch told Jo that they had already been prepared for this turn of events. She glanced down at her body, and at the triangle of short, wiry hair that covered her pubis. To lose it would seem extremely odd, she thought.

As the evening had been progressing, however, Jo had begun to guess what this ordeal was all about. The previous ones had been concerned with her ability to stand pain, culminating in the agony of the whipping. Today's exercise, though, was more to do with humiliation.

The nipple clamps stung terribly. More perhaps than the cut of the whip. Yet it was the manner in which they had been applied, with her body tethered and displayed before an audience, that had been the motive behind their application. The fact that they had chosen to display her clothed initially, albeit scantily, then had systematically stripped her naked had been to the same end. Now, the intention to remove even her pubic hair was a final, deliberately humiliating, laying bare of her body to those watching.

In a sense, this was the worst challenge of all. To be treated thus before people who were exactly her peers was harder than any of the previous ordeals, where simply the age difference had been enough for her to concede power over her body. These were the sort of people she met in everyday life, and whose opinions and lifestyles she shared. Yet she was being shamed before them, forced to display her body and to allow them to treat it as they wished. And, like the beatings before, she was beginning to find the experience powerfully arousing.

Tom had climbed up on to the stage, and the waiter followed him, passing him the soap and razors. The second waiter mounted the stage as well, and the pair of them moved round behind Jo.

'Lean back against the men and bend your legs,' ordered Clarissa.

At the same moment, Jo felt the men's hands on her back. Tentatively, she allowed her body to rest against theirs.

'Lean back further and press your hips forward,' urged Clarissa.

Jo did as she was told, bending her knees and thrusting her open sex towards the crowd, bringing another hubbub of comments as she displayed herself so blatantly. She knew they would be able to see the wetness inside her now, and the thought filled her with a perverse excitement.

Tom moved to stand right beside her, and placed his hand flat on her belly. Then she felt the unmistakable sensation of the soft shaving brush on her pubis as he began to rub the suds into her nether hairs. She stayed as still as she was able as he covered her dark triangle with the foam, then moved down further, coating her slit. The hair down there was still sparse after her previous depilation, but it was clear that he intended to ensure that even this stubble should be removed.

When he had completely covered her crotch, he put down the brush and took something shiny from the leather pouch. Jo peered down between her breasts, watching as he pulled out the straight razor and opened it up. She shivered slightly when she saw the silver blade glint in the harsh stage lights. He stropped it carefully, honing the blade to a fine edge, then knelt down between her open thighs.

A tremor ran through Jo's body as the blade touched her flesh and began scraping across her skin. She watched, fascinated, as it swept away the hairs, leaving the skin smooth and virgin. In no time he had completely denuded her pubis and was working down her sex lips, his fingers resting on the chain, every movement causing the metal to rub against her clitoris and send another surge of excitement through her.

It took him no more than five minutes to complete the task, after which he dabbed away the remaining foam with a cloth. Once he was content with his work, he stood back, and Jo was aware of the crowd leaning forward to view his handiwork. There was another murmur of approval from the watchers and somebody produced a mirror, holding it between her legs to allow Jo herself to see the results. Jo gave a little gasp when she saw how totally bare her sex now was, her slit prominently displayed, the lips cruelly split by the chain.

Once the watchers had had their fill, Jo was allowed to stand once more, and the two waiters carried away the shaving gear. Meanwhile the crowd moved in to stare at their naked captive. Jo had never felt so totally exposed before, and even the pain from the nipple clamps was momentarily forgotten as she thought of how wanton she must appear.

'What about a dance?' asked a voice.

'Yes, let's see her perform,' said another.

The man called Peter climbed on to the stage once more. 'I understand you wish to see Jane here dance for you,' he said.

The audience called out its assent.

He turned to Jo, running his eyes up and down her form. 'Unfortunately she's a bit handicapped at the moment, but I'm sure she'll do her best. After all, there's nothing to prevent her moving her hips. Put on the music.'

Almost at once a low beat began and the sound of a disco record filled the room. Jo looked about her nervously. The order was quite unexpected, and not at all welcome. She would almost have preferred another whipping to this. To be asked to dance naked before all these people filled her with embarrassment. Once again she recognised the subtleties of this, her forth ordeal. In many ways this humiliation was far worse than any pain the Society had imposed on her before.

Peter then pulled a thin horsewhip from his belt and he brought it down suddenly across her buttocks, making her cry out with surprise.

'Dance,' he ordered.

Jo began to move her body in a smooth, swaying action, her hips swinging from side to side in time to the music. It was only then that she thought of the chain between her legs. Whilst she had been standing still, the metal had been no more than an unwelcome distraction. Now, as she moved, it began a smooth sawing motion back and forth inside her slit, creating an exquisite friction against her already swollen love-bud. She stopped moving at once, her face crimson as she fought down the passion that was already beginning to rise within her.

Peter brought down the whip across the top of her behind once more, leaving a stinging stripe. Jo's first impulse was to object and to beg to be spared from this new humiliation. Then she remembered the importance of this ordeal and said nothing. Instead, taking a deep breath, she recommenced her dance.

She swayed her body from side to side, trying to blot from her mind the extraordinary passions that the action was arousing in her. Every movement caused the chain to rub against her love-bud. It was as if she was frigging herself with a rough object, something she sometimes did in the privacy of her bedroom, utilising a hairbrush or possibly a leather belt. But this wasn't her bedroom. This was on a brightly lit stage, before an audience of young people, and they were all watching her. It was like one of her recurrent dreams, where she found herself the only one naked amongst a crowd of fully clothed people. Except that this was no dream.

'Move faster,' ordered Peter, waving the whip in front of her face.

Jo increased her tempo, and with it the friction on her clitoris. Every movement sent a fresh surge of excitement through her and she felt her wetness begin to leak on to the chain. She knew that this would be visible to those watching, and she tried not to catch their eyes as she danced, wishing that her passion was not so obvious.

The more Jo danced, the more her desires overcame her. Soon she was grinding her hips down on to the wet metal, moans of passion escaping her lips as the heat in her belly increased. She tried desperately to control her emotions, but in vain. With every minute she was losing control, the swaying movement of her hips becoming an overtly sexual one, her bare pubis jabbing forward as if she were impaled on the penis of some invisible lover. Her breasts bounced up and down with every stroke, the chain between her nipples jangling, the pain of the clamps almost totally forgotten now, such was her passion.

The orgasm caught her by surprise, surging through her body and bringing hoarse cries from her as the passion of her climax shook her frame. She drove her sex down hard against the chain, extracting every ounce of pleasure that she could from it, her entire being consumed with lust.

It was some time before she realised that the music had stopped, and that the only sound in the room now was her own voice. Gradually her movements slowed as her senses returned and she realised the enormity of the display she had been putting on. She forced herself to stand still, her face glowing as she stared round at the sea of faces below her. Some had amused expressions, others were wide eyed. Most of the men's crotches were bulging. For a moment there was silence, then Peter was beside her on the stage once more.

'This is clearly a girl who enjoys dancing,' he said.

Jo dropped her eyes.

'Now,' he went on, 'the raffle. The winner gets to strap Jane to the frame and give her a dozen strokes. Second prize is a blow job. Has everyone got a ticket?'

Jo took a deep breath. Clearly it was going to be a long evening.

Twenty-One

Lucy stood in the reception room staring up at the cabinet in which the book rested. Not for the first time she contemplated the power of the volume, and the effect its words and pictures could have on a young woman. And nobody could know of those powers better than her. For the previous two weeks she had been reading extracts from the book aloud into a tape recorder, and had experienced the full effect of it.

Reading the book had been both a pleasure and an ordeal. She had taken it in stages, managing to read no more than three pages at a time before the effect of the words had overcome her. At such times she had been forced to reach for one of the sex toys provided by the Society, bringing herself to numerous noisy orgasms in her cell before she was able to read further. On more than one occasion she had called Haddow into the small room, and he had bent her over the bed and thrashed her before fucking her with gusto, the room ringing to her cries of pleasure.

Lucy had never known such prolonged and passionate arousal. By the time she had done all that was required of her, she was quite exhausted. On handing over the completed tapes she had returned to her cell and slept for a solid twenty-four hours, a sleep haunted with erotic dreams so that she felt sure she had achieved orgasms whilst still unconscious.

That had been three days ago, and now she found

herself summoned once again to the room where the book was kept. She was wearing only a leather G-string and high heels, her magnificent breasts bare, and she waited, her hands pinned behind her, for the overlord to appear.

When he did arrive, his manner was almost cheerful, and she could see that there was a spring in his step.

'Ah, Miss Stone,' he said. 'I've been listening to your tapes. An admirable performance. Your feelings come through perfectly to the listener. I've seldom heard such passion.'

'Thank you, sir,' she muttered.

'Tonight is the big test,' he went on. 'I've arranged for a number of female Society members to gather here this evening, ostensibly for a social event. Then we will see the true power of the book. It is my intention that we expose them to its powers soon after they arrive. A number of male staff will be on hand to assist, and you too will be required.'

'Me, sir?'

'Yes. Some of the girls respond better to a female taking charge of them. You will be spared the readings, however, if that is your wish. From what I hear you would prefer some respite from the book's powers at the moment.'

'Thank you, sir.'

'Good. You are dismissed. You will be called upon in good time.'

So it was that, some two hours later, Lucy found herself, resplendent in black leather uniform and cap, standing in an upstairs room looking down through a sheet of glass at the reception room. It was empty, but she knew that already the 'guests' had begun to arrive, and that they would soon be let into the room. She glanced sideways at Bruno, who was inserting a cassette tape into a machine beside her, whilst across the room, Haddow was fiddling with the focus on a large projector. The whole thing was being organised with almost military precision.

Lucy's own emotions were a mixture of curiosity and excitement. Having seen the powerful effect that the book had had on her, she was anxious to see whether it could have the same effect on others. At the same time, though, she knew that this was precisely the use to which Jo hadn't wanted the book put. If it worked today on these women who were, in effect, volunteers, Lucy knew the next victims would be completely innocent, and that was something she had to prevent at all costs.

The women were beginning to file into the reception room now, and she leant forward, watching them enter. There were about a dozen of them. They all wore smart clothes, some in cocktail dresses, others in longer gowns. There were a few she recognised from her encounters in the Society. All were young and beautiful.

On the far side of the room a waiter was serving drinks, and soon all the visitors held a glass. Most were chatting happily together, although Lucy saw one or two glance about themselves, clearly curious about what was to happen. The window was soundproof so she couldn't hear what was being said, but that was, in a sense, a bonus, since she knew it would prevent her hearing her own voice when they played the tapes.

All at once the women turned in her direction and she realised that the overlord had entered the room directly below her. The faces of the guests told her how surprised they were to be in the great man's presence, and many of them seemed quite apprehensive, aware that this was no ordinary party.

The overlord spoke for about two minutes, then departed. Almost at once, Bruno pressed the start button on the cassette recorder and Lucy saw the women glance about themselves, clearly searching for the source of the sound. The bright orange lights danced up and down the console in front of Bruno, and Lucy knew that it was her voice that was causing the lights to flash. Down below all talking had stopped, and the women's faces were suddenly serious as they listened to the recording.

There was a sudden flash of light, and Lucy saw that Haddow had switched on the projector. Its powerful beam speared across the room and an image appeared on a screen below and to the left of where Lucy was standing. She could barely make it out from this acute angle, but could just recognise it as the illustration from the front of the book. She studied the girl's faces in the reflected light. All were staring in fascination, some with their mouths wide open. She saw one girl reach up and almost absent-mindedly begin to rub her breasts through the material of her dress.

For the next ten minutes the group in the reception room were held spellbound by the sound of Lucy's voice and the ever-changing images on the screen. And, as they watched, they became ever more animated. At first it was only one or two of them stroking their bodies over their clothes. Then Lucy noticed one slide her hand into the top of her dress, her fingers clearly visible through the thin material as they worked on her nipples. Another had hitched her skirt up and was running her hand over the gusset of her panties, her legs slightly spread as she caressed herself.

A pretty, dark-haired girl standing opposite Lucy reached behind her for the zipper on her dress and pulled it down, letting the garment drop to the floor. Beneath she wore only black panties and hold-up stockings, her firm young breasts having no need of support. Lucy watched as she began to caress herself, rubbing her firm, brown nipples between her fingers and sliding her other hand down the front of her panties, her face a picture of arousal.

Others began to follow suit, pulling off their dresses

and tossing them aside, revealing an extraordinary display of sexy underwear. One woman, a tall blonde of about twenty-two, wore nothing whatsoever under her dress. To Lucy's astonishment, even her sex was shaved clean of hair, and she leant back against a pillar, her legs spread, her knees bent, sliding two fingers into her open slit.

A movement on the far side caught Jo's eye, and she saw that a petite brunette wearing matching bra and pants, had turned to the redheaded beauty beside her and was undoing her bra. As soon as the girl's large breasts spilled out she began to suck greedily at them, placing her arms about the girl's waist and burying her head in her chest.

Lucy knew that the tape was still running, since she could see the lights on the console flashing, but nobody seemed to be paying it heed any more, though some were still watching the pictures that Haddow was continuing to flash on to the wall. All around the room women were masturbating or turning to one another for relief. In one corner a woman lay, her legs spread wide whilst another crouched before her, her face buried in her crotch, her own fingers flashing in and out of her sex. On the other side, three naked beauties lay in a circle, lapping urgently at one another's cunts. One stunningly beautiful girl of about twenty had snatched a wine bottle from the drinks table and lay on the floor working it in and out of her sex, oblivious to the red wine that spilled from it on to her thighs. Every woman had discarded her underwear now, and Lucy watched in rapt attention as a veritable orgy took place before her.

All at once the doors to the reception room swung open, and in came a small army of men, some in evening dress, others in the uniform of the Society. They stood, staring about them at the extraordinary spectacle of female arousal that met their eyes. For a moment, nothing happened – the women continued to writhe about on their own, in pairs or in threes. Then she saw one of the smartly dressed men point to the beauty with the wine bottle and say something. At once two of the staff grabbed her arms and pulled her to her feet, snatching the wine bottle from her. Then a pair of cuffs were snapped on to her wrists behind her and she was led away, struggling.

Almost at once more of the men went into action. Pairs of girls were pulled apart and shackled, then taken from the room. Sometimes two were taken together, their wrists attached by short chains. Some resisted vigorously; others went quietly. One girl had her captor's trousers open and was sucking at his cock even before he was able to manacle her and pull her from the room. In a couple of minutes the area was empty, the only evidence that the girls had been there the half-full and empty wine glasses and clothes strewn all over the floor.

A hand touched Lucy's shoulder, and she turned to see Bruno standing behind her. He gestured her to follow him, then set off down the stairs. As he pushed the door open at the bottom, the sounds of the girls and their captors met her ears for the first time.

All about there were shrieks and gasps as the men took advantage of the girls' arousal. Emerging into the room that led off from the reception area, the first thing to meet Jo's eyes was the shaven blonde, who was bent over a narrow table, her backside projecting on one side whilst her breasts hung over the other. A man in evening dress was fucking her hard from behind whilst repeatedly striking her buttocks with a thin, cruel-looking whip. Her cries were muffled by the cock of one of the guards, which filled her mouth at the other end. On the far side of the room, a girl lay on her back on a table, her knees tucked up to her chest whilst a man slapped her backside hard with a wooden paddle. At first, Lucy couldn't make out how she was maintaining her awkward position, but as she came close she saw that the girl's nipples were trapped in the jaws of painful-looking clamps which were joined to straps about her knees by short chains. Any attempt to straighten her legs put what must have been unbearable tension on the tender flesh, so that the girl had no choice but to offer the smooth cheeks of her bottom to her tormentor.

Lucy moved out of the room into a corridor, on either side of which were cells. In the first a girl stood, her wrists attached to rings high in the wall whilst one of the guards beat her backside with a cane. Next door the dark-haired beauty who had first attracted Lucy's attention was shackled astride a low bar, her sex forced down against the wood, her face a picture of arousal whilst a guard whipped her backside.

For a moment, Lucy felt a pang of guilt. After all it was partly her doing that had caused these women to come here tonight, and had brought about these scenes of punishment. But she drove the thought from her mind. All these women were fully fledged members of the Society, and all had come here of their own accord in the full knowledge of what might be required of them. And of all the reactions she had seen that evening, sheer sexual excitement was without doubt the dominant one. These girls were submissive by nature. All she had done was to participate in bringing them to a state of sexual arousal that had left them barely in control of themselves. There was no doubt that they would masturbate for weeks over the images that had been presented to them tonight.

She was distracted by Bruno grabbing her arm once more and pulling her into one of the cells. Inside, in a recess on the far wall, were two girls. Lucy recognised them as the petite brunette and redhead who had been the first to start pleasuring one another's bodies. Now they stood, their hands pinned behind them and locked to rings on the wall, facing each other no more than a foot apart, the sexual hunger in their expressions unmistakable as they stared at each other's naked bodies. One of the men in evening dress was seated by the wall between them, evidently enjoying their frustration.

Bruno bowed to the man, then gestured at Lucy to remain before withdrawing to the door. The man beckoned Lucy forward and she pressed between the two gasping women to stand before him.

'Right, young lady,' he said. 'I'm told you have some skill with the whip.'

'Yes, sir.'

'Good. I shall need some assistance with these two minxes. I intend to have them simultaneously thrashed, but first I want them joined together.'

'Joined, sir?'

'That's right. And to make it all a little more intimate, we'll start with this.'

He reached into a bag and pulled something from it, holding it out to Lucy. She stared at it. She had never seen anything quite like it. It consisted of two long, thick dildos, shaped exactly like erect penises, complete with bulging veins and a thick glans. They were joined at the centre so that they formed a vee shape. Just above the join on each one was a small horn that curled back, clearly designed to come precisely into contact with the girls' clitorises. From the centre hung a series of thin straps.

'A pretty little device, I'm sure you'll agree,' said the man. 'I think the little brunette can have it first. Insert it and strap it on, please.'

Lucy reached out and took the object from him. It felt warm and rubbery under her fingers, and she felt a slight shiver of pleasure as she imagined it inside her. She turned to the dark girl, who was staring at the thing with a mixture of apprehension and arousal.

'Make her lubricate it with her saliva first,' ordered the man.

Lucy moved between the two women. She could feel

196

the hard nipples of the redhead brush against her back as she raised the phallus up to the other girl's lips. The girl didn't hesitate, opening her mouth and taking the thick, rubber object inside, sucking and licking at it as she might a real cock. Lucy pressed it as deep into the captive's mouth as she was able, ensuring that almost its entire length was coated with a sheen of saliva.

'Now insert it.'

Lucy dropped to her knees. The girl's sex was right before her eyes now, the thick pink lips revealed. She had already spread her legs in anticipation of receiving the dildo, and Lucy could hear low moans escaping from her mouth as she thrust her pubis forward. She positioned the bulbous glans against the shining opening of the girl's sex, then began to force it forward. The flesh resisted for no more than a second, then the object was sliding into the girl's vagina, forcing its way deep into her and making her gasp aloud. Lucy felt the muscles of the girl's sex tighten about the object, as if trying to draw it in even deeper, then heard her sharp intake of breath as the little horn came into contact with the pink swelling of her love-bud. A loop of leather hung down from the bottom of the object and she pulled this back between the girl's legs, threading another strap through it as she wrapped it about the girl's waist and buckled it tight.

She checked that the straps were fast. The phallus was well and truly embedded in the girl, the other end standing proud from her groin, to all intents and purposes like a stiff erection.

'Right,' said the man. 'Loosen her chain and give her companion the other end.'

Lucy moved behind the redhead and, taking hold of the chain, slackened it just enough to allow the girl's body to touch her fellow captive's. The smaller girl's breasts pressed upwards against the other's, her stiff nipples brushing the soft underside of her friend's bosom. The phallus was pressed against the redhead's belly, and Lucy could see the hungry expression on her face as she gazed down at it.

Lucy dropped to her knees once more. This time, she knew, it was up to her to lubricate the object, and she took it into her mouth with relish, suddenly excited by the scent of feminine arousal from the two panting women. She went down on the phallus as she would a man's cock, sliding it in and out of her mouth whilst sucking hard at it. She gazed up at the dark girl's face as she did so, and was pleased to see an expression of pure lust on her face as the phallus moved back and forth within her.

'Enough. Join them.'

Lucy immediately withdrew the object from her mouth, then touched the redhead on the thigh. The girl required no second bidding, spreading her legs and pressing her thighs forward whilst lifting herself on to tiptoe. In no time, Lucy had the second knob as deeply inserted in her as it was in her companion, and was tightening the straps to the sound of a chorus of groans from the two captives.

Once the pair were firmly joined, the man held out a long, thick belt to Lucy. She fastened it about the girls' waists, cinching the buckle so tight that their bellies and breasts were pressed hard together. Then she joined their collars at the front so that their faces touched. Finally she undid their wrists in turn, fastening each girl's hands behind the back of her partner and attaching them to the rings at the back of the other's collar.

Lucy turned to the man, who rose and inspected her handiwork. He nodded his approval. The girls were well and truly locked together, their naked bodies joined in the most intimate manner possible, and both were completely at the man's mercy.

'Bring them to the centre of the room,' he ordered.

The girls' progress was slow and clumsy as they shuffled across, struggling to keep their balance. At last they were where he wanted them though, standing in the dead centre of the room and staring into each others' faces. Both were trembling slightly, a faint sheen of perspiration glistening on their young bodies, their expressions tense with obvious excitement.

'Fetch those,' ordered the man, gesturing to a rack on the wall. As Lucy approached it she saw that it bore two horse whips, both made of leather, and both no thicker than a pencil. She picked them up and bore them across to the man. He took one from her and tested it, swishing it through the air.

'Good,' he said. 'Five strokes each, then we change over. And mind you mark her, or you'll feel the lash yourself.'

Lucy could see the expressions of anxiety on the girls' faces, but mixed with that anxiety she could also clearly detect an air of excitement and anticipation of what was to come. She reminded herself again that these two were voluntary members of the Society, and were no strangers to the lash, though she doubted they had ever been as aroused as they were now. She moved round behind the redhead and tapped her whip against the girl's backside. Then the man nodded, and she drew back her arm.

The two whips came down in unison, striking the girls' bare behinds simultaneously and bringing a cry from each. Lucy watched as the thin line she had laid across the girl's creamy flesh turned dark red, then pulled back her arm again.

Once again the whips struck with perfect timing, thrusting the two girls together as the leather bit into their soft behinds.

Lucy wielded the whip expertly, each stroke laying a fresh stripe across the redhead's behind and bringing a yelp of pain from her lips. Yet such was her timing that the girls remained precisely where they were, the force of the two whips exactly balancing themselves out.

The fifth blow fell, then the man nodded and he and Lucy circled their captives so that they were positioned behind the partner of the girl they had been beating. Lucy examined the brunette's backside. The pattern of stripes was as precisely grouped as the ones she had laid across the redhead's. She knew the man would be pleased with her. She drew back her arm.

The sound of the blows echoed about the room, along with the shrill cries of the tethered pair.

The slight sheen of sweat that Lucy had noted on the bodies of the pair had now become a positive shine, and each blow of the whip raised a tiny spray of moisture as it dislodged it.

Then Lucy noticed something else. What had apparently been a reflex action in their hips, an attempt by each girl to pull in her backside away from the fall of the whip, was turning into a more regular motion; the girls' behinds were beginning to thrust forward in unison. She paused, as did the man, and they watched for a moment as the moaning girls pressed their hips together. There was no doubt about it, the pair were, once again, succumbing to the power of the book, and to the whip, and were beginning to screw one another, taking full advantage of the thick dildos that filled their vaginas.

The moans of the two women were growing louder now, the thrusts of their hips becoming more violent as they pleasured one another with renewed vigour. Lucy watched the brunette's backside pump back and forth, the angry red stripes across it serving to make the sight even more erotic. She raised her arm again.

As the final blow fell the two women screamed aloud. But this time their screams were of pleasure as the pair climaxed simultaneously, their violent orgasms threatening to overbalance them as their bellies slapped wetly together. Lucy stood transfixed by the sight of their bare bodies locked together so intimately as they swayed back and forth, their heads thrown back, their mouths open in a keening cry of release. So spellbound was she that Bruno had to take her arm to get her attention.

He pulled her from the cell, still staring back over her shoulder at the two lovers bound together in the centre of the room. They crossed the corridor and entered another cell, where they found a girl strapped face down over a vaulting horse, her legs pinned wide apart. The red-wine stains on her thighs told Lucy that this was the girl who had been using the bottle on herself. Now her behind bore a lattice of cane marks. As they entered, her punisher was dropping his trousers to the floor to reveal a thick, stiff cock. Lucy looked from this great truncheon of flesh to the girl's gaping love hole, then turned questioningly to Bruno.

'Just a little lubrication required,' he said. 'First the girl's cunt, then the gentleman's penis.'

Lucy licked her lips and stepped forward.

Twenty-Two

Jo knew she was no ordinary initiate into the Whipcord Society. No girl had ever made such rapid progress towards membership of the group. Now, as she sat in the back of the cab that was taking her, once more, to the premises that she now knew so well, she was almost in sight of her goal.

Once again Lander had been sceptical of her ability to take the test so soon, and, if Jo was honest with herself, she knew that she herself felt close to exhaustion after what she had been through. As on previous occasions, she was still a little sore where she had been whipped and caned, and it had only been in the last few days that she had felt able to wear a bra again, such was the effect the nipple clamps had had on her. But when Lander had told her that an opportunity had unexpectedly arisen for her to complete her final ordeal and to gain full admission, she had not hesitated. Apparently a girl had had to pull out at the last minute, owing to illness, and Jo had been given less than twenty-four hours notice to make up her mind whether she was ready to attend. Despite all her misgivings, she had known that she couldn't let the opportunity pass. Now here she was, the weekend stretching before her, a weekend that would finally confirm or deny her suitability to become a fully fledged member of the Whipcord Society.

A whole weekend! She had scarcely believed it when

Lander had told her. Even to someone with her stamina and stoicism it seemed an incredibly long time to subject herself to the whims of the Society's members. She wondered what could possibly lie in store for her. Once again, under her coat she wore only her straps and collar. Lander had made it clear that she was to bring nothing else with her, and she knew better than to disobey. She gazed out of the window of the cab at the passers-by on this busy London evening. They would be going home, or to the theatre or cinema, perhaps on for dinner afterwards. She could join them if she wanted. There was nothing to prevent her stopping the cab and climbing out, walking away from the Society and its cruelties. But, deep inside, she knew that she would do no such thing. She had come too far to consider turning back now. Besides, she couldn't deny the feeling of intense excitement that was already filling her as she contemplated what was to come.

The cab pulled up outside the Society's building and she paid the driver. Then she knocked on the door and was admitted.

The doorman took her coat, pausing to admire the swell of her young breasts, the curve of her hips and the sparse stubble that now covered her pubis. He reached down and ran his hands over her mound, his fingers straying between her nether lips. It was a most intimate gesture, one that any normal girl would only have allowed her lover to make, yet Jo made no complaint, simply standing stock-still whilst he fingered her.

'Looks like you need shaving,' he said, gazing closely into her eyes whilst his fingers explored her in the most intimate way possible. 'Go in there.'

He indicated the room beside the entrance hall, where Jo had first been fitted with her straps and collar. So well trained was Jo that she didn't hesitate for a second. She went in and, at his directive, lay down on the table, her legs spread, whilst he prepared the foam and razor.

He was just removing the last of the short, dark hairs from about her sex when Lander entered. Her guide glanced down at her as she lay, her lovely young body open to his gaze, and for the first time she wondered if she detected a spark of lust in his eyes as he took in her nakedness.

The doorman declared himself satisfied with her shaven sex, and Jo climbed to her feet, standing passively as her arms were pinned behind her. Then Lander attached a chain to her collar and led her out. She expected to be taken to one of the large rooms in the building where she had previously undergone her ordeals, but instead she was led down a corridor she was not familiar with. A door led into a narrow passageway, with neither carpets nor wall hangings, then into a kitchen. A man stood at the stove stirring a saucepan whilst two others, who wore the uniforms of waiters, stood by. All three watched with interest as the naked, shaven girl was led past them toward another door.

Jo got her first surprise when Lander opened the door and she found herself stepping out into the open air. Immediately she glanced about herself, suddenly afraid someone would see her in her naked state and wishing fervently that she could, at least, cover her nudity with her hands. Lander seemed quite unconcerned, however, dragging her across the open courtyard towards a gate on the far side. The courtyard itself was strewn with beer crates and empty barrels. To Jo's relief there was nobody in sight.

The gate led into a back alley lit by a single streetlamp. Parked at one end was a van with a man behind the wheel. As they approached he flashed his headlights, making Jo feel even more exposed as he illuminated her naked form in the powerful beams. For a second she wanted simply to escape, to get as far away as possible from the unfriendly spot. But Lander dragged her onward, clearly quite unbothered by the vehicle's lights.

He took Jo round the back and opened up the doors. It was brightly lit inside, and quite empty apart from a carpet on the floor. From the centre of the ceiling hung a chain, and Jo eyed it warily as he pushed her on board.

He reached behind her and freed her arms, then immediately attached her wrists together again and locked them on to the chain, pulling her arms up until her hands were touching the van's roof. Then, without a word, he turned and jumped down, closing the doors with a bang and locking them. At the same time the light went out and Jo found herself plunged into darkness. For a moment there was silence, then the van's engine came to life and the vehicle lurched forward, throwing its unwilling passenger off balance and making the straps dig into her wrists.

Jo's mind was a whirl. She hadn't anticipated this. Where were they taking her? The thought of being driven away like this was extremely unnerving, particularly since she had not a stitch of clothing. She stared about her for some kind of window, but there was none. Wherever they were taking her, they didn't want her to know.

The van drove on for what seemed like ages. As so often on these occasions, deprived of any outside stimulus, Jo soon lost track of time. Before long the stop-start of London's roads gave way to a smoother, more regular ride and she guessed they were heading out of the city. She was very uncomfortable, forced as she was to stand with only the chain to support her, and her mind was mostly occupied with maintaining her balance.

After some time, the van slowed and she felt them turn off. The new road was altogether slower and more winding, adding to her discomfort. Then she felt them bumping along a track and heard the scrunch of gravel beneath the wheels, before they finally came to a halt and the engine died.

A door slammed, then she heard the back of the van being unlocked and there stood Lander once more. She tried to peer past him out of the van, but he pulled the door to and set to work unfastening her wrists and securing her arms behind her once more. Then, to her dismay, he placed a blindfold about her head, leaving her in darkness once more.

She stepped carefully from the van on to the gravel which felt hard beneath her bare feet. She could sense from the silence, broken only by the distant bleating of sheep, that she was in the country, though where precisely she had no idea. She wondered if anyone could see her. If there was anybody about she knew she would present the strangest sight to them, her body quite nude, her sex devoid of hair, her hands pinned behind her so that the soft protrusions of her breasts were accentuated.

A tug at her lead told her to move forward, and she followed Lander as he led her away. All at once the gravel gave way to soft grass under her feet, then to paving stones.

'Steps,' said Lander shortly, and she found herself climbing a long, shallow flight of stone steps.

Ahead of her she heard a door open and Lander brought her to a halt.

'This the one?' asked a low male voice.

'This is her.'

'I'll take her from here.'

Jo sensed her lead being handed over, then a sharp tug almost dragged her off her feet.

'Inside,' ordered the voice, and she heard the door bang behind her. She couldn't tell if Lander had entered with her, but guessed he hadn't, since she could hear no sound from him. That made her feel even more uneasy. He wasn't exactly a great companion, but Lander was, at least, a familiar face. Now she found herself alone and naked in a place she didn't know accompanied by a complete stranger who she couldn't even see. At once the extreme precariousness of her position struck her. They had her totally in their power now. Nobody knew where she was or what she was doing. She was currently no better off than was Lucy, and the thought brought a knot of fear to her stomach.

She didn't have much time to contemplate her situation, however. All at once she was pulled up short, and strong, male hands on her shoulders turned her and pushed her forward. She felt the cool, hard edge of a wooden table against her pubis, then found herself being forced down over the table top, her breasts pressed flat against the wood. Her feet were kicked apart.

'Lift up your arms.'

It was difficult, but she managed to raise her hands clear of her backside. Then she felt a thin, wooden cane touch her flesh and a shiver ran through her.

She gave a shout of pain, dropping her palms instinctively to cover her behind. A hand slapped her thigh hard.

'Lift up your arms, I said.'

She obeyed.

Another stroke lashed across the tender flesh of her behind. This time she was ready for it, and managed to keep her mouth shut and her hands off.

The cane was thin and cruel, and wielded with considerable force – each blow excruciatingly painful. Even after all her previous punishments, Jo always forgot just how terribly a cane could hurt, and the tears welled in her eyes as the pain overtook her.

Two more rapid blows, then she heard the man place the weapon on the table beside her and felt another tug at her lead.

'Come on.'

Jo rose stiffly, her backside smarting, and it was all she could do to stand straight. As her hands came into contact with her behind she could feel the heat from her flesh and knew that it must be glowing red. Still she suppressed her tears and walked quietly behind her captor as he led her away.

He took her down a number of corridors, and suddenly she detected a change in her environment. The carpets beneath her feet were replaced by hard wooden floors, and the surroundings began to echo in a way that suggested a lack of furniture or wall hangings. All at once she heard sounds ahead, the clattering of crockery and cutlery and loud chatter. Then a door was opened and the sounds became suddenly louder. Along with them came the smell of cooking.

The kitchen was clearly a large one, manned by a number of people. It was humid and noisy inside, the noise amplified by the echoing walls. As she entered, though, the talking and movement stopped momentarily and she sensed eyes turning her way. Someone whistled.

'Get on with your work.'

The voice was that of her escort, and almost at once the chatter began again, though at a somewhat reduced volume.

Jo followed the man across the room, her senses filled with the sound and smell of the cooking. She was brought to a halt on the far side and turned with her back against the wall. Then her wrists were tugged downwards and there was a click as she felt them attached to a metal ring set low down in the wall. The position of the ring was such that she was unable to stand upright, being forced to bend her knees in an awkward and uncomfortable posture. When she felt her ankles kicked apart she knew that the position was designed to show off her sex to the maximum.

Time passed, and the clatter and bustle of the kitchen went on. The doors opened and closed continuously, and Jo could tell that a meal was being served, the waiters bustling past her as orders were shouted. Her escort seemed to have left her, her lead hanging loose between her breasts, and once again a sense of loneliness and vulnerability descended on her as she simply waited to see what would happen next.

At last she sensed that the meal, wherever it was, was coming to an end. The aroma of coffee filled her nostrils, and the clatter of dishes being washed had become the dominant sound. Still they left her where she was, her legs aching from the awkwardness of her enforced stance, her behind still throbbing from the caning she had received. Yet her thoughts were dominated, not by shame or embarrassment, but by the sheer eroticism of her situation: bound and blindfold; her body mercilessly displayed to the workers, as if she were the final course in the meal they had been serving, simply waiting her turn to be set before the diners. She tried to rid her mind of the sight she must make, her legs open, her hands powerless to prevent herself being ravished by any or all of these servants but she couldn't, and the image brought a new warmth to her belly and a wetness inside her.

All at once someone was beside her, and she felt her hands freed from the place to which they had been anchored. She straightened her legs gratefully, moving from one foot to the other as she eased the stiffness in her joints. Then she felt herself being pulled forward.

'Step up.'

She did so, and found herself standing on a low, wooden platform about six inches high. Hands grasped her arms from both sides and she was forced into position on to the platform.

'Kneel.'

She did as she was told. At once her thighs were grasped on either side and dragged apart, then her body was pressed downwards until her backside rested on her heels. Behind her she felt a chain attached to her cuffs, pulling them downward and anchoring her to the platform. The chain was tightened, forcing her to straighten her back. She knew this left her body perfectly displayed, her breasts thrust forward, her sex lips parted, revealing her hard little love-bud and the wetness inside her.

Suddenly a hand snatched her blindfold away. She shut her eyes, momentarily blinded by the brightness of the kitchen. Then something descended from above, and she was plunged into darkness once more. She barely had time to absorb this, however, when she suddenly felt the platform on which she was sitting rise and begin to move forward. It swayed as it moved, and she realised that it was being carried manually, like some kind of litter.

All at once she understood what was happening. Her sense of being the final course at the meal had been completely apt. She was that course. The object that was covering her was dome shaped, like a dish cover, and the litter on which she sat resembled a platter. She was being served up to the diners in the same way they would some exotic dish. A shiver of excitement ran through her as she contemplated what they would see when the cover was raised.

The doors of the kitchen closed behind them, and for a moment there was quiet, the only sound that of the waiters' footfalls as they carried their exotic delicacy along, and the constant thump, thump, thump of her heart. Jo's mind was a whirl: on the one hand apprehensive about what trials might lie ahead of her; on the other totally aroused by her situation, so that she longed to be able to touch her most private places and bring herself some relief from the tension that was building inside her.

As they progressed her ears discerned a murmur of voices ahead of them. With every sway of the litter the voices grew louder, and the pace of her heart increased. This was her final ordeal. Already her backside bore the stripes of these cruel people. Now she was about to learn the full extent of their depravity, and of her own. As she heard the doors open ahead of her, and the murmur became the clear sound of conversation, her stomach tightened.

And this was just the first evening.

Jo had heard the expression 'deafening silence' before, but this was the first time she had fully understood its meaning. Since the litter had been put down, and the waiters had shuffled out, she had heard not a sound. Yet the atmosphere was electric.

She knew that she was surrounded by people, and that, from the way they had lifted her litter just before putting it down, she was on a surface some way above the ground, probably a table. Now, as she waited to see what would happen next, all she could think about was her nudity and vulnerability amongst these people. Yet still, the dominant emotion in her remained one of sexual arousal, and she knew this would be apparent as soon as the cover was lifted.

The silence had descended on the diners the moment she had been carried inside, and she knew that the 'dish' that had just been served was the centre of all attention. Now, as she heard the scrape of a chair being drawn back, she knew that her ordeal proper was about to begin.

'Ladies and gentlemen, welcome to the Whipcord Society.'

The voice was that of a man. The words were enunciated with a clarity that betrayed a privileged upbringing.

'Tonight's final course is Jane,' he went on. 'She has already received six strokes in order to ensure that she understands the nature of this evening. In a moment I shall reveal her to you and we'll explain the rules of this evening's little game.'

Jo listened from her strange location. As usual, the whole thing would be choreographed, with a master of

211

ceremonies presiding over her ordeal. There was something strangely ritualistic about these affairs. She knew they were designed to place the maximum stress on her.

The man talked on for a minute more. Then Jo froze as he gave the order:

'Lift the lid!'

It took no more than two or three seconds for the waiters to grasp hold of the cover and raise it above their heads, carrying it back and depositing it on the floor behind her. Once again, the sudden brightness momentarily blinded Jo, and she blinked her eyes as she stared forward, her body rigid.

She found herself in the centre of a large, circular table. Bright lights shone on her from all sides, illuminating her pale, naked flesh and offering her no escape from the hungry eyes of the diners who sat all around her. It was difficult to make them out through the glare, but she could discern at least four faces within her line of vision, and it was clear that there were more to her sides and behind her. She wanted to gaze around and see exactly where she was, but her instincts told her that she was required to stay still until ordered to do otherwise.

There was a general murmur of approval as the men took in their plaything for the evening. Jo felt her nipples stiffen with excitement as the men surveyed her charms. Not for the first time she wondered at the perversity of her own nature as the excitement within her grew.

For a full two minutes nothing was said, then she felt a hand at her wrists and she was suddenly freed from the platter.

'Stand up, Jane.'

Jo rose slowly to her feet. It was difficult to move gracefully with her wrists and elbows tethered as they were, but she managed to stand without too much difficulty, carefully planting her feet apart and holding her head high.

'Very nice,' said a voice next to her.

'A real beauty,' said another.

'Is her cunt wet?'

'Find out.'

'Come forward.' It was the voice of the man in charge again. He was sitting directly in front of her, a middle-aged man, his hair receding, his face aristocratic. Jo stepped toward him.

'Down. Present your cunt to me.'

Jo hesitated, uncertain what was meant.

'Down!'

This time the order was barked in a military tone that brooked no argument. Jo dropped back to her knees just in front of him, spread her legs and thrust her pubis forward. Clearly this was what he wanted, as he gave a little nod of approval.

He reached out his hand and placed it flat on her thigh. The contact of his flesh against hers was electric, sending a shock of excitement through her rigid body. He glanced at her sharply.

'She's certainly excited,' he said.

'Yes, but is she turned on? Check her cunt.'

He moved his hand upwards and his finger touched the hard little nut of her clitoris, bringing a gasp from the trembling girl, a gasp that changed to a low moan as he slid two fingers into her vagina. He probed deeply, twisting them as he did so, making her muscles convulse and tighten around his fingers. For a second, Jo feared that she would come, then he withdrew, and she bit her lip as she tried to bring her body back under control.

The man held up his fingers, and once again his companions murmured their approval at the way her juices glistened upon them.

'I think the young lady is excited,' he said, unnecessarily, then turned back to Jo. 'Now, lick my fingers clean.'

He held the fingers up in front of him, and Jo was

obliged to lean forward to take them into her mouth. The taste and smell of her own arousal filled her senses as she sucked at them, her breasts dangling delightfully in front of him.

Once he was satisfied that his fingers were clean, he withdrew them from her mouth and wiped them across her belly, leaving a shiny streak of saliva just above her pubic mound.

'Back on your feet,' he ordered.

Jo struggled back to a standing position in the centre of the table. As she did so, she took the opportunity to glance about her. There were about twelve of them, she estimated, all men, their ages ranging from mid-thirties to early fifties. As seemed to be the custom at these events, all were smartly dressed in dinner suits, making a stark contrast with her own total nudity.

'Now,' said the man. 'Let me explain this evening's little game. Before you were brought in, we drew lots. Four of us now have the right to satisfy our desires on your body in four different ways. In short, four of us are going to fuck you.'

The words were spoken quietly, almost casually, but the effect they had on Jo was extraordinary, her heart suddenly thumping against her chest as his words penetrated. It was all she could do to concentrate as he went on.

'The four ways are as follows. One of us will come between your breasts, one in your mouth, one in your cunt and one in your backside. Do you understand me so far?'

'Yes sir.' Jo understood the words, but their implications were slower to sink in. Fuck her backside? No man had ever penetrated her there; that orifice was virgin. Tonight she was to lose that particular virginity to one of these men. She feared the pain such a deflowering might cause. Yet, at the same time, the prospect was one that seemed apt, almost symbolic, a final loss of inno-

214

cence that would form the first chapter of her ultimate ordeal.

'However,' the man went on. 'It's not as simple as that. First there are a number of rules you must understand, so listen carefully.'

'Yes, sir.'

'You must first find out who the four men are, and how they are to enjoy your body. You will choose one of us and ask, "Would you like to fuck me?" Just those words. If he replies yes, he is one of the four. You must then ask how he is to take you, by asking, for instance "Would you like to fuck my arse?" If he again responds positively you are to take up the position he instructs you to and allow him to have his way. Do you follow so far?'

'Yes, sir.' Jo was shocked, but not surprised by what was being asked of her. Clearly the whole exercise was aimed at humiliating her. She was being made to offer herself in the most blatant manner, like some common whore. Worse, she was likely to have her offers refused. Not for the first time she felt a sneaking admiration for the way in which the Society imposed its will on its young initiates.

'Right,' the man went on. 'However, there is another complication. Each man who replies to you in the negative will be obliged to punish you for your sluttish behaviour in offering yourself so blatantly. He will deliver a stroke across your behind with the instrument of his choice.'

Jo glanced down and, for the first time, noticed that beside each place at the table was a weapon of punishment. One man had a cane, another a horse whip, yet another a belt. So pain was to be mixed with humiliation in this extraordinary test. She looked likely to have a good deal more stripes across her behind before the evening was over. And this was only the first night!

'There's one more thing you should know,' the man

went on. 'We will be making a tally of the number of refusals, and strokes, you receive. For each one you will also receive a black mark. Score less than twenty, and you will spend the night in the relative comfort of a cell. Score twenty or more, and you will have to work a little harder for your accommodation.'

Jo stared at him, quite unable to understand his meaning. He gave a little smile.

'The servants of this place have a canteen to which they retire after the rigours of a day's work. It's a rather sordid little tavern after the splendour of this place, but they find it fills their simple needs. Some of them will already be there, enjoying a well-earned glass of beer. The only thing the place lacks, as far as they're concerned, is a waitress. Score twenty or more this evening, and you will be obliged to fill that post. Is that clear?'

'Yes, sir.' There was a tremor in Jo's voice now. The whole thing was totally diabolical. No wonder it took so long for most girls to qualify for membership to this extraordinary organisation. Not for the first time, she found herself doubting whether she would succeed in surviving the whole weekend.

All at once she found herself being lifted down from the table by two of the waiters who had carried her in. Then the catches at her wrists and elbows were undone, and her arms were free at last. She wanted to stretch, and to ease the aching of her limbs, but decided against it, allowing her arms to hang at her sides.

'Right,' said the man. 'Begin.'

Jo stood, staring round at the men as they sat, waiting expectantly. It was an impossible task, she thought. There was no way of knowing where to start. All the men's faces were impassive, giving no clue as to which were the lucky ones. Eventually, having no better plan, she approached the man closest to her.

'Would you like to fuck me, sir?'

He stared at her for a moment, then shook his head.

'No. Bend over the table and take your punishment for making such a suggestion.'

She moved forward to the edge of the table, then prostrated herself over it, shivering slightly as the hard, cold wood came into contact with her bare flesh. She spread her legs, then looked expectantly at the man. He lifted a long, thin cane from the table and tapped it against her backside.

Then he brought it down hard, the thin weapon biting deep into her flesh and bringing a cry of anguish from her, and he regained his seat.

Jo straightened, clenching her teeth as the pain in her behind burned with a terrible intensity. She moved round the table and stopped in front of another of the men.

'Would you like to fuck me, sir?'

'No.'

This time it was a belt that thwacked into her soft rear, the end wrapping round and delivering a stinging blow to the inside of her thigh. Then she was moving on once more. Her third attempt had no more success, nor did her fourth, and the agony in her backside was increased by a stroke from a leather tawse and another from a length of thick rope. Fighting back the tears, Jo turned to the next man.

'Would you like to fuck me, sir?'

The man smiled. 'Yes.'

Jo's emotions were a mixture of relief and apprehension as she stared at him. He was in his mid-forties, his hair flecked with grey, his eyes deep-set and inscrutable. She took a deep breath.

'Would you like to fuck my arse, sir?'

'No.'

He picked up the thin leather horsewhip that lay on the table before him. Without waiting to be told, Jo bent over the table.

The man wielded the weapon with force, bringing it

217

down just below the cheeks of her behind and leaving a thin red stripe across the tops of her legs. She straightened once more.

'Would you like to fuck my cunt, sir?

'No.'

It was all she could do to force herself to bend over the table once more and receive another stinging blow.

'Would you like to fuck my mouth, sir?'

'Yes.'

Jo could have cried with relief at the thought of getting a respite from the dreadful pain of the beatings. There was almost an air of urgency about her as she stared down at the bulge of his fly.

'Kneel.'

She obeyed at once, her eyes fixed on his crotch as he moved closer to her.

'Unzip me.'

His orders were short and, in truth, unnecessary. Jo knew what was wanted of her, and she reached for his fly with trembling fingers, sliding down the zip and delving inside. His cock already felt hard, straining against his briefs, and she dragged them downwards, releasing his stiff rod so that it stood out proudly from his fly. She placed her hands about it. It was not long, but thick, the uncircumcised end bulging. It felt rigid, yet alive, beneath her fingers and she watched as it twitched in anticipation of the delights to come.

'Suck me.'

Jo glanced up at his face momentarily, then moved her head forward, opening her mouth and taking him between her lips, savouring the taste of him as she began to suck. One hand slid down and closed about his balls as she did so. The sac had tightened against the base of his erection and she squeezed it gently, feeling his large testicles through the puckered skin.

All at once Jo forgot the pain in her behind and the shame of her nakedness. The feel of a hard cock between her lips held her full attention, and she began to work the man's shaft up and down, her face moving back and forth and she sucked hard at him. She raised her eyebrows and glanced up through her lashes at his face. It was contorted with pleasure, and she could hear his grunts as she worked at him, her breasts bouncing up and down with each movement of her head.

As she fellated him, his cock seemed to grow even thicker, and the pulsations within it became more frequent, so that she was spurred on to increase her pace, gobbling greedily at his engorged penis.

He came suddenly, a spurt of thick semen splashing against the back of her throat and causing her to gag momentarily, allowing a trickle to escape and run down her chin. Then she was back in control, wanking him hard, gulping down his creamy spunk as it continued to leap from the end of his cock. She tightened her grip on his balls, feeling the way the sperm was being pumped from them into her willing mouth. She sucked harder, determined to drain every drop she could from him as he gasped and moaned in ecstasy.

At last the pumping slowed, then stopped altogether. Jo reduced her motions gently, savouring the taste of him, her own body alive with arousal at the smell and taste of his orgasm. When he finally withdrew from her mouth his cock was already softening. She wiped the trickle of sperm from her chin and rose slowly to her feet.

Three to go, and five black marks recorded.

It took her six unsuccessful attempts, and six more strokes across her smarting behind, before she was forced to prostrate herself on the floor and squeeze her delicious breasts together whilst the man thrust his cock back and forth between them. His sperm was copious, covering her face and neck and matting her hair. But she was given no time to clean herself off, and soon she was prostrated over the table once more as they used their canes and straps on her.

By the time she discovered the man who was to bugger her, she had used eighteen of her black marks and her behind was a mass of blood-red stripes.

Being fucked in the backside was a new experience for Jo. The man made her take up the same position as she had for the beating, then a finger rubbed grease into the tight hole of her anus. Jo shivered as she felt the hot, stiff tip of an erect penis slide down the crack of her backside, then begin to press against her rear. It pushed insistently, and she fought down the natural reaction to tighten her sphincter, willing herself to let him enter her. And enter her he did, his cock sliding into her rectum as she bit her lip against this new pain.

He fucked her with hard, determined thrusts, banging her hips against the table with every stroke, his thick weapon stretching her behind. She wondered if a woman could ever find pleasure in such an act. It was certainly an extremely erotic and intimate way to couple, and she knew that, were he to use his fingers on her clitoris, she might even find a way to enjoy it.

He came quickly, the tightness of her rear hole ensuring the maximum sensation for him as he filled her rectum with his spunk. Once he was spent he withdrew, and Jo felt a trickle of sperm escape from her burning anus.

Now there were only three men she hadn't spoken to, and she could only afford two more black marks if she wasn't to spend the rest of her evening in the hands of the servants. This time she knew, at least, that it would be her vagina that was penetrated, and a new surge of wetness suddenly filled it at the thought. Suddenly she realised how totally aroused she was. The nakedness, the beatings and the unsatisfying sexual acts had raised her to a peak of sexual tension, and the thought of finally being properly fucked made her almost gasp with desire. She eyed the three men: one was the master of ceremonies; one was a distinguished looking man in his fifties; the third a younger, arrogant-looking man who eyed her with disdain.

'Would you like to fuck me, sir?

The distinguished looking man replied in the negative, and used a thin cane to lay a stinging blow across her bare globes. Then there were two.

She chose the master of ceremonies.

'Would you like to fuck me, sir?'

'No,'

Jo's heart sank. That was it. She'd had her twenty attempts. It looked like it was going to be a long night. Without waiting to be asked, she prostrated herself across the table and accepted the crack across her behind with a belt without a murmur. Then she turned to face the man who was to screw her.

'Would you like to fuck my cunt, sir?'

A faint grin appeared on the man's face. 'Sit on the table, then lie back,' he ordered.

Jo hoisted herself up, wincing with pain as her tender backside came into contact with the hard wood. Then she lowered herself until her shoulder blades touched the surface.

'Move forward and spread your legs.'

She obeyed, peering down between her breasts at the man, who showed no emotion as he dropped his trousers to the floor.

Jo licked her lips. His cock was large, easily the largest she had encountered tonight. He stood, working the foreskin back and forth and staring at her bare sex.

Jo moaned and thrust her hips forward. There was no room in her emotions for coyness now. She was totally turned on, and ready to be screwed. Already she could feel the involuntary tightening of the muscles inside her sex as she anticipated the penetration that was about to occur. Yet still he held off, clearly enjoying her frustration, the grin still playing about his lips as he contemplated his partner's naked body.

At last he moved forward between Jo's open thighs. She watched as he used his hand to guide the tip of his cock toward the open hole of her sex. When his stiff rod came into contact with her slit, her entire body jerked suddenly and she gasped aloud. He took his time, running his glans over her clitoris, watching the passion on her face as he played with her. Then he moved lower, and began pressing himself home, sliding his thick penis into her, forcing himself deeper and deeper until she felt the hard bone of his pubis come into contact with her own.

He thrust once, twice, then she was coming, thrashing about on the table in front of him as all her pent-up emotions were released in a single wave of orgasmic joy. Her cries echoed about the room as she thrust her hips against his.

He continued to fuck her, his hands grasping her thighs, his backside pumping back and forth. There was no expression on his face, no sign of love or passion. He was simply using her cunt, treating her as he might a blow-up doll laid out for his pleasure. But Jo didn't care. He could have been any man, as far as she was concerned. All she required right now was a long, stiff cock inside her that would relieve the extraordinary sexual tensions that had been building in her all evening.

He came without warning, with no change to the pace of his screwing, his cock suddenly twitching as he spurted his semen deep into her vagina. Almost at once Jo came for the second time, screaming with passion as yet another glorious orgasm coursed through her. Her sex lips tightened about his stem as she came, as if trying to draw him deeper inside her whilst the contents of his balls was emptied inside her body.

He continued to thrust until the last drop of his semen had been transferred into her. Then he withdrew, leaving her still squirming about on the table top, her backside clear of the surface as she thrust her hips forward in a lewd and overtly wanton gesture.

All at once there were two men beside her, gazing at her naked body. They were two of the waiters who had brought her in, and now they were waiting to take her away again. She glanced down at herself. Her neck and breasts were still shiny with semen as, she knew, was her face. Between her legs she could feel more of the substance trickling from her vagina on to her thighs to join that which had already leaked from her still stinging backside. Her face reddened; all at once she wanted to hide herself, to cover the obvious evidence of her debauchery. But she knew she had forfeited all such rights when she had submitted herself to the Society that evening. So, when the men took hold of her arms and dragged her to her feet, she made no complaint, standing passively as they locked her arms behind her and attached the lead to her collar.

She took a last look around at the diners, most of whom had turned away, having apparently lost interest in their plaything. Then there was a tug on her lead, and she followed her new captors out of the door and off in what she knew must be the direction of the servants' canteen.

Twenty-Three

When Jo awoke, she wasn't certain for a moment where she was. She stared about in confusion at the dull grey walls of the small room in which she lay. Then she glanced down at her naked body and it came back to her in a rush. The ordeal. She was here to undergo the final ordeal. And it was still going on.

She lay, gazing at the ceiling, going through the events of the previous evening in her mind. The servants' canteen had been in a separate building in the grounds of the house. She had been led, naked and dirty, up to the building by the two men, to be greeted by a chorus of approval from those inside. The canteen had proved a sort of dingy tavern, with strip lighting and formica-topped tables at which sat the men and women who worked at the house, now out of their uniforms and in casual dress.

Jo had been made to stand on a table whilst the stripes of her punishment were examined. The evidence of what else had happened to her at the house was also clear, and was the subject of many ribald remarks as they inspected her. Then she was put to work waiting on the tables.

Once again she had felt a perverse sense of arousal at the humiliating way she was treated, forced to work naked before these men and women who were themselves merely servants. As she scurried between the tables, her hands occupied by a laden tray, no opportunity was lost to slap her bare behind or squeeze her succulent breasts. Later they had put on music and made her dance for them, standing on a table, her legs spread, her hips pumping back and forth to the beat. As a finale they had made her swig down a bottle of beer, then thrust the neck of the bottle into her vagina, using this makeshift dildo to bring herself to a shuddering orgasm to the cheers of those watching. Only then was she allowed to leave, and was taken to this cell, where they had thrown her on to the bed and locked the door, leaving her to fall almost at once into a deep, dreamless sleep.

She glanced across at the door, and realised with a start that it was ajar. Someone must have come along whilst she was asleep and opened it. She rose cautiously to her feet. She was still completely naked, and there was nothing in the cell for her to wear. She pushed the door open and stepped through.

She found herself in a bathroom, painted the same bleak grey colour as her cell. It was a dull, functional room, with a stainless steel toilet and sink and a shower cubicle in the corner. Nevertheless it was welcome, and she stepped gratefully under the shower, allowing the cascading water to wash away the night before's grime.

She completed her ablutions, drying herself on a towel that was attached to the wall by a strong cord and cleaning her teeth with the toothbrush provided. Once she was satisfied with her appearance she looked about her. As well as the door that led back to her cell, there was another on the far side of the room and she crossed to it and tried the handle. It opened into yet another room, decorated in a similar manner to the previous ones. In the centre was a single table and chair, on which had been laid a meal. There was fruit juice and coffee, fresh fruit and an array of rolls and cold meat.

All at once, Jo realised how hungry she was, and soon she was tucking into a simple but very welcome meal.

Once she had eaten, Jo's curiosity returned. She had seen and heard nobody since leaving her cell. It was all very strange. The place had the appearance of a prison, yet none of the doors was locked and there were no warders. This room too had a second door, and it was towards this that she made next. Once again it was unlocked and she stepped through, then stopped short in surprise.

She was in a very odd room indeed. It was divided almost exactly down the middle, and the two sides were in total contrast to one another. On her left, the room was carpeted, the walls covered by expensive flock wallpaper. The furniture was extremely fine, with low, soft easy chairs and top-quality hardwood tables. The whole resembled nothing more than the living room of a country house.

The other half of the room, by contrast, was painted in the now familiar grey, with no carpet or furniture, apart from a simple wooden table in the centre.

She stepped on to the carpet and gazed about her. There were flowers on an occasional table by the window, and a door led on to a driveway on which a shiny car was parked, the driver's door open. Beyond it was a pair of large wrought-iron gates that stood open, and in the distance Jo could just discern a busy highway, with cars flashing by.

Turning back into the room, she saw that there were some clothes laid out on the sofa. There was a small, elegant dress bearing a designer label, a set of good quality underwear and a pair of shoes just her size. On the coffee table beside them was a set of car keys which, she had no doubt, would fit the car outside.

Jo turned her attention back to the bleaker side of the room. That, too, had an exit, beyond which she could see a path that led to a tall, forbidding looking manor house, where she assumed she had spent the previous evening. She moved across to the table. On it was a long, thin cane and a scrap of paper. She picked up the paper and read the single sentence inscribed on it.

'Bring this cane to room 117 in the manor, where someone is waiting to use it.'

Jo retreated to the door through which she had entered the room and stared from one side to the other. The message was clear. This was her opportunity to escape from this place. All she had to do was don the clothes, take the car keys and drive out on to that highway and home. In an hour she could be in her own flat. She could spend the afternoon in London's West End, and take in a show in the evening, just like any normal girl. She could regain her clothes and her dignity and leave this dreadful place behind her. The alternative was continued nudity, bondage and the cane. She had no illusions as to whom whoever it was in room 117 wanted to use it on.

There was a full-length mirror on the wall, and she stood in front of it, turning her back to it and gazing over her shoulder. Her backside was a mass of criss-crossing stripes, and when she ran her fingers over the soft flesh she winced at the tenderness. She swung round to face it once more, her eyes taking in her bare breasts and her shaved pubis. She glanced across at her clothes. More than anything she wanted to cover herself, to regain her modesty and to hide her most private places from the prying eyes of the Society members and their servants. The temptation to put on the bra, pants and dress was almost overwhelming.

Then she thought of the book, and of her friend Lucy still held somewhere, and she knew she had no choice. She sighed, then turned her back on the clothes and car, crossed to the table and picked up the cane. She flexed it in her hands, imagining how it would feel cracking down on her tender behind. She slid a hand down her belly and delved into her slit, rubbing her finger over her clitoris and shivering slightly at the frisson of pleasure this intimate contact gave her. She thought again of the men who would see her nakedness and would use her body that day, and a sudden surge of excitement swept through her.

Then, still masturbating, she set off through the door and up the path towards the manor.

Twenty-Four

Jo fought to retain her balance as the van bounced along a rutted road, rattling and banging as it negotiated what was clearly a little-used track. She was in the same position as she had been when they had taken her to the manor, her wrists locked together and fastened to the chain in the van's roof

They had been travelling for more than half an hour now. At first she had thought they might be returning to London, but it soon became clear that they were taking a quite different route, down narrow, winding roads. Then they had turned off on to this track.

The van lurched again and Jo staggered to one side, tugging hard at the chain that was her only support. At least the journey was taking her mind off the pain in her behind, she mused. That was some consolation.

On returning to the manor, a grinning servant had shown her upstairs to room 117. There three men were awaiting her. None had been at the meal the night before, and all took in her lovely young body with interest, making her stand with her legs spread whilst they examined her and probed her most intimate places.

They had laid her over an old vaulting horse, the hard leather chafing against her bare skin. Then they had taken it in turns to lay four fresh stripes each across her backside with the cane. Afterwards they had made her suck them off, each one coming in her mouth, forcing her to gulp down their semen. Only after the last one had shot his load between her lips had she been allowed to leave. A servant had been waiting for her outside the door, and had led her straight down to the van.

With a final lurch, the van drew to a halt, and Jo had the luxury of being able to stand unaided for the first time in what seemed ages. A few moments later she heard the van door being unlocked and a man climbed in. She didn't recognise his face, but his voice was that of the man who had brought her into the manor the day before, and had laid the first six stripes across her behind. Now she studied his face with interest. He was about thirty-five, tall and dark with a goatee beard. His face was expressionless as he released her wrists and indicated the door.

Jo stepped out on to soft, cool grass and gazed about her. They were in a wooded area, the van having been parked in a small clearing. The track they had driven down was narrow, and scarcely looked drivable, yet there were at least ten other vehicles also parked in the lonely spot. Jo glanced up and down, afraid that someone might see her, but all the cars were empty.

The man dropped down beside her, and she immediately placed her hands behind her head and her legs apart. The gesture was almost automatic now, she reflected, illustrating how she was becoming conditioned to the subservient demeanour required of her by the Society. The man sat down on the tailgate.

'Can you swim?'

'I beg your pardon, sir?'

'I asked if you can swim.'

'Yes, sir.'

'Good. Come with me.'

He jumped to his feet and headed off along a path between the trees. Jo followed at once, picking her way carefully in her bare feet. It was a hot day, the sun beating down through the trees. In any other circumstances this would have been a pleasant spot, but naked as she was, and fully aware that she wasn't simply here to enjoy the setting, Jo found herself far to nervous to enjoy the surroundings.

They walked for about five minutes, then suddenly broke clear of the trees. Ahead, Jo saw the edge of a cliff, and beyond it the blue of the ocean. The man beckoned her to the edge.

Jo stared down. Beneath them was a wide strand of sandy beach. Dotted about on it were human figures. Jo noted with surprise that some of them were naked. Most were men, but here and there were couples enjoying the sunshine. One or two were swimming in the sea.

The man turned to Jo.

'Pretty spot, isn't it?' he mused. 'It's not officially a nudist beach, but nobody minds. Some of them are genuine sun lovers, though I suspect some of the guys are just along to look at the scenery. They're going to enjoy getting a look at you.'

'Me, sir?' Jo was taken aback.

'Certainly. You won't be too out of place down there, will you?'

Jo stared down at herself. Even on the front of her body, on her belly and thighs and the sides of her breasts, the marks of her beatings were visible. She knew that her back and behind were striped with marks. Anybody seeing her couldn't help but remark on the fact that she had been recently whipped. Add to that the fact that her sex was quite devoid of hair, and she knew that she made a most unusual, and extremely erotic sight, naked as she was. She looked up at her escort, who was grinning broadly.

'I see you've grasped the implications. Displaying yourself naked down there could well prove an interesting experience for you, and for those watching. They aren't Society members by the way, just some genuine nudists and a bunch of peeping toms. Even I don't know how they'll react. However, it would be in your interest if they do react.'

'Sir?'

'It would be a pretty cold fish that didn't get aroused at the sight of you,' he went on. 'That's why I want you to get fucked.'

Jo gasped, staring at him with wide eyes.

'Don't go all coy on me,' he said. 'You didn't expect this weekend to be some kind of picnic did you? Now go down there and take a swim, then look for someone who'd like to get his dick in you. You have one hour to come back with your cunt full of spunk, or you've failed. Understand?'

'Yes, sir.'

Jo could scarcely believe what he was proposing. She wondered at the ingenuity of the Society in dreaming up ways to punish and humiliate her. Every time she thought that there was nothing they could suggest that could shock her more than she already had been, they found some new, fiendish way to get to her. Simply walking naked on the beach was an idea that she would have found shocking, but to do it with her sex shaved and her back and behind covered in stripes was almost beyond the pale. And even that was not enough for them. She ran her eye over the bodies prostrated on the beach, and a tight knot formed in her stomach as she imagined the seduction she was to perform.

The man moved close to her, reached out a hand and ran it over her breast. At once the nipple puckered to a hard point. He moved his finger up and stroked her collar.

The collar! Jo remembered with a start this emblem of submission and the straps that accompanied it. They were badges of her subservience, the uniform of a slave. With these, she could never be mistaken for a mere nudist. It would be clear to any observer that her motives were sexual. She swallowed hard as she contemplated this new realisation, remembering of the clothes and the car keys she had found that morning. To think she could have been safely at home now, leading the life of any normal girl. Instead here she was, about to put on the most lewd of displays and to seduce a complete stranger.

Yet even as she turned and began to make her way down to the beach, the apprehension in her was already giving way to an intense excitement. Somehow, here amongst these strangers, she was able to abrogate all responsibility for her actions. Nobody knew who she was, or what her motives were. She could behave as outrageously as she wished, and simply walk away.

The path wound down the side of the cliff to some sand dunes, beyond which was the beach. Already she could see that she was an object of interest for a number of the male sunbathers as she approached them. She wondered if, from this range, they could discern that her crotch was shaved. If not they would soon do so. Then there were the stripes on her behind. She felt her face glow as she thought about the sight they must make.

As she reached the foot of the cliff, the dunes hid the beach momentarily from her view. She skirted round one, then another, and was brought up short by the scene in front of her.

A man, in his early twenties, lay on his back in the sand. He was quite naked, his head towards her. Astride him was a naked woman, a blonde of about twenty. For a second, Jo couldn't make out what was going on. Then she realised that the man's long cock was buried deep inside the girl's sex, and that she was moving her body up and down with regular movements, fucking him hard. Jo stood there, unable to take her eyes off the scene as the girl screwed the man with vigour, her pert little breasts bouncing up and down with every stroke. As Jo watched, the blonde looked up and caught sight of the silent watcher. Jo's face turned scarlet as she realised she had been caught out, but to her amazement the girl simply smiled and winked at her, before setting about her task with increased vigour.

Jo retreated behind one of the dunes. The sight had powerfully aroused her, and she paused for a moment to recover her composure. It seemed she wasn't to be the only one to seek sexual relief down on this beach today.

She wound her way round the dunes in the opposite direction, until she broke clear of them and found herself stepping on to the beach.

There was no doubt about the interest she engendered amongst the young men, and she was amused to see some of the naked ones roll over on to their stomachs to hide their reaction to the lovely youngster as she strode across the sands. Jo suddenly felt very exposed and self-conscious, her straps, shaven crotch and striped behind making her an odd, and extremely erotic vision to anyone watching. She could see the shock on the faces of some of the women, but she tried to appear composed as she made her way to the water's edge.

The water felt cool and refreshing as it lapped about her ankles. She strode in deeper, letting it come up to her knees, then her thighs. Then, in a single movement, she dived forward into the water. It enveloped her in a sudden green silence, and she allowed herself to sink to the bottom, before her natural buoyancy carried her to the surface once more. She struck out strongly for the open sea, enjoying the luxury of having her body concealed from view for the first time since she had left London.

She swam for about ten minutes, relishing the warmth of the sun and the coolness of the water. Then she began to consider her next move. Up on the cliff she could see her escort. He was lying prone on the grass, and a glint of sunlight told her that he had a pair of binoculars trained on her. Reluctantly she turned towards the shore, swimming slowly as she contemplated what to do.

If she was honest, she wasn't certain where to start. It was all very well him telling her to get herself screwed, but how to make the first move? She couldn't just go up to the first man and offer him her body. As she got closer to the shore she surveyed the figures lying there. Which one was it to be? And how would she start the conversation? She was right in the shallows now, and could swim no further. She rose slowly to her feet, only too aware that she was, once more, the centre of attention.

As it was, she had neither to choose her man nor to make the first move. The first man she passed at the water's edge he spoke to her.

'Interesting swimming costume.'

She stopped and turned to him.

'I beg your pardon?'

'The costume. Never seen one quite like it before.'

'You mean my straps and collar?'

'Yeah. Real sexy!'

For a moment Jo was reminded of her encounter by the river, when the fisherman had caught her masturbating. Then she had been quite unnerved by the whole occasion, and if it hadn't been for the extreme arousal that the book had kindled in her she would have almost certainly run away. Now, though, she felt in control of herself. Calm almost, although she couldn't deny the arousal that was beginning to germinate inside her.

'They're slave's straps,' she said.

'You're a slave?'

'Sort of.'

'And the person who put those straps on you, did he thrash your behind as well?'

'A few men have been thrashing my behind. It's what they do to slaves. As well as make them shave their cunts.'

The man gave a low whistle and shook his head. 'You're quite something.'

She smiled at him. He was about thirty years old, slim and tanned, his hair bleached by the sun. He wore a pair of black swimming shorts and nothing else. She sat down on the sand beside him.

'Mind if I join you?'

'Be my guest.'

They began chatting. He was fascinated by her subservient role, and she answered his questions frankly, though she told him very little about the Society and the precise reason she was there. As they talked she saw his eyes roving over her body, and she positioned herself with her legs slightly spread so as to give him the view she knew he wanted.

Time was passing, though, and her hour would soon be up. It was time to make a move. She decided a direct approach would be best.

'Listen,' she said. 'Having all these guys staring at me is making me feel really horny. Do you fancy going behind the dunes with me?'

His eyebrows rose. 'You mean . . .'

'You know what I mean.'

He shook his head. 'You really are some girl.'

'I know,' she said, rising to her feet. 'Coming?'

She set off toward the dunes, not looking back. She couldn't believe how forward she was being. To think, a couple of months previously she had been unable to allow a man to touch her. Now here she was, brazenly naked, her intentions obvious to all as she led the man to the seclusion of the dunes.

He came alongside her and she took his hand.

'This is all a bit unexpected,' he said.

She smiled. 'Believe it or not, it's unexpected for me too.'

As they approached the dunes they passed the young couple she had encountered earlier. The man watched them with undisguised interest, but failed to notice the knowing grin and wink that his girlfriend gave Jo as they passed. This time the gesture was returned.

Scarcely were they out of sight of the beach than Jo

turned to her companion. He moved in close to her, wrapping his arms about her and planting his lips over hers. Jo was already extremely aroused, and the kiss sent new spasms of excitement through her as he pressed his strong body against her own, his tongue snaking into her mouth. He ran his hands down her back, taking the soft flesh of her backside into his palms and squeezing gently, making her wince slightly as she was reminded of the numerous stripes that covered her tender flesh.

She placed an arm about his neck. He was taller than her and she found herself stretching upward to meet his lips. Meanwhile her other hand strayed down the front of his shorts, feeling for the bulge that was already forming there.

The kiss went on for minutes. His hands left her behind and began to range over her body, grasping her breasts and rolling the solid nipples back and forth between finger and thumb. At the same time his other hand reached down for her crotch, cupping her pubis, his index finger tracing the soft wetness of her nether lips.

Jo fumbled with the cord that held his swimming shorts up, pulled it undone, then slid a hand inside. Her fingers closed about his penis, which was growing and thickening by the second. She manoeuvred it round so that it stood upwards, running her small hands up and down its length, feeling it throb with excitement as she did so.

All at once she broke the kiss, staring up into his eyes.

'I want to taste you,' she said.

'Go ahead.'

'Lie down then.'

He dropped on to the sand, lying back, his hands tucked behind his neck, staring up at the naked beauty who had ambushed him so unexpectedly. Jo dropped to her knees beside him and reached for the waistband of his shorts. He raised his backside, allowing her to pull them off in a single movement. She tossed them aside, then turned to him, sitting back on her heels for a moment to admire his physique.

His body was slim and muscular. His chest was broad, with only a sparse coveting of hair, the pectorals bulging. His legs were sinewy, like those of an athlete. But it was his manhood that drew her attention. Long and slightly curved it rose proudly from his groin, the ball sac at the base contracted into a tight brown sphere that hugged close to him. Every now and again the end of his tool would twitch, making it bob up and down in a way that fascinated her. She took hold of his shaft, feeling the pulses run through it. Then she leant forward and opened her mouth.

He let out an audible gasp as she took him between her lips, savouring the smell and taste of his rigid knob. At once she began to suck him, working his foreskin up and down with her fist whilst she slurped greedily at the swollen end. He responded instantly, pressing his groin up at her face as she closed her other hand about his balls.

There was no doubt about his arousal. His breath was coming in short bursts and the spasms of his penis were increasing in frequency and violence. It occurred to Jo that he might come in her mouth at any moment. Whilst she had no objection to tasting his spunk, she had her orders, and they were to have a man come inside her cunt. Reluctantly she released his cock and sat back, staring down at the thick rod, now glistening with her saliva.

'I want you inside me now,' she said.

He smiled. 'You're certainly a lady who knows what she wants.'

'Let's do it doggy fashion.'

'Whatever you say.'

Jo dropped forward so that she was on all fours, her succulent breasts dangling beneath her. She placed her knees wide apart in the sand and pressed her backside up and back, deliberately presenting him with a perfect view of the wetness inside her sex.

He rose to his knees and moved round behind her. His fingers began gently to trace the stripes that crisscrossed her pert behind. Then they slid down the crack of her behind, lingering for a moment on her anus before moving lower still and sliding into the heat and moisture of her sex.

'Ah!'

Now it was Jo's turn to gasp as he delved deep into her vagina, his long fingers twisting about inside her, bringing the most delicious spasms of desire. Her bottom pressed still further backwards as she tried to coax him even deeper into her, the lust in her knowing no bounds.

He withdrew his fingers, leaving her panting hard. Then she felt the thick tip of his penis probing at her sex.

She almost screamed aloud as he plunged his cock into her. So wet was she that it slid in with a single thrust. The muscles inside her contracted about it, as if trying to hold it within her.

He began to move his hips. Slowly at first, clearly savouring the sensation of his knob being enveloped in the warm wetness of her sex. She groaned quietly as his meaty weapon slid back and forth within her, pressing in until she could feel his pubic bush against the tender flesh of her behind, then drawing back, the friction bringing her a pleasure that was exquisite.

She glanced upward. At the top of the cliff she could just discern a face, peering down at her. She wondered how clearly he could see her as she gave herself so freely to this man.

Her lover's movements were increasing in tempo now, as his passion grew. His hands grasped her thighs, pulling her back towards him as he plunged his rigid cock into her love-hole. Jo was almost crying aloud with pleasure, her entire body on fire with desire as he fucked her hard. Every stroke now rocked her body forward, causing her dangling breasts to shake deliciously.

All at once she felt his grip on her tighten and his thrusts became suddenly more urgent. Then he gave a gasp and she felt her cunt flooded with his semen, rhythmically spurting from him as he climaxed within her. Two more strokes and she was coming too, waves of passion coursing through her as a delicious orgasm overtook her. The pair were locked together, their bodies moving in rhythm as they milked pure pleasure from one another.

He continued to thrust into her until his semen was spent. Then he withdrew, pulling his erection from inside her and flopping down on to the sand, dragging her down on top of him.

'Was I good?' she asked mischievously.

'Great. The best.'

She kissed him on the cheek. 'I'm glad,' she said. Then she untangled herself from his arms and rose to her feet. 'Got to go.'

He grabbed for her ankle, but she avoided him.

'Can't I even have your number?'

She shook her head. 'You were the right guy, in the right place at the right time, that's all,' she said. 'Now I've got to go.'

And, without another word, she set off round the dunes and was soon lost to view.

Twenty-Six

Lucy sucked hard at the long, hard erection that filled her mouth, and her hand worked back and forth along the man's shaft. Her partner gazed down at her, unable to either assist her or stop her, since his hands were attached to chains that hung down from above him. He was naked, his back and behind bearing the marks of a recent whipping, his face and body bathed in perspiration as he stood, watching his beautiful warder fellate him.

Lucy was clad in a tight-fitting PVC leotard and hold-up stockings, her feet encased in one of the highest pairs of heels imaginable. She sucked hungrily at the cock in front of her, her head jerking back and forth as she rewarded her victim for his good behaviour in accepting his punishment.

This was not the first time that Lucy had been called upon to deliver a beating to one of the male Society members. Since she had been incarcerated at the Lodge, she had had a number of visitors seeking a relief that she was almost uniquely qualified to offer.

Virtually all the female members of the Society played a submissive role with the males. Their duty was to submit to the cruel whims of their masters, in return for which they were able to satisfy their own sexual desires. Lucy, though, was different. There were a number of male Society members whose preference was to take on the submissive role, and, quite early on in her relationship with the Society, the men had discovered Lucy's talents as a dominatrix, a role she played with some enthusiasm. She was still subject to the strict rules of the Society, which dictated that the men always held the upper hand, but it suited them to allow her to wield the whip on occasions. When word had got around the Society that she was being held captive at the Lodge, a number of the male members had availed themselves of her services.

This particular man was in his early fifties, his white hair giving him an almost distinguished appearance. His current position, though, naked and spread-eagled whilst his young punisher sucked hard at his rigid cock, was far from dignified. Still, she could tell that he was extremely aroused by the harsh treatment he had received at her hands, and now his gasps told her that his climax was near.

He came with a moan, his cock jumping as a gob of spunk flew from the end into Lucy's throat. She kept her lips firmly clamped about his glans as she drank down his seed, swallowing every drop as it squirted into her mouth.

When, at last, he was spent, she rose to her feet, taking his cheeks between her palms and kissing him on the lips.

'That better, you evil man?' she asked.

He nodded. 'Thank you, mistress.'

'Good.'

She left him there in his cell, still tethered. No doubt someone would be along to release him eventually. Outside the corridor was deserted, and she began to make her way back to her own cell.

Suddenly she noticed a door ajar. She stopped short, her heart thumping. The area she was in was a secure one, with all doors to the outside world locked. She would have been in her cell at this time of day, if it hadn't been for the summons to attend to the man.

Haddow had been off duty that afternoon, so she had been taken to the punishment room by a warder she didn't know. He had left her with orders to make her own way back to her cell once she had finished. Now, though, she paused, staring at the open door.

She knew that it led into one of the warders' offices, a place out of bounds to a prisoner such as herself. It should have been locked, but it looked as if someone had been careless.

Lucy glanced about herself to reassure herself that she was alone. Then she tiptoed across and peered inside. The office was, indeed, empty. Lucy's eyes surveyed the scene, alighting on a telephone that stood on the desk. Her heart leapt when she saw it. Since being brought here, her only contact with other humans had been with Society members. She had racked her brains to try to think of a way to get a message out to Jo, and to warn her of the forthcoming evening, when the innocent girls would be exposed to the power of the book. Now, here was her chance.

Taking a final look about her, she stole into the room. She reached out for the receiver and lifted it gingerly. To her relief she heard the dull purr of a dialling tone.

She punched in the number of Jo's flat, then listened, her heart beating, as the connection was made. It rang once, twice, then there was a click.

She drew her breath to speak, then hesitated as a short silence was followed by the obvious hiss of an answering-machine tape.

'This is Jo,' said a strangely disembodied voice. 'I'm afraid I'm not in at the moment. Please leave your name and number after the tone, and I'll get back to you.'

The instrument bleeped, and Lucy began to speak, trying to keep her tone measured.

'Listen Jo, this is Lucy. The Society has me prisoner in the Lodge. I don't know where it is, but the book is here. They're going to use it this Wednesday night.

They've lured a gang of innocent young girls here, and they're going to subvert them just like you feared. You've got to try and get here, Jo. I've . . .'

She broke off. She had heard a sound outside. The sound of a door being opened.

Quickly she replaced the receiver in its cradle, careful to make no sound. Then she tiptoed to the door, slipping quietly through and back into the corridor. She wasn't a moment too soon. At that very moment a warder rounded the corner.

'What are you doing here?' he demanded.

'I'm going back to my room, sir,' she replied.

'Where have you been?'

'I've been with the gentleman in room thirty-seven, sir.'

'I see.' He eyed her suspiciously for a moment. 'Well you'd better get a move on back to your cell, then. And don't let me catch you wandering about the corridors again.'

'Yes, sir.'

And, with a sigh of relief, Lucy headed back in the direction of her cell.

Twenty-Six

The sound of the bolts on the door behind her being shot back made Jo start. She had been so long alone in the dark chamber she had begun to doubt that she would ever see the light of day again. Now, as the heavy door swung open, the shaft of light that it allowed in was more than welcome to the girl. Less welcome were the blinding beams of the spotlights in the ceiling that suddenly flooded the room with so bright a light that she was obliged momentarily to close her eyes against it.

As she blinked them open again, the first thing she saw was her own image, reflected in the mirror opposite her. As in so many parts of the Society's establishments, provision had been made for the unfortunate victim to witness her own suffering at the hands of its sadistic members.

The sight that met Jo's eyes was an extraordinary one. The position in which she had been placed was one of extreme discomfort, fiendishly contrived to both display her and to bring her pain. She was astride a narrow bar that was suspended between two posts about four feet above the ground. Her legs were clear of the floor, spread wide apart and attached to the ground by chains. The bar itself was no more than half an inch wide along its upper surface, so that it intruded painfully into her sex. There was no way for her to ease this pain by raising her body, since her wrists were locked to the ring at the back of her collar, causing her plump young breasts to be thrust forward. Her jailers had taken full advantage of this vulnerability. Attached to her nipples were a pair of vicious clamps, the teeth curved back so that any attempt to pull them off simply resulted in them digging even deeper into the hard, brown flesh. Chains ran from these clamps to a ring set in the wall in front of her, stretching her breasts almost conical, the tightness being maintained by another chain that ran from the back of her collar to a ring behind her. The sum total was an extraordinary tension, obliging her to stay rigidly still, since every movement brought new agony to her breasts and crotch. Yet staying still was the difficult thing. She estimated that she had been in this position for two hours now, and the effort to maintain her balance had exhausted her. Her limbs felt impossibly stiff, and every attempt to move them simply increased her agony.

The door closed and somebody stepped into the light. It was her guard. The man who had taken charge of her since she had arrived at this strange place. He stood in front of her, admiring his charge. Jo said nothing, simply staring ahead at her own reflection.

It had been this same man who had had her placed in this extraordinary position in the early hours of that morning. The previous evening had been spent serving on tables at a large dinner party, along with the rest of the servants, the difference being that they had worn their uniforms whilst she had been obliged to be naked throughout, forced to endure the slaps on her behind and the pinches and prods of the diners as she endeavoured to serve them. Compared to many of her experiences, however, it had been relatively mild, clearly designed to give her a slight respite after the games of the night before.

Soon after midnight they had taken her to a cell and left her there, and she had fallen asleep almost at once. She wasn't certain what time they had come for her, but the sky outside had been barely light when three men had arrived in the cell, pulling her out of bed and dragging her unceremoniously down to this damp chamber deep in the bowels of the building, where they had put another dozen stripes across her behind with a cane, before placing her in this terrible bondage.

Now, with the prospect of finally being released, the pain was suddenly even worse, and she gritted her teeth as she waited for him to make a move.

'Remarkable,' he said at last.

'Sir?' she whispered.

'Your resilience. Most women scream the place down after less than an hour in that position. Your pain threshold must be very high.'

'Yes, sir.'

He moved close to her, running his hand over the stretched flesh of her breast.

'I can see you will be quite an asset to the Society,' he said. 'But, for now you have other duties to perform.'

He took hold of one of the nipple clamps and squeezed the catch, making the jaws open. At once her flesh sprang out, making her gasp with relief. He released the second one, and as the circulation began to return to her swollen teats, a new pain hit her. She longed to be able to rub them but, even as he released her hands, she knew she dare not.

He undid the chain at the back of her neck, then set about freeing her legs. Soon she was off the awful bar, flexing her arms and legs in an attempt to relieve the stiffness in them.

He allowed her a mere five minutes to recover from the torture of the bar. Then her arms were secured behind her, a lead attached to her collar, and she was on the move once more.

He led her up a flight of stone steps to a heavy door. When he opened it, Jo was astounded to find herself outside, in the grounds of the manor. She followed obediently as he led her across a patch of grass towards some buildings set apart from the main house. As she approached them she saw that they were stables, relics of bygone times at the house. She could see no sign of horses now, though.

He took her down a row of stalls, pausing outside one of them. The door was in two halves, the upper one open, and inside were two servants who were working on some kind of pony trap. As Jo arrived they rose to their feet.

'All set?' asked Jo's companion.

'We're ready for her,' came the reply.

Her escort pushed open the lower door and indicated for her to enter.

As Jo stepped into the stable, one of the men gestured her across to him. He took hold of her shoulders and, turning her round, positioned her between the shafts of the trap. It was quite a small vehicle, with a double seat and large wheels. For a moment, Jo was at a loss as to what they wanted of her, then she saw the thick leather belt the man was carrying, and it dawned on her. She was to be the pony.

The servant approached her and placed the belt around her waist. It was about three inches thick and made of hard, thick leather, like a real horse's harness. It fitted snugly around her, and he pulled it tight, squeezing her waist in until it was almost painful. From each side hung a chain, and he used these to attach her to rings on the shafts of the pony cart, making her grip the handles and hold them horizontal.

The two servants made a final check that her chains were securely fastened to the trap, then stood back.

'Outside,' said her escort tersely.

Jo moved forward, pulling the trap behind her. It wasn't heavy, and the large wheels were smooth running, so that it required surprisingly little effort to tow it. She pulled it clear of the stable door, then stopped, awaiting her next order.

The man pulled something from the trap. At first Jo had thought that the upright post was part of the structure, but now she saw that it was a long whip, slotted into a hole beside the seat. It was about six feet long, made of leather, tapering to the thickness of a piece of string a the end.

'This is the driver's steering whip,' the man said. 'If he taps you on the right thigh, turn right, on the left, turn left. Understand?'

'Yes, sir.'

'Good. Now take this thing to the gatehouse. Straight down this road, and get a move on. They're waiting for you.'

He slotted the whip back into its stand, then slapped her backside. At once Jo set off at a run in the direction he had indicated, dragging her burden along behind her.

Once again the Society had surprised her with its ingenuity in finding new ways to humiliate her. Now she was to be a pony girl, and she had no doubt that, before long, they would find her a passenger.

The road was a long one, the tarred surface hard on her bare feet. The day was beginning to warm up now, and her breathing became heavier as she trotted along. She had gone almost a mile before she spotted the building ahead, and the large metal gates beside it.

She ran as far as the entrance to the building, then stopped. Clearly she couldn't go in, there was no way she could have got through the door with the trap. Instead she turned the trap round so that she was facing back the way she had come, then waited, still panting slightly from her run.

It was about five minutes before the door to the building opened and somebody stepped out. There were two people, and Jo recognised them at once. It was the overlord, and his ever-present assistant Bruno. This was the first time she had encountered the Society's chief since her ordeals had begun, and she was surprised to find him taking an interest in her. She said nothing, however, simply staring forward down the road.

The overlord paused in front of her, his eyes travelling up and down her naked form. Then he nodded. 'I have heard good reports of you, Miss Larwood,' he said. 'It seems you were quite serious in your intention to pass the ordeals in so short a time. It is possible you may prove an asset to the Society.'

'Thank you, sir.'

'Now, my companion and I would like to go to the house.'

'Yes, sir.'

Jo eyed the pair of them with some trepidation. Carrying the overlord would be hard enough, but to have the combined weight of the burly Bruno as well was going to make this very hard work indeed. She clung tightly to the shafts, just able to hold them horizontal as the two men climbed aboard.

Once they were seated, they were actually less of a burden, since the seat was balanced just above the axle. But she knew already that getting the trap moving would be a different matter.

She heard Bruno slide the whip from its stand, then felt a tap on her bare behind.

'Walk on.'

Bracing herself, Jo tugged hard at the trap. For a moment it didn't move, then the wheels began to turn, slowly at first, but gathering momentum as she stepped out.

The whip came down suddenly and unexpectedly on her backside, stinging dreadfully and bringing a cry from her lips.

'Faster,' shouted Bruno.

Jo strained against the shafts, pulling as hard as she was able, and gradually the trap began to gain momentum. Fortunately for her the road was level, and soon she had it moving along quite nicely, or so she thought.

Bruno's aim was near perfect, and once again her bare behind was stung by the crack of the whip as she strained forwards.

'Trot!'

Summoning up all her reserves, Jo dug her feet in and hauled, just about managing to break into a trot. She was beginning to sweat now as the strain told on her young body, but still she gritted her teeth and went on.

Still Bruno kept up his onslaught, the whip cutting into her tender behind and proving a spur to her to keep moving as fast as she was able. They were approaching a fork in the track now, and she waited to see which way they would send her.

The end of the whip snaked round her right flank, the stinging tip catching her on the underside of her breast, leaving a mark that immediately darkened to an angry red. The pain was excruciating, but Jo put it to the back of her mind, dragging the trap round to take the right-hand fork. Then she was trotting on again.

Jo was starting to feel the strain now, the sweat pouring from her face, a thin rivulet running down her neck, through the valley between her breasts and down to her crotch. Her breath was beginning to rasp in her throat as she gasped for breath, whipcrack after whipcrack raining down on her burning behind.

This time the lash came across her left flank, the end actually catching her nipple, already sore from the cruel clamps that had held it such a short time before. Jo wanted to cry aloud, but she shut her mouth firmly, veering off to the left on a track that took them back towards the manor.

As they skirted round the walls of the building, Jo's energy was almost completely drained. She knew that if they took one more detour she would not be able to make it. As it was, her lungs were burning as she sucked in the air, and her legs felt like jelly, each step an enormous strain on her. Yet still Bruno did not let up with the whip, and she knew that her two passengers must be staring at a bare behind that positively glowed red with the punishment it was receiving.

They were approaching the front entrance to the manor now. A hundred yards to go, though to the exhausted Jo it looked more like five hundred. Still she trotted on. Fifty now. Surely they weren't going any further?

At the last moment, Bruno swung the whip so that it wrapped about her neck, giving a sharp tug as it tightened. Jo didn't need the command interpreting, and she drew the trap to a halt just at the entrance to the manor.

For a moment there was silence, broken only by the laboured rasping of Jo's breath, her heart pounding against the wall of her chest. Behind her she felt her passengers dismount, but she was too exhausted to turn. Instead she simply stood, her body soaked with sweat, her hair dishevelled, her breasts rising and falling as she struggled to regain her breath.

Suddenly she realised that the overlord was standing in front of her, and she raised her head to stare into his eyes. He shook his head.

'You really are quite a remarkable woman, Miss Larwood,' he said, running a hand over the soft swelling of her breast. 'Once you have returned the trap I intend to fuck you, as does Bruno here. Then you have only an afternoon in the torture chamber to look forward to before you're officially invested. I'm sure you'll have no problem with that. Now off you go back to the stables and get rid of this thing. Once you've done that, I've given orders for you to be bathed and shackled to a couch, where I intend to enjoy your charms.

He slapped her hard on the backside, and Jo set off wearily in the direction of the stables.

Twenty-Seven

When Jo arrived back at her flat that evening, she was almost completely spent. She staggered through the front door and slammed it behind her, dropping her coat on to the floor. In the bathroom she examined her body. It was covered in red marks where the whips had landed. Some of the early marks had already darkened to purple bruises, whilst others were bright and fresh and too tender to touch.

Being screwed by the overlord and Bruno had been almost a respite from the ordeals of the day. She had been tied face up on a couch in the front room, and they had taken it in turns to ravish her. Afterwards, her escort had explained that it was most unusual for the overlord to fuck one of the girls, particularly a novice. Jo hadn't been quite sure how to take that piece of news, though she had enjoyed an orgasm with both of the men.

The afternoon had been spent in the same chamber in which she had begun the day, her body being clamped, stretched, prodded, caned and whipped in all manner of ingenious devices until the overlord had finally declared himself satisfied. Afterwards there was no ceremony, no welcome to the Society she had worked so hard to become a member of. She was simply taken out to the van and strapped in as before, the door were closed, and she was carried back to London.

She spent a long time in the shower, washing the

manor from her body both actually and symbolically. Once she felt clean she ran a bath, pouring in some salts and relaxing in its steaming waters, feeling the aches and pain soak away. As she lay there she contemplated her weekend. In her wildest dreams she would never have imagined that she could behave in such a way. It had been painful, humiliating and exhausting. Yet, at the same time, it had been one of the most exciting and exhilarating experiences of her life, leaving her feeling more vital and alive than she could possibly have imagined. And it had left an indelible mark on her. Never again would she be the shy, diffident young woman who had bought that book. The new Jo was fully aware of her own sexuality, and of how to use it.

She stayed in the bath for an hour, then hoisted herself out, dried herself and poured herself a stiff gin and tonic. Sipping at her drink, she wandered into the living room. Only then did she notice the light flashing on her answering machine. She moved across and rewound the tape. Then she pressed the start button.

Moments later she was staring open mouthed at the machine, scarcely able to believe the message she had heard. So she had been right about Lucy all along. Her friend was being held prisoner by the Society, and the book was being used for precisely the purpose she had feared. There was only one thing for it. She must get to the Lodge and find a way to gain entry to the ceremony. But how? Wednesday was only three days away.

The next morning, sitting behind her desk at work, Jo was still indecisive. She needed to be at the event, but to ring the Society and ask would arouse suspicion. She knew there must be a way, but what was it?

Jo had never been superstitious, or believed in fate. Life was simply a gamble according to her philosophy, and coincidences were just that. However, in the days and weeks to come, she was to look back at what happened next and wonder whether her scepticism was well-founded.

What happened was that the telephone rang.

Jo snatched up the receiver.

'Hello.'

'Jane? It's Lander here.'

'Lander . . . sir?'

'I had good reports from the overlord. You seem to have done well.'

'Thank you, sir.'

'In fact the overlord has taken a particular interest in you. You should be honoured.'

'Yes, sir.'

'The notice is short, so I can't order you, but you are required on Wednesday night. Can you be there?'

'Where?'

'I can't tell you. Suffice to say it's some distance, and you will be very late back.'

'What is it for, sir?'

'I can't tell you. Simply that it's a very special evening, and that the overlord wants you to attend.'

Jo could hardly believe her ears. Here she had been, fretting over how she could possibly be involved in the initiation, and now she was being invited.

'I could take the day off,' she said quietly.

'Good. All the better. I'll have you picked up in the morning. That'll give you time to learn the ropes. Wednesday morning at ten o'clock.'

There was a click, and then silence. Jo shook her head in disbelief, then a smile spread across her face.

Wednesday was going to be quite a day.

Twenty-Eight

Jo stretched out in the back of the limousine as it sped up the highway. Despite her blindfold she knew they were on a fast road from the sound of the wheels, and of the other traffic. At least it was a good deal more comfortable than her trip to the manor. This car was long and expensive and smelt of leather.

The car's windows were darkened – a good thing in Jo's eyes, since they had once again made her travel naked, her hands cuffed behind her. She didn't mind, though. She was becoming accustomed to the practice and, if she was honest with herself, she had to admit that she was turned on by the thought of men seeing her naked body.

She must have dozed off, for all of a sudden she realised that they had left the busy roads and were moving slowly along a track. Then she felt the car draw up, and moments later her door was opened.

'I trust you had a comfortable journey?' The voice was Lander's.

'Yes thank you, sir.'

'Good. I don't think you'll need the blindfold for the time being.'

He pulled the black velvet band over her head and she stood, blinking to try and restore her focus. They were standing on a wide gravel driveway outside a large house, even bigger and grander than the manor. As well as the limousine there were a number of other vehicles parked there, though there was nobody in sight. She waited patiently whilst Lander attached a lead to her collar, then followed him inside.

Everything about the building was on a grand scale. The ceilings were high, the rooms long and wide. The walls were hung with old tapestries and expensive-looking oil paintings. The furniture was antique. Lander led her through the main entrance hall into a large reception room. There Jo pulled up short. In the centre of the room, in a glass cabinet set high up, was the book. Her book. There for all to see. She felt her heart thump in her chest when she saw it. At last she had found it. It was like greeting an old friend. Even the sight of it kindled a familiar sensation in her groin as she thought of what it contained.

But finding it was one thing. Getting it back quite another. She knew it wasn't going to be easy.

'The women who are visiting tonight are all newcomers,' Lander was saying. 'None of them is as yet familiar with the Society or its aims. That is why we need some experienced members, as well as some new ones like yourself, to assist them in understanding the aims of the Society.'

Jo scarcely heard what he was saying, though. Her mind was entirely occupied in working out how she would retrieve her book. Even with the assistance of a chair to stand on she would only just be able to reach it, and then she would have to consider the noise she would make in breaking the glass to get at it.

She gazed about the room. As well as the entrance through which she had been brought, there were two other doors. Somewhere in the building, she knew, was Lucy. She would need her friend's help if she was to get away with the book.

'Have you any questions?'

She turned to Lander, her face blank for a second as she tried to remember what he had been saying. Then it occurred to her that he had given her a rare opportunity to question him and she knew she must take advantage of it.

'Who will show these new girls how the Society intends to treat them, sir?' she asked.

'We have a number of men, some of whom you will already have met during your initiation. And one woman.'

'A woman?'

'Yes.'

'And she administers punishment?'

'Certainly.' He eyed her closely. 'That seems to interest you.'

She glanced down. 'It's just that ... Well, I've never had a woman touch me.'

He stared at her for a second. 'It could be arranged.'

Jo said nothing.

Lander smiled. 'Wait here.'

He went back through the door they had come through, and she heard his voice on the telephone. Two minutes later he was back.

'Follow me,' he said, taking up her lead.

He knocked on a door on the far side of the room, and it was opened by a guard in the familiar black uniform. They passed through and he closed the door behind them. This part of the house was quite different from the one she had just left. The floors were bare, the walls painted a grey colour. It reminded her of the cell they had put her in at the manor. As Lander led her along the corridor, she stole a glance to the right and left. The rooms seemed more like cells, the doors having heavy locks with small spyholes in them. Lander took her on down the passage to a door at the end, which he opened.

The room was quite a large one, the walls painted the same grey colour as the corridor. Spread about the room were a number of devices that she recognised from the chamber at the manor, mainly frames designed to restrain a miscreant whilst she was being punished. The mirrors were there too, reminding Jo of her own nudity, as if she could forget it.

Lander undid her wrists, then fastened them together at the front again. He attached them to a chain that hung down from the ceiling beside the wall, hauling her hands high above her head and stretching her young body taut. He made a final check of her bonds, then turned and left the room.

Jo was left alone, with only her own reflection in the mirror opposite for company. She surveyed her body. The marks of her weekend ordeal were only too visible, the stripes from Bruno's whip curling round her upper torso and across her breasts. She shuffled round as far as she was able, examining the lattice of stripes that covered her behind, back and legs. She could scarcely credit the fact that she was back so soon in one of the Society's torture chambers.

There were footsteps outside, and she looked up as a warder entered. With her was Lucy.

Lucy stopped short at the sight of her young friend, standing naked and chained against the wall. For a second Jo was afraid that she was about to give the game away, but she pulled herself together and turned to the guard.

'Thank you, sir,' she said. 'I think I can take care of the young lady from here.'

The guard took a long look at Jo, his eyes travelling slowly over her charms. Then he turned and left, closing the door behind him.

Lucy was dressed in her dominatrix outfit of black leather, with long boots and fishnet stockings, the military style cap perched rakishly on her head. There was a whip hanging from her belt. Jo opened her mouth to speak, but Lucy shushed her with a finger to her lips.

'So, little beauty,' she said, moving close to the tethered girl. 'It seems you've already felt the whip recently.'

'Yes, mistress.'

'I'll wager not from a woman, though.'

'No, mistress.'

'Hmm.' Lucy ran the end of the whip over Jo's breasts, teasing the nipples to hardness. 'A sensitive little thing, aren't you? Turn round and let me see your backside.'

Jo obeyed, and she felt her friend's hand run down her back, tracing the stripes.

'How did you get here?' The tone of Lucy's voice was completely different now, as she spoke close to Jo's ear.

'They just brought me. Is it safe to talk?'

'It's okay as long as the red light is out on that camera.'

Lucy indicated a small video camera set high in the ceiling. Jo hadn't noticed it before, but even as Lucy spoke a small red light illuminated on the front and the camera panned round with a low whirring sound.

'Such lovely, soft flesh,' purred Lucy, reverting to her dominatrix role. 'And so beautifully striped. I can't wait to add to those marks. Let's have you over the horse, I think.

There was an old leather vaulting horse in the centre of the room that had been fitted with chains and manacles. Lucy undid Jo's wrists and led her across to it. As she did so the light on the camera went out.

'That's security,' she confided in a low voice. 'They scan every room periodically. We just have to keep an eye on it. How did you get here?'

'I'm a member of the Society now,' said Jo. 'I completed my final ordeal on Sunday.'

Jo stared at her in admiration. 'That's incredible,' she said. Then she ran her hands over her friend's backside once again. 'I see they put you through it.'

'I can take it. Shouldn't you be tying me to that horse?'

'Lie across it then.'

Jo levered herself up on to the horse. It was so high that her legs were clear of the ground as she prostrated herself across it. Lucy set about attaching the manacles to her arms and legs.

'It's happening tonight,' she said.

'I know. Tell me the details.'

'The girls are all from nearby towns. They answered an advert in the local papers. They think they're auditioning for a show.'

'I knew something like this would happen once the Society got hold of the book,' said Jo. 'How do they plan to expose the girls to it?'

'They made me read extracts from it on to tape,' said Lucy, still busying herself with the bonds. 'The plan is to play the tape and project images of the illustrations onto the wall from a control room just above the reception. The girls will be in there having a welcome drink.'

'What kind of drink?'

'Some sort of punch I think.'

'Good. Where will you be?'

'I'll be up in the control room helping.'

'Who else will be in there?'

'Two guards. One working the tapes, the other the projector.'

'And down in the reception room?'

'Just a couple of waiters. You'll be waiting outside to join in the fun once the book has taken effect.'

'That's great. Now ...'

'Stop complaining you little slut,' said Lucy suddenly.

Jo craned round to see that the red light on the camera was illuminated once more. Then she noticed that Lucy was pulling the whip from her belt.

'Let's see what a few more stripes on that pretty behind will do,' she said.

She brought the whip down with considerable force across Jo's rump, reawakening all the pains of her weekend experience as the flesh darkened to red.

It was clear that Lucy was pulling no punches as she brought the whip down on Jo's behind once more, the blow stinging terribly as it bit into her flesh.

Swish! Whack!

Then the hand stroking her flesh once again.

'Sorry about that. I have to make it look realistic.'

'Don't worry,' said Jo through gritted teeth. 'Listen, Lucy I want you to do something for me.'

'Anything.'

'Feel inside my cunt.'

'What?'

'Just do as I say. Right up inside.'

'Jo, this is no time to ask me to frig you.'

'Don't be silly. There's something in there.'

'Something in there?'

'Go ahead and see.'

Lucy hesitated for a second, then reached out tentatively for Jo's sex, which was easily accessible, her legs having been spread wide by the chains.

'Go on. Push right inside.'

Lucy slid her fingers into her friend's love hole, probing deep into the hot dampness. As she did so Jo felt her muscles tighten involuntarily in a spontaneous reaction to so intimate a gesture.

'Deeper,' she urged.

'Oh Christ,' said Lucy, suddenly. 'There's something there.'

'I knew they'd bring me here naked,' said Jo. 'There was nowhere else to put it.'

Lucy pulled the small parcel from her friend's vagina. It was circular, about three-quarters of an inch across. As she examined it she saw that it was a condom wrapped about something soft.

'What is it?' she asked.

'A couple of Mickey Finns. I've got a friend who's into that sort of thing. Apparently there's enough there to fell a dozen grown men in about three minutes.'

'Wow!'

'Yeah. And all we have to do is find a way to get it into the punch.'

'The punch? I don't understand.'

'Just listen and I'll explain.'

But at that moment the light on the camera came on again, and Jo braced herself as her friend drew back her arm.

Twenty-Nine

Jo stood quietly with the four black-clad guards listening as the sound of chatter in the reception room next door increased. She checked the clock on the wall. The timing was exactly right. The girls, who had all arrived about fifteen minutes earlier, had been given a preliminary chat by the overlord and were now being shown into the reception room for their drink and, ostensibly, a chance to meet one another. At any minute the audio visual display would commence and the influence of the book would soon become evident. Even as the thought passed through her mind, she heard the speakers come to life and the sound of Lucy's voice. Her heart beat faster as she realised that her plan was about to come into operation.

Once she had been released from Lucy's company, Jo had spent much of the afternoon in a cell. Lander had come in and briefed her on her role in the evening's proceedings. She was simply to assist the guards as they took the girls into the various treatment rooms and torture chambers in order to take advantage of the effect that the book had had on them. Now, as she waited, wearing only her straps and collar, she prayed that Lucy had been able to carry out her part of the plan and laced the girls' punch with the powder she had smuggled in.

She glanced at the clock again. Nearly three minutes had passed. The stuff was supposed to have taken effect by now. If it didn't work soon, the danger was that the book's words and pictures would have had their effect, and the innocent girls might be affected permanently.

Then she heard a thump and a scream, shortly followed by the sound of footsteps and another thump. The men with her stared at one another in consternation as more voices began to be raised in the next room.

'What the hell's going on?' asked Lander.

One of the other guards shook his head. 'I dunno.'

The volume of sound increased. Someone was shouting, then the words just seemed to die away.

'Better take a look,' said Lander.

The sight that met their eyes on opening the door was one that gladdened Jo's heart. At least half the girls were already slumped unconscious on the floor. As she walked in, one of those still standing turned to face her, and the girl's jaw dropped as she saw Jo's state of undress.

'Where are your . . .' The girl's voice trailed off and her eyes seemed to glaze over. Then she slumped to the floor, unconscious.

All at once, Jo pulled up short. From outside the room, Lucy's voice had been muffled, the words impossible to discern. Now she heard them clearly, and at the same time was confronted by one of the book's illustrations projected on the wall opposite. The picture showed two naked girls, their bodies tied together so that they hugged one another close whilst a pair of burly men stood on either side whipping the pair. In the background a third girl was tied in a kneeling position, a man thrusting his long cock into her mouth whilst another whipped her back.

Jo stood, rooted to the spot, her mind filled by the image and by the words that came from the speaker. Words that described the pain and pleasure being experienced by the women as they were so savagely beaten. Oblivious to the pandemonium about her, Jo found her fingers dropping to her crotch as the words rang in her head.

Then, suddenly, the voice stopped in mid sentence and the picture before her went dark. For a moment longer Jo stood where she was. Then, as if waking from a dream, she shook her head and glanced up at the control room. There she saw Lucy's face gazing out through the window. She was holding something in her hand. It was an audio cassette.

All at once Jo remembered where she was and what she was doing. Lucy was telling her that the men in the control room had also collapsed, due to their coffee being laced with more of the powder. Lucy had removed the tape from the machine and switched off the projector. Even as she watched, Jo saw her turn away from the window and begin gathering up all the tapes and slides in the room.

Jo glanced about her. None of the girls was standing now, and apart from one or two who were still gazing blearily about themselves, nearly all were unconscious. The guards were gathered around them, anxiously slapping their hands and faces in vain attempts to revive them. She knew she didn't have long. Already Lucy would have grabbed all the pictures and tapes and would be on her way to the car park at the front of the building. Her plan was to purloin the car keys of one of the men in the control room, and to wait by the door for Jo to appear.

Jo moved quickly. There was a chair beside the wall and she carried it quickly across to the centre of the room, above which was the cabinet containing the book. Picking up a heavy ashtray from a nearby table she climbed up on to the chair and hurled the object against the glass, smashing it into tiny fragments. She reached inside and snatched the book from its resting place.

'Hey!'

She turned to see Lander heading towards her.

'What the hell do you think you're . . .'

But he got no further as Jo lashed out with her foot,

catching him square in the jaw with her heel and sending him reeling. Then she had jumped from the chair and was heading for the door, the book tucked under her arm.

As she ran into the entrance hall, she saw the car pull up outside and discerned Lucy's face peering anxiously through the window. She made a dash for it, but even as she did so two figures appeared in the doorway.

The overlord and Bruno.

The overlord stood, his hands outstretched, blocking her way, whilst Bruno made a dive down the steps toward the car. Lucy did not hesitate, and the tyres shrieked as she roared away down the drive, leaving the burly man watching helplessly.

Jo was on her own now. She had known this might happen. Both girls had agreed that the important thing was that at least one of them escape, and Lucy had grabbed her chance. Now Jo heard the sound of footsteps behind her, and she knew she had to move fast.

There was a corridor off to her right, and it was for this she headed even as Bruno dashed back into the building. Jo ran as fast as she was able, still clutching the book. At the far end was a door, and she grabbed the handle and pushed. To her relief it opened. Even better, there was a key in the door on the other side. She slammed the door shut and turned the key just as Bruno reached it, crashing against it so hard that the door post shook. He began hammering on it, and Jo could see that it wouldn't last long under his onslaught. She stared around her. On the far side was another door and she ran across and tried it. It led into a small room with a table in the middle, on which was a motorcycle crash helmet and a set of keys. Behind her she heard splintering wood. In no time Bruno would be through. On a whim she snatched up the keys and ran to the window, dragging it up in a single movement. She jumped out and found herself on a lawn with a car park beyond.

There, standing on its own, was a large, gleaming motorcycle.

A loud crash told her that the door had finally given way. Saying a little prayer she sprinted across to the machine, straddling it and sliding the key into he ignition. At the same time she saw the shape of Bruno appear at the window. She turned the key and searched frantically for the starter. The first button sounded the horn, the second switched on he lights. Bruno was out the window by now and sprinting across toward her. Then she pressed another button and the engine roared into life.

Jo just had time to slip the book underneath her, so that she was sitting on it, then she kicked the bike into gear, twisted the throttle and was off, with less than a second to spare.

She thanked her lucky stars that her brother had once taught her to ride a motorcycle as she sped across the car park, through a pair of open gates and off down a narrow country lane. She kept her speed up until she had put a good two miles between herself and the house, then eased back the throttle and sighed with relief. She had made it!

A mile later, the engine stuttered and gave out. It was only then that she glanced at the fuel gauge and realised that it read empty.

She drew the machine up at the roadside and climbed off. Her relief at having escaped with the book was tempered by the situation she found herself in. She was lost, miles from home, and quite naked.

Then she realised something else. Until now, the excitement of escaping had driven her arousal from her mind. Now, though, in this sudden silence, she remembered the words and the pictures from the book, and the way they had been affecting her in the reception room, and all at once the heat returned to her belly.

She slid a hand down her stomach, over her bare mound, and found her slit. Her clitoris was wet and swollen, and she gave a sharp intake of breath as her finger ran over it. All at once her mind went back to the occasion in the wood, on the day she had first found the book, and how she had masturbated there beside the stream. She began moving her finger in a circle about her love-bud, shuddering at the delicious sensation it gave her. For a moment she forgot her situation, so intent was she on giving herself pleasure. Her mind was filled with the image of the fisherman, and the wonderful fuck he had given her, stretched out on the grass in the open air. She began to rub all the harder, moaning softly as she did so.

Then she heard the vehicle approaching.

It was still some distance off, but already she could see the glow of its headlights in the night sky. Her first thought was that she was being pursued by the Society, and she looked about wildly for somewhere to hide. Then she realised that it was not a car's motor that she could hear, but a heavy diesel. What was approaching was a large truck.

Jo's mind raced. She was in trouble, there was no doubt about it, and she was going to need someone's help to find some clothes and to get home. At some stage she was going to have to approach someone and ask for assistance. Who better than a truck driver?

A shiver of anticipation ran through her as the thought struck her. If she stood in the road and hitched, there was no doubt that the truck would stop. But what would be the reaction of a macho lorry driver and his mate to finding a horny, naked beauty on the road?

Jo felt her stomach knot. She knew the answer to the question only too well, and, as she ran her fingers over the cover of the book, she knew too what her own response would be.

As the truck crested the rise and came into view of where she was standing she took a deep breath. Then she stepped into the road and stuck out her thumb.

Thirty

Jo glanced across the table a the young couple in front of her. Both looked nervous. The girl in particular was continuously playing with the ring on her finger, an engagement ring, Jo suspected. The man, too was clearly uncomfortable. It was hardly surprising, Jo mused. After all it wasn't so long since she had been in the same situation as the girl. She glanced down at the file on he desk in front of her, then addressed the girl again.

'And you really think that we at Passion Incorporated are your only chance?' she asked.

The girl nodded. 'We've tried everything else. Counsellors, books, you name it. I just can't seem to cope with the physical side of it.'

'Yet you want to have sex?'

The girl's face reddened. 'Of course we do. I'm just frigid, that's all.'

Jo smiled her most reassuring smile. 'Frigid isn't a word we like to use here,' she said. 'It implies that you have a cold nature, and if that was the case, you'd hardly be talking to me now,'

'It's just that Jennifer can't stand being touched,' said the man. 'She's fine up until then. There just doesn't seem to be anything anyone can do.'

'I think we can help,' said Jo. 'Our success rate is extremely good, and we don't charge unless we're successful.

'How many treatments will it take?' asked the girl.

'Most people only visit us once,' said Jo. 'Occasionally they come back a second time, but that's not all that common.'

'Just once?' The girl was incredulous. 'That's extraordinary.'

Jo smiled again and reached into a drawer in her desk. She pulled out a video cassette and a key and put them down in front of her.

'Go down the corridor to room nine,' she said. 'This is the key. You'll find a video player by the bed. Put this into it, and turn on the television. You can get straight into bed if you want to, or wait until the moment seems right. Take as long as you like.'

The girl picked up the tape. 'And that's all there is to it?'

Jo nodded. 'Trust me,' she said. 'And remember, no success, no charge. Off you go.'

The pair, still looking nervous and embarrassed, rose to their feet.

'Turn right out the door,' said Jo. 'You can't miss it.'

They went, leaving her alone.

Jo glanced about her office. It was very well appointed. Luxurious almost. In the six months since she and Lucy had started Passion Incorporated it had gone from strength to strength, until now it had an international reputation, with couples flying in for treatment from as far afield as the USA and the Far East.

She looked across at the cabinet on the wall in which the book was kept. She was convinced that this was the best use for so powerful an object. She and Lucy had selected readings and illustrations from the volume and had made up three audio visual presentations, each one slightly stronger in content than the last. It had taken some time, and their vibrators had been put to a good deal of use as they had worked through the volume, but the results had been exactly what they had expected. In fact they had never had to use the third tape, such was the power of the first two.

Jo glanced at her watch. She was due to meet Lucy in room eight in five minutes for a routine test of the equipment. With a slight smile she pulled tape three from her desk and slipped it into her pocket. From another drawer she took a long, black vibrator. Then she headed up the corridor. At the door of room nine she stopped and listened. A woman's voice could clearly be heard, moaning noisily.

Jo smiled and pulled the key to room eight from her pocket.

Bonded by Fleur Reynolds
September 1997   Price £4.99   ISBN: 0 352 33192 5

When the beautiful young Sapphire goes on holiday and takes photographs of polo players at a game in the heart of Texas, she does not realise that they can be used as a means of revenge upon her cousin Jeanine. As the intrigue mounts, passions run ever higher – can Sapphire hope to avoid falling prey to the attractive young Everett, or will she give in to her libidinous desires?

Silent Seduction by Tanya Bishop
September 1997   Price £4.99   ISBN: 0 352 33193 3

Bored with an unsatisfying relationship in her home village, Sophie enthusiastically takes a job as a nanny at a country estate. She soon finds herself embroiled in sexual intrigues beyond the furthest reaches of her imagination. A series of passionate encounters begins when a mysterious, silent stranger visits her at night, and she sets about trying to discover his true identity.

There are three Black Lace titles published in October

French Manners by Olivia Christie
October 1997   Price £4.99   ISBN: 0 352 33214 X

Gilles de la Trave persuades Colette, a young and innocent girl from one of his estates, to become his mistress and live the debauched life of a Parisian courtesan. However, it is his son Victor she lusts after and expects to marry. Shocked by the power of her own lascivious desires, Colette loses herself in a life of wild indulgence in Paris; but she needs the protection of one man to help her survive – a man who has so far refused to succumb to her charms.

Artistic Licence by Vivienne LaFay
October 1997   Price £4.99   ISBN: 0 352 33210 7

Renaissance Italy. Carla Buonomi has disguised herself as a man to find work in Florence. All goes well until she is expected to perform bizarre and licentious favours for her employer. Surrounded by a host of desirable young men and women, she finds herself in a quandary of desire. One person knows her true gender, and he and Carla enjoy an increasingly depraved affair – but how long will it be before her secret is revealed?

Invitation to Sin by Charlotte Royal
October 1997   Price £6.99   ISBN: 0 352 33217 4
Beautiful young Justine has been raised in a convent and taught by
Father Gabriel to praise the Lord with her body. She is confused
when the handsome wanderer Armand offers her the same pleasure
without the blessing of the church, and upon sating her powerful lusts
is banished in disgrace from the convent and put into a life of servitude. She must plan her escape, and decide whether to accept
Armand's invitation to sin. This is the second Black Lace novel to be
published in B format.

NEW BOOKS

Coming up from Nexus and Black Lace

There are three Nexus titles published in September

Amanda in the Private House by Esme Ombreux
September 1997   Price £4.99   ISBN: 0 352 33195 X
When Amanda's housekeeper goes missing, she travels to France in an attempt to find her. During the search she meets Michael, who awakens in her a taste for the shameful delights of discipline and introduces her to a secret society of hedonistic perverts who share her unusual desires. Amanda revels in her new-found sexual freedom, voluntarily submitting to extreme indignities of punishment and humiliation.

Bound to Submit by Amanda Ware
September 1997   Price £4.99   ISBN: 0 352 33194 1
The beautiful submissive Caroline is married to her new master at a bizarre fetishistic ceremony in the USA. He is keen to turn his new wife into a star of explicit movies and Caroline is auditioned for a film of bondage and domination. Little do they know that the film is being financed by Caroline's former master, the cruel Clive, who intends to fulfil a long-held desire – to permanently make her his property.

Eroticon 3
September 1997   Price £4.99   ISBN: 0 352 32166 0
Like its predecessors, this unmissable collection of classic writings from forbidden texts features some of the finest erotic prose ever written. In its variety of people and practices, of settings and sexual behaviour, this exhilarating anthology provides the true connoisseur with the flavour of a dozen controversial works. Don't miss *Eroticon 1, 2* and *4*, also from Nexus.

Sherrie and the Initiation of Penny by Evelyn Culber
October 1997   Price £4.99   ISBN: 0 352 33216 6
On her second assignment for her enigmatic master, Sherrie acts as instructress to the unhappy writer Penny Haig, initiating her into an enjoyment of the depraved and perverse games the writer has never before dared to play. Penny soon becomes a fully-fledged enthusiast, revelling in humiliating ordeals at the skilled hands of expert disciplinarians.

Candida in Paris by Virginia Lasalle
October 1997   Price £4.99   ISBN: 0 352 33215 8
Naughty Candida has a new mission – one very much in keeping with her lascivious sensibilities. She is sent to investigate a clandestine organisation providing unique sexual services for wealthy Parisians, and soon finds herself caught up in a secret world of orgies and hedonistic gratification. She cannot resist the temptation of sating her prodigious lust – but does she underestimate the danger of her task?

NEXUS BACKLIST

All books are priced £4.99 unless another price is given. If a date is supplied, the book in question will not be available until that month in 1997.

CONTEMPORARY EROTICA

THE ACADEMY	Arabella Knight	Oct
AGONY AUNT	G. C. Scott	Jul
ALLISON'S AWAKENING	John Angus	Jul
BOUND TO SUBMIT	Amanda Ware	Sep
CANDIDA'S IN PARIS	Virginia LaSalle	Oct
CANDY IN CAPTIVITY	Arabella Knight	
CHALICE OF DELIGHTS	Katrina Young	
A CHAMBER OF DELIGHTS	Katrina Young	Nov
THE CHASTE LEGACY	Susanna Hughes	
CHRISTINA WISHED	Gene Craven	
DARK DESIRES	Maria del Rey	
THE DOMINO TATTOO	Cyrian Amberlake	
THE DOMINO ENIGMA	Cyrian Amberlake	
THE DOMINO QUEEN	Cyrian Amberlake	
EDUCATING ELLA	Stephen Ferris	Aug
ELAINE	Stephen Ferris	
EMMA'S SECRET WORLD	Hilary James	
EMMA'S SECRET DIARIES	Hilary James	
EMMA'S HUMILIATION	Hilary James	
FALLEN ANGELS	Kendal Grahame	
THE TRAINING OF FALLEN ANGELS	Kendal Grahame	Dec
THE FANTASIES OF JOSEPHINE SCOTT	Josephine Scott	
HEART OF DESIRE	Maria del Rey	

EROTIC SCIENCE FICTION

RETURN TO THE PLEASUREZONE	Delaney Silver	

ANCIENT & FANTASY SETTINGS

CAPTIVES OF ARGAN	Stephen Ferris	Mar
CITADEL OF SERVITUDE	Aran Ashe	Jun
THE CLOAK OF APHRODITE	Kendal Grahame	
DEMONIA	Kendal Grahame	
NYMPHS OF DIONYSUS	Susan Tinoff	Apr
PYRAMID OF DELIGHTS	Kendal Grahame	
THE SLAVE OF LIDIR	Aran Ashe	
THE DUNGEONS OF LIDIR	Aran Ashe	
THE FOREST OF BONDAGE	Aran Ashe	
WARRIOR WOMEN	Stephen Ferris	
WITCH QUEEN OF VIXANIA	Morgana Baron	
SLAVE-MISTRESS OF VIXANIA	Morgana Baron	

EDWARDIAN, VICTORIAN & OLDER EROTICA

ANNIE AND THE SOCIETY	Evelyn Culber	
BEATRICE	Anonymous	
CHOOSING LOVERS FOR JUSTINE	Aran Ashe	
DEAR FANNY	Aran Ashe	
LYDIA IN THE BORDELLO	Philippa Masters	
MADAM LYDIA	Philippa Masters	
MAN WITH A MAID 3	Anonymous	
MEMOIRS OF A CORNISH GOVERNESS	Yolanda Celbridge	
THE GOVERNESS AT ST AGATHA'S	Yolanda Celbridge	
THE GOVERNESS ABROAD	Yolanda Celbridge	
PLEASING THEM	William Doughty	

SAMPLERS & COLLECTIONS

EROTICON 1		
EROTICON 2		Jun
EROTICON 3		Sep
THE FIESTA LETTERS	ed. Chris Lloyd	
NEW EROTICA 2	ed. Esme Ombreaux	

NON-FICTION

HOW TO DRIVE YOUR WOMAN WILD IN BED	Graham Masterton	
HOW TO DRIVE YOUR MAN WILD IN BED	Graham Masterton	Jul
LETTERS TO LINZI	Linzi Drew	

Please send me the books I have ticked above.

Name ....

Address ....

....

....

.... Post code ....

Send to: Cash Sales, Nexus Books, 332 Ladbroke Grove, London W10 5AH

Please enclose a cheque or postal order, made payable to Virgin Publishing, to the value of the books you have ordered plus postage and packing costs as follows:

UK and BFPO – £1.00 for the first book, 50p for each subsequent book.

Overseas (including Republic of Ireland) – £2.00 for the first book, £1.00 for each subsequent book.

If you would prefer to pay by VISA or ACCESS/MASTER-CARD, please write your card number and expiry date here:

....

Please allow up to 28 days for delivery.

Signature ....